To Debby
Best wishes

Brenda Marder

The Greek Dream

by

Brenda L. Marder

Bloomington, IN

authorHOUSE™

Milton Keynes, UK

AuthorHouse™
1663 Liberty Drive, Suite 200
Bloomington, IN 47403
www.authorhouse.com
Phone: 1-800-839-8640

AuthorHouse™ UK Ltd.
500 Avebury Boulevard
Central Milton Keynes, MK9 2BE
www.authorhouse.co.uk
Phone: 08001974150

First published by AuthorHouse 5/25/2006

ISBN: 1-4259-2557-X (e)
ISBN: 1-4259-2556-1 (sc)

Library of Congress Control Number: 2006902872

Printed in the United States of America
Bloomington, Indiana

This book is printed on acid-free paper.

Eliminated

He disappeared at the end of the road.
The moon was already high.
A bird screeched in the trees.
Simple, the usual story.
No one noticed a thing.
Between the two lampposts
a large spot of blood.

Heard and Not Heard

A sudden movement, unexpected; his hand
grasped the wound to staunch the blood,
but none of us heard a shot
nor the whistle of a bullet. Soon
he put down his hand and smiled,
but again he raised his palm slowly
to that same place; he took out his wallet,
kindly paid the waiter and left.
At that moment his coffee cup cracked on its own,
that at least we heard clearly.

Poems by Yannis Ritsos

Translated by Everett J. Marder

Permission: Ery Ritsou

Disclaimer

November 17, the Greek terrorist organization, whose first action was the murder of CIA Station Chief Richard Welch in 1975, does actually exist in history. It is also true that the American Embassy in Athens, Greece, as well as other American and foreign agencies were engaged many years with Greek authorities in an effort to track down the murderers. I have used that terrorist organization as a hook on which to pin this tale. However, with the exception of Richard Welch, none of the characters in this novel are based on any character living or dead. It is true that an American naval attaché was assassinated at a time, and under other circumstances, than those related in this book. Any other assassinations described in this book are fictitious and any resemblance to actual events or persons is purely coincidental.

Author's Note

Richard Welch, CIA station chief in Athens, was returning home from a Christmas party at the residence of the United States Ambassador to Greece on the evening of December 23, 1975. In the car with Welch were his wife and driver. Three masked men lurking at his gate, approached the American as he stepped out of his car, and with a pistol, shot him dead. The terrorists sped off in a dark-colored sedan. Not until December 1976, when the revolutionary organization November 17 sent a letter to a French newspaper claiming credit for the assassination, did Greek authorities receive any information about the killers. At that time, November 17 also claimed responsibility for its second victim, a Greek police officer convicted of torturing political prisoners during the period 1967-1974, when a military junta had governed the country.

The organization went on to assassinate fifteen Greek, five American, one British, two Turkish citizens, including a banker, a newspaper publisher, a ship owner and some Greek politicians. In May 1977, the State Department renewed an earlier offer of a two million dollar reward, appealing to "the Greek people for information regarding terrorists acts against American citizens and American property."

November 17, the last of the far left anarchist organizations from the 1970s operating in Europe (such as Baader Meinhof and The Red Brigades), stated that it was acting on behalf of the working class. Not a single leader or member was identified until the summer of 2002, when a terrorist was caught in Piraeus as an explosive went off accidentally in his hand. Subsequently, nineteen members of the group were rounded up. The trial began in Athens in March 2003. In December 2003, a court found fifteen members guilty of a string of assassinations, car bombings and rocket launchings. Six members received multiple life sentences; at this writing, the court decision is under appeal.

This book is inspired by real events.

After the murder she had never expected to return to Greece. But here I am, she was thinking, some thirty years later circling over the Mesogio. Dismayed, she couldn't orient herself; the coastline, the whole lay of the land, was unintelligible. Foolishly, she expected the contours would be the same as the approach to the familiar old airport at Hellenikon: first the descent over the ancient ruin at Sounion, then the bleached shoreline, marinas chock-a-block with yachts, the green turf of the Glyfada golf course, a landscape she had known intimately. Wait, she reminded herself, this was the Greece of the 2004 Olympics, not the country she had known decades ago as home. She was dizzy, shaky, her heart pounded. She felt an odd detachment, an alienation from this strange place below. Was she herself the phantom or had she entered some spectral space? This was, in fact, a ghoulish trip. And it certainly was not the Olympics that had drawn her; certainly she was not among the millions of careless spectators who were descending on this impossible city. Already overrun and polluted by its own citizens, this bedeviled ancient precinct was now reduced to a construction site in preparation for the games. She wondered what was worse, the daunting circumstances that had drawn her back or experiencing the chaos of twenty-first-century Athens.

At the state-of-the-art Eleftherios Venizelos airport, she stepped from the plane onto a walkway that led her straight inside the airport. Where was the Greek earth, steps leading directly down from the airplane to the ground, so you could place your feet immediately on Greek soil— that electrifying moment, the thrill of homecoming? She left the building, anonymous and dazzling in its newness, and signaled a cab.

"Korydallos Prison," she said to the driver in Greek. The driver didn't start the motor. He stared at her through the mirror. "Korydallos?" he asked, as if to clear up a mistake. "The prison, you said?"

"*Malista,* just as I said."

She was not surprised by his reaction. Most Greeks, familiar with Korydallos' sordid reputation, knew from the newspapers—television had been banned from the proceedings—about the great drama being staged there at the moment: the trial of nineteen people alleged to be members of the terrorist organization called November 17. He must have been thinking, "What in the name of God would an American tourist want at Korydallos?"

She knew full well what she wanted to achieve at Korydallos Prison. Whenever she dwelt on the repercussions, she grew nauseated. Her unique and sensational testimony would crackle throughout Greece and bolt over to the States. It was not every day that a person coming from her background brought testimony against November 17.

She was haunted by the powers at Langley and the State Department who had forbidden her to appear before the Greek court, hinting at a possible loss of

Robert's pension from the State Department or her pension from DIA, along with other veiled threats, some ridiculous, others plausible. The kind of information she had volunteered to report to the tribunal was categorized as "sources and methods," and therefore mandated never to become declassified; the damage to Greek-American relations would be not only extensive but "irreparable," as one State Department officer, a young wise guy on the Greek desk, had warned her.

Over time, she and Robert had ceased discussing the murder at all, their positions so contrary and emotional. Her decision to testify in Athens had reignited the antagonism between them after all these years. And, to add to the misery, she experienced a stab of self-revulsion for having to turn on Stavros, an act many would consider the worst kind of treachery.

She stepped from the taxi and approached the prison. Two armed guards came forward to accompany her down the airless, endless cement corridor toward the courtroom. The prison stank of powerful disinfectant and some other pungency, not unlike decaying seaweed on a polluted beach.

Chapter 1

The airplane carried the letters BALKAN in green across its fuselage. Beyond the Athens airport stretched the bay at Glyfada, the turquoise water gathering the glow of sunset as the orange sphere slid into the Aegean. Barbara and Robert Baldwin's three children raced past their parents up the gangway, two steps at a time.

"Destination then? St. Moritz? Val d'Isère?" she joked as she kissed Robert goodbye on the tarmac. "Don't tell me you've never heard about the truly in place to ski for the 1979 season."

"Don't be funny, Barbara," Robert said, his straight, black hair plastered to his forehead by the cold January gusts blowing from the bay.

"Listen, wow, it's Vitosha in Bulgaria, just outside Sofia. Never mind that there's a Cold War going on. How do I look? My Bogner ski pants? My Christian Dior sunglasses?" she laughed, pointing to the yellow plastic paperclip that pinned together her unremarkable glasses.

"How do you look? Just don't look like Mata Hari. And for God's sake and mine be careful. Do only the absolute minimum. No heroics. Please." He pointed to the magazine she held under her arm. "This has got to be the worst decision you've ever made." He blew kisses

4

up to the three children, who stopped a moment to yell, "Bye, Dad, bye," and wave to him. He waved back, his lips compressed, as he watched them disappear into the cabin.

She felt his arms tightened around her, holding her back. She saw his frown, the corners of his mouth turned down, his gray eyes narrowing with worry.

"Think of this simply as a ski trip, dearest, Robbie. That was the original intention, and it still is." She stretched up against his tall frame, kissed his cheek, hesitated, pulled away and followed the children up the gangway. "See you in five days," she called down keeping her voice steady. She tucked the current issue of *Paris-Match* more tightly under her arm. The dingy plane reeked of diesel, bitter tobacco, and a suggestion of feta cheese. Although the brochure had described the aircraft as propeller-driven, she hadn't expected the cabin to be so confining, so shabby. Two lanky Danish teenagers and their mother banged their heads on the low ceiling as they entered. The older boy rubbed his head and swore.

A narrow aisle cut through the center and a dozen rows of two seats ran along either side. The members of the ski party, all wives and children of the Athens diplomatic community, were filing into the cabin—all Western Europeans, except for her and her three children. The passengers squeezed into their narrow seats, the upholstery frayed. She was amused by Gerda, the Austrian military attaché's wife. Overweight, she got her rump caught between the two arms despite her forceful gyrations to edge down between them. In this position she would be unable to fasten her seat belt.

Luckily the Bulgarian crew members wouldn't be sticklers for safety regulations.

She was recalling that all Bulgarian aircraft were manufactured in the Soviet Union, the very reason that Bulgaria's Balkan Airlines was a laughingstock among the diplomats posted in Athens. They had chuckled, similarly, over the scandal surrounding the Greek government's purchase of the yellow trolleys from the Soviets—trolleys that stalled in their tracks, snarling traffic in Syntagma Square. And they knew about the ensuing brouhaha over the total lack of spare parts that consigned the rusting Russian behemoths to the car barns. Of course they had the luxury of laughing: what diplomat ever traveled by trolley? Certainly not her compatriots at the American Embassy.

From her window seat, she glanced out at the wing, where the propeller had just twirled into action. Simultaneously, Bulgarian folk music, all treble, no bass, blasted from the loudspeakers. The tremulous voices, singing in a minor key, accompanied by piercing clarinets, scratchy string instruments and shallow drums, grated on her nerves. Against the music, the propellers' clatter held its own: the music, Turkic, primitive, but human; the engine, powerful, relentless, mechanical. For a moment, she thought the engine sputtered oddly, as if stalling.

"Hey, Mom, is there a propeller out your window too?" Her sixteen-year-old son, Roger, yelled over to her from his side of the aisle. "Or are we flying with just one prop till the spare-part shipment comes from Siberia?"

She excused herself to the woman sitting next to her on the aisle seat as she leaned across to address the boys. "Shh, they'll hear you. Don't be obnoxious."

"The crew doesn't understand a word of English," Roger said. He motioned to the stewardess by touching his fingers to his lips in a crude Balkan gesture that meant, "Come here, I need to talk to you." The stewardess, wearing thick red lipstick, fixed him with a sulky expression. In Greek, he asked with exaggerated politeness, "Mypos servieretai coca cola, Kyria?" She shrugged and ambled to the galley. His brother Freddy, three years younger, popped his gum and snickered.

Catherine, her nineteen-year-old daughter, home on winter break from Dartmouth, seated herself triumphantly one row in front of Barbara, beside the French Consul General's son, Albert, a thin, pimply-faced university student, whom she had met on a diplomatic family cruise the previous summer. She claimed he reminded her of Alain Delon. Catherine always harbored this thing for the French. Just let someone say *enchanté* and she was smitten. With the skill of a Greek bazaar vendor, she had wangled this seat next to the French boy through complicated negotiations among three people. Barbara pursed her lips and frowned at Catherine, who was now staring into a hand mirror, fluffing out her long, honey-colored hair with her fingertips, ignoring her mother. The European children had taken their seats dutifully as assigned, and wouldn't dream of causing such a hubbub over seating arrangements.

But why be annoyed over Catherine, who, after all, possessed a roving and independent spirit much like her own? When she herself was still in high school, she had studied a map of Paris until she knew the location of the streets and the monuments as well as if she'd already traveled there. It wasn't until college, when she read in

Madame Bovary that Emma, fed up with the provinces, likewise had traced with her finger the map of Paris, that she realized many people, in this way, are Madame Bovarys.

Catherine. The boys. American third-culture kids as they were called by sociologists. Their growing up abroad in the womb of the diplomatic corps had not really polished them or broadened their horizons. The experience had merely turned them into privileged, spoiled kids living beyond ordinary conventions and even, thanks to diplomatic immunity, beyond the law. They were cultural eccentrics who, having lived in Greece on and off for over seven years in the course of Robert's State Department postings, had acquired Greek habits and humor, layered over a sloppy American informality. And, oh, God, their sense of superiority, like Rudyard Kipling's. She buckled her seat belt and, according to her habit whenever she analyzed her children, reversed herself in mid-thought: her children were good, healthy youngsters, loving, curious, humorous, ever-becoming.

Had she acted irresponsibly? On the phone a few nights ago her mother had objected to the trip—"in the midst of the Cold War. . . behind the Iron Curtain. . . Bulgaria of all places. . . the end of the world. . . please, go to Switzerland to ski like the rest of civilization." Barbara had defended the trip as "educational for the kids."

She had pictured her mother standing stiffly at the table in her front hall, fortressed in her home in New Bedford, Massachusetts—a white Cape Cod colonial with blue shutters, the American flag fluttering on the lawn—and decided not to argue further. She merely added that they were going on a specially arranged tour with other wives and children from the diplomatic community in Athens and that Robert was not able to accompany them, given his official status and his high security clearance. She omitted that she and the children would have to travel on tourist passports—the Bulgarians would not accept their diplomatic passports—and that they were the only Americans going on the trip. Other American families spent a vacation or two lolling on the Greek islands or cruising around the Aegean Sea, but they never ventured, as the Baldwins often did, north of Athens into rougher border areas, Macedonia, Epiros, Halkidiki, and even behind the Iron Curtain to the Eastern Bloc countries, to Yugoslavia and Hungary.

In 1979, Bulgaria did not represent everyone's ideal substitute for a winter frolic in Switzerland. As she well knew, the country was a backward, agrarian police state, on the margins of Europe, enthusiastic about its satellite status, separated from the Soviet Union only by the Black Sea. But with three demanding kids to bring up on a State Department salary, a romp to Bulgaria was considerably cheaper and truly intriguing. "Bulgaria," she mouthed, noting the four strong consonants, sounds that somehow evoked that distant country, clinging to the fringe of Europe.

At times, she drew comfort from picturing her parents in the sanctuary of their home. A home was what she had traded for a life of wandering. She had given up what most women craved: the brass front-door latch, the sun-streaked patio, the vegetable garden, the view of hill or pond from a second-floor window.

On the other hand, she exulted in the state of exile, as if exile were her true domicile, an exotic kingdom of exquisite anonymity, freedom, where you had no past, so no one could foretell your future; of autonomy, where you were free from stifling hometown conventions that cramped your vision, where boredom— a condition akin to death—was unthinkable. But you paid a stiff price for your citizenship in that kingdom of exile: you were often in danger, you were always a sojourner

What aliens, all five of them. Many of their relatives and most of their friends in the States had forgotten them. Since they were granted home leave only once every three years, the children visited the States rarely. Freddy, for instance, had been home so seldom, he held a cockeyed view of what it meant to be American, but he clung to his confection with a kind of desperation, with the pathetic stubbornness children have when they conjure up an image they know to be faulty, but lack the wit to replace it.

She looked at her watch. The trip, less than a thousand miles from Athens, up over Greek Macedonia and into Bulgaria, wouldn't last more than three hours. Now, she reckoned, the plane would be skimming the ice-fogged peaks of the Rhodope mountain range in Bulgaria. Strung out along the border, armed patrols, land mines, gun emplacements and barbed wire, a segment of the Iron Curtain, separated Greece and Bulgaria. How did so many defectors scuttle miraculously across that hostile strip of no-man's-land into Greece?

Suppose the plane crashed. Who would ever find them? Brown bear and wild boar would root through the wreckage and easily sniff them out. The plane was rolling from side to side, plunging and rising, like a plastic ball in the ocean. As if jerked on a string, the stars and moon swung about the sky. Pressing her face against the cold window, she watched the Big Dipper bob up and down; the normal pattern of constellations was askew. She left her book on Bulgarian grammar shut in her lap.

She had deliberately chosen to live a life of fear. She found herself recalling a harrowing incident in 1955 in Vienna, a forlorn city occupied by the four allied forces. She was still furious for those hours of fright she'd imposed on herself there. Any prudent young woman would have stayed in the American or British zone. On purpose, she chose to stay in the Russian zone to experience the atmosphere in that sinister sector. A poor tourist, on a trip through Europe after college, she slept in a rundown hotel, where, as was customary, the desk clerk took her passport to register it with the authorities. When she tried to retrieve it in the morning, the clerk muttered that "they" had not returned it; she had not encountered such a situation in any other European country, since all over the continent you were obliged always to carry official identity documents. In the course of the day, she returned four or five times, her hands trembling, to ask for her passport. The clerk shrugged, "Later, *fräulein*." In between she traipsed the gritty, downhearted streets, gripped by the fear that she was as vulnerable as any one of the thousands of displaced persons confined to special camps in postwar Europe. Up and down the sidewalks stomped the Russian patrols, searching for people exactly like her, desperate vagrants without official identity papers. Yet she was stunned when two soldiers on patrol shoved her into a doorway. One, a sloe-eyed blond giant, slammed her against a wall; the other, a runt with filthy hands, grabbed her shoulder bag and searched it. She cowered against the wall, sure they would drag her off when they couldn't find her passport. Much to her disbelief, they handed back her bag, turned and marched off, leaving her terrified. Just before midnight the clerk knocked at her door to inform her that "they" had returned her passport. Ironic, how misplaced the frothy strains of a Strauss waltz would have been in this cast-off sector of postwar Vienna, improbable as the voices of angels singing in a coal mine.

As the plane continued to zigzag, she admitted that even now, some two decades later, she was still courting danger. Yet, look at the others. What about Gerda stuck between the arms of the chair with her seat belt unfastened? Look at the rest of her companions: battle-scarred Europeans, used to the rape of the Sabines, invasions of Visigoths, crusades, wars of religion, bubonic plague, guillotined royalty, trench warfare, concentration camps, socialized medicine, votes of confidence, caretaker governments. Look what cool travelers these hausfraus were. How could they be so idiotically relaxed? Well, why not? As far as they were concerned, they were just on a short jaunt to visit some European neighbors.

Under her left arm she was clutching the magazine so tightly that pain began to stab at her shoulder. Shifting it to her right arm, she made a mental note to hold it in a more relaxed grip. In these close quarters, though, it might rub against her seatmate. She checked the angle of the magazine.

In the window, reflected like a hallucination, her own blurred face was set among the tipping stars: even features, high cheekbones, well-drawn lips, slightly jutting square chin—her grandmother had often told her, "Your Edwardian chin gives you a strong face"—and light brown hair, by now disheveled. In the haze of reflection, her age lines had been smoothed away; she was a girl, as adolescent as Catherine, as vulnerable. "Courage," she said to herself. "This is what you asked for. This is what you want. This is the life you chose. So, courage."

She started when her seatmate, turning to her, extended her elegant hand, the fourth finger bedecked with a beautiful, gold antique ring.

"I am Louisa Borromeo. Attaché wife from Italy. Your children?"

"Yes, they're mine."

"Ah, very nice boys. Very strong, *sì*?"

"Yes."

"You like skiing?"

"I love it. But I'm no expert. I go for a half day only, and spend the rest of the time with a good book."

"I hate skiing," Louisa said, screwing her oval-shaped face into a sneer. "Cold. Wind. Ice. Ah horrible, such climate is for wild animals, boars, bears, *animale*. I come on the trip to look through the windows. See mountains, sky, clouds traveling close by. Beautiful." She stressed the *u's* in "beautiful," and chuckled at the idea of her own preferences. "No children. Very free." She pointed a thumb at her chest as if to make a grand proclamation.

Barbara smiled in answer. Odd an Italian woman would announce her childless condition so blithely. The striking sonority in her voice, delightfully pitched, made

Barbara think she might be a professional singer. Her hair, black as ebony, and pulled back, was fastened by a gold cloisonné clip at the neck, her complexion glowed with a copper tint, her dark eyes full of an expression that Barbara couldn't interpret. Something. A glimmer of irony, perhaps? Barbara had seen her someplace before. Yes, of course, at a formal reception at the Italian Embassy in Athens accompanied by her husband, he, slim and elegant, a brass sword strapped to his side, an extravagant anachronism in his dress uniform. The couple resembled leading characters in a nineteenth-century Viennese operetta.

"One afternoon after you finish your ski, you and I, we sit by the fire and drink a glass of *Glüwein* together. You have been to Italy?"

"I love Italy, and I adore opera," answered Barbara, jabbing her own thumb at her chest in joking imitation of Louisa. Louisa tilted her head up against the back of her chair and delivered a scale of laughter that seemed to begin on middle C, and then climb half an octave.

"Good. We'll sing together."

"Where did you come from originally in Italy?"

"Although we live in Italy, I was born in Trieste. A long, long story. A tragic story." She shook her head slowly and made a clucking sound with her tongue.

Barbara wanted to say something kind, but being familiar with how the Triestinos had suffered as pawns in the Great Powers' struggle for control of that region, she was afraid of saying something trite, so she didn't comment. She started to move the magazine back to her left arm, but decided to let it be. If her intuition was right, she and Louisa had, in this short exchange, through some particular chemistry that friendship works, indeed become friends. She closed her eyes to the quivering constellations.

Although the no-smoking signs were aglow in Russian and English throughout the cabin, two stubble-bearded stewards, were puffing their cigarettes with the detachment of people sitting at their own kitchen tables. The acrid smoke floated through the cabin. A few passengers coughed.

The stewardess lurched down the aisle bringing Roger an orange drink.

"No. Cok-aaa-Co-la," he intoned through the deeper range of his unpredictable adolescent voice, as the thick, yellow liquid trickled down the sides of the overfilled glass. The stewardess answered "No, no," and, finally, switched to a more preemptory "*Nein.*"

Barbara signaled the boys to take off their baseball caps. She had forbidden them to bring the caps; as she had anticipated, the other youngsters were all dressed in proper ski attire. Roger called over to her, his blue eyes squinting in mock seriousness, "Hey, Barbara, O, Barbara, I don't think we're in Kansas any more."

After a surprisingly smooth touchdown, the group shuffled into passport control, a barren room with a few tables. At one, a scowling officer with thick eyebrows and a luxuriant mustache the density and color of beaver fur studied the documents. Louisa offered a musical "*Buona Sera*" and waved airily at the official, then handed him her passport. He turned the pages warily, as if they were infectious.

"You come to Bulgaria twice before. You come to Rumania, too, and once this year, Yugoslavia." She

15

smiled, nodded her head in agreement, and hummed as she tapped her fingers on his desk. He rose and examined her from head to foot. "I ask you what's your business in the People's Republic of Bulgaria." He raised a thick eyebrow.

"Tourist, like my friends here. We love the snow, the scenery, love to ski. So healthy, the out-of-doors." She laughed up the scale again, the same laugh as before, but more muted.

He remained on his feet, fingering through yellow index cards in the small wooden box, checking her name against whatever was written on the smudged cards for what seemed to Barbara, who stood next in line, an eternity. She tightened the scrolled magazine under her arm; a muscle behind her shoulder blade contracted. Louisa stood there unruffled, still humming and smiling at the Bulgarian, who called over to another official. The second man, wearing stripes of a more senior official, picked up Louisa's passport, examined it, leafed through the cards, eyed Louisa carelessly as if he had more important duties pressing him someplace else, and nodded to the first official, who stamped her through.

Barbara and the children stepped forward. The official scrutinized each of their faces, including Freddy's, stained with the orange drink that Roger had refused, and without ceremony pounded the stamper. She quickly grasped the passports.

Roger grinned, "*Mnogo ste lyubezan. Nadyavam se da se vidim ottnovo,*" a couple of the phrases they had memorized in preparation for the trip.

"Roger, shut up," she said, through clenched teeth.

"Why? It just means, You are very kind; I hope I'll see you again."

Dominating the otherwise bare walls was a larger-than-life photograph in black and white of the Communist Party's first secretary, Todor Zhivkov, gazing above and beyond the smoothly functioning bureaucracy, wearing the same expression of vacuity as the airplane stewards. He had been in full possession of this country since 1962, jarred only once by an attempted military coup in 1965, and now, in 1979, it seemed he would rule forever. His professed desire was to make his country, "the Japan of Europe," a mantra that promised industrial and technological advances, but western commentators had also noted the implied corollary of a controlled and submissive citizenry.

Freddy pointed at the photo. "Hey, who's *that* guy?" She pushed her younger son ahead through the exit; under her ski jacket, her body was wet with sweat. Gerda, clumping behind, was pulled out of line, as she fumbled in her pockets and shoulder bag for her passport.

Chapter 2

Well, the inn could have been worse. Haunted by their uncomfortable ski trip to Yugoslavia last year, when the toilets had frozen over, she steeled herself this time for a frosty, damp room, warmed only by a puny wood stove that had to be refilled every ten minutes, a service not provided by the hotel during the night. As promised in the brochure, though, the room she was sharing with Catherine actually possessed central heat: two silver radiators like boilers on an ocean-going ship were spraying jets of tepid water and hissing. The room was lit by a low-wattage bulb dangling on a wire from the ceiling—no reading lamps on the night tables. She would ask for reading lamps in the morning, but she knew it would be useless, that reading in bed was not a Balkan pastime. How many futile evenings had she spent in Yugoslavia, Hungary, and even Greece, straining to read under a fifty-watt yellowing bulb. The beds, simple wooden slats supporting mattresses stuffed with a lumpy cotton fill, sagged. A gigantic, dark armoire leaned like a sulking presence against the wall. She was thankful for the bath they had to share only with the boys, whose room was adjoining, and prayed for hot water. Striped green and red wool blankets, folded at the foot of each bed and red flokati rugs on the floor, redeemed the room. A colorful photo on the wall featured a group of smiling men and women, peasants standing in a field of pink roses.

"Not so bad after all," she said to Catherine, as they undressed for bed.

"Next year, maybe we could go to France," her daughter answered.

Exhausted, she buried herself under the blanket and rough muslin sheet, her head on the skimpy, sour pillow. The sensation of motion, of being tossed about the bed as if still airborne, annoyed her. She reached over to the night table to assure herself that she had placed the magazine there, a ridiculous gesture since she knew every second where it was, could never get her mind off it, or off the CIA station chief, Dana Franklin. She was seeing him now in her mind as if he had stepped suddenly from the armoire in his full sartorial splendor: white, initialed shirts, Hermes ties, and Savile Row gray suits.

She was swept by the fleeting madness that insomnia brings; an image of Puccini's malignant Scarpia, flamboyant in his scarlet lined cape, floated through her head. In spite of her dread and the time of night, the comparison with Franklin made her smile. She and Robert had wondered if Franklin used his couturier display for deep cover—a beautiful act of deception, Robert decided, since in the common perception, which couldn't be more mistaken, CIA agents were regarded as part thug, part colorless bureaucrat, part stumblebum. Or perhaps Franklin possessed some quirk, an irrepressible theatrical flair. Yes, like Scarpia, although Franklin's thin, steel framed glasses and pallid face gave him an almost prissy air. Could he actually command a hit squad?

Franklin's predecessors, anything but natty, had been inconspicuous in their drab suits and crew-cut hair. In fact the station chief in 1975 had been a football star in college and had played pro before joining the Company. In one spirited game, his right ear had been flattened against his head, and in another, his nose had been broken. He looked more like a prizefighter than a Harvard graduate who had, of all things, majored in Classics. Four years ago, he had been gunned down in Athens by the terrorist group known as November 17, whose members the Greek government had been unable to identify or apprehend. Franklin had been reassigned as station chief, transferred from Tel Aviv to Athens in 1976, charged with finding the terrorists, who since that initial murder had been killing not only American officials, but Greeks as well, and were bound to strike again.

"He's theatrical, his wife, a cipher," Robert had said, when the Franklins first arrived on station. The couple had immediately instituted "occasional" insufferable dinners at their residence with colleagues from the Embassy – "just the Embassy family where we can let our hair down, no foreigners," Matilda, his redhead wife, was fond of saying. Not a word of Greek was uttered, though some of the dinner guests spoke the language well. From her commanding position at the foot of the table that sparkled with Lenox china and crystal, and was attended by three waiters, Matilda held forth on the dynamics of the PTA at the American school, unmistakably her consuming interest. At the last get-together just before

Christmas, the cultural attaché had tried to elevate the level of conversation:

"The new bureau chief from the *New York Times* is writing a book. He's investigating some sensitive issues to do with the fate of Greek children, thousands of them—both their abduction into the neighboring Balkan countries by Greek communists and also their flight to those countries with their leftist parents during the Civil War."

"Sensitive material," the economic counselor said. "Has he got a publisher?"

"A New York press. The repercussions here in Greece could . . ."

The cultural attaché was cut short by Matilda. "Oh, the journalist with the lovely wife? She's joined the PTA. I'm trying to nab her to serve on the International Dinner Committee."

Franklin, installed at the head of the table, had prescribed a precedent-shattering seating pattern; he had put Robert to his right—defying protocol, which demanded the placing of the senior wife to his right—and the cultural attaché to his left. Thus, isolating himself from the women's chatter, he ate contentedly, never initiating conversation. But he answered the cultural attaché's remarks in a confidential tone, nearly a whisper, ignoring Robert entirely, as if someone of Robert's rank were far beneath him. Robert flushed with humiliation. He was, after all, the counselor for political affairs, the third ranking officer in the Embassy, and since the deputy chief of mission was in Washington for congressional hearings for his nomination for an ambassadorship to Nigeria, Robert was actually the second ranking officer.

But it was known that Franklin was fascinated by music and theater, and hence enjoying himself enormously in the company of the cultural attaché. "Just exactly like the atmosphere at the home of a British colonial in India before World War I," Robert remarked when they had left.

Later that week, when Franklin heard Barbara was going to Bulgaria, he called Robert into his office and asked if he thought she would do the station a favor.

"What kind of favor?"

"Just some courier stuff."

"What kind of courier stuff?

"The courier chain to Bulgaria has broken down, and we need to get a message to an agent in Sofia immediately. We do have a courier to run it to the Bulgarian agent, but only after the message is carried through passport control. However, that courier is tainted and might get hassled by the passport officials. So that's the problem. We don't have anyone to take it through passport control. What a piece of good luck for us that Barbara happens to be going there at this time."

"She's taking the children with her. I don't think . . ."

That's not a problem."

"Hey, hold on. I see it as a definite problem. I wouldn't subject them to any risk, no matter how minimal."

"It's a hundred percent risk-free. I guarantee it. You don't think I'd suggest this otherwise, do you?"

"Keeping it totally risk-free has to be impossible."

"Not at all. We do risk-free missions all the time. Couldn't operate if we didn't. Hell, imagine the kind of flak I'd have to face from Washington if anything happened to your wife or kids."

Robert stood up to go. Franklin put a hand gently on his shoulder, and smiling all the while, sat him back down, displaying a cordiality he had withheld at table the other night. "Listen, Rob, my friend. We'll put her on a need-to-know security classification. We'll give Barbara no details, no names. No one will know about her mission but the other courier, one of my best operators. That individual will not discuss it with her or anyone else no matter what happens. Barbara will be innocent, as pure as the driven Bulgarian snow. She'll simply tuck a magazine under her arm and off she'll trot to ski. Think of her as doing just a little business on her pleasure trip. She won't even know who's coming to get the magazine until the person approaches her and asks for it. That simple."

"Sorry. Anything for the mission," Robert smiled sardonically, "but my wife doesn't do your kind of work."

"I bet she'll love it. If I know her at all, she's dying for a chance to do something. Restless. It's written all over her face. Bored as hell. She's got her Defense Intelligence Agency stuff but that's just analysis, not action. She's not the kind to sit on her duff all her life, pouring tea. You know, Robert, not everyone can trudge along in lockstep to the bureaucracy."

He came home that night furious. As he told her about his meeting with Franklin, he grew angrier. "I don't even want you to discuss it with him. He got so personal, insinuating, the arrogant bastard. He all but called me a pusillanimous bureaucrat." Robert complained that Franklin was being egged on constantly by Paige Gardner, the Ambassador, a naive political appointee, who got his jollies from being associated with the CIA in their rogue adventures. Gardner was the perfect accomplice for Franklin, who tended to get carried away, picturing himself a John le Carré figure.

She went over to the drapes and slowly drew them shut against the night. Then she answered softly, restrained, trying to keep the stridency out of her voice.

"Well, he's edgy. Suppose one of your predecessors was shot in the face by November 17? You'd be arrogant, too. Facing that kind of violence doesn't make a man meek. You know danger must stalk him."

They had noticed when he appeared in public, at non-official gathering —at the American School or the American Youth Club—Franklin would always stand with his back against a wall, for safety, a habit he'd picked up someplace in his long career. Maybe, she suggested, his stance was an instinctive adaptation like the possums' playing dead.

"Just for kicks, suppose I go see him? Learn more about it. That can't hurt," she said.

"You don't have to do that. I'll tell him for you that you're not interested."

"I'd enjoy talking with him professionally, observe close up how his mind works. Besides, I've never been in his office, certainly never dreamed I'd ever enter the Bubble. He can't do anything worse than patronize me." By now her tone had become decisive.

"You'll come away from that encounter feeling like shit. You'll degrade yourself. . . and me. For God's sake, Barbara, sweetheart, be reasonable. That mission he wants to give you is petty crap. Hackwork. You can't want to risk anything for *that*."

"No, not for *that*."

"If not for that, then for what?"

"You never know what might come from it, do you? I view the whole caper as a way to maybe—somehow—to get in."

"Given any thought as to how this could impact on my career? Your status on station derives from my position. Your antics with the agency could ruin it."

"The State Department is pretty much a tool of the CIA."

"That remark is one of the grossest simplifications I've ever heard," he said, throwing up his hands in disgust.

She knew that Franklin, who was trained to read people infinitely more complicated and devious than she, had guessed how she chafed. Confined to operating as the wife of a foreign-service officer, attending the lethal cocktail parties and the Embassy wives coffees, she functioned on the same level as a restaurant hostess. Despite her Ph.D in Balkan Studies, her scholarly reputation in the field, her position as analyst at the Defense Intelligence Agency before she was married, her many publications and the occasional papers she was writing now on the Balkans as consultant for DIA, she had no official status on station.

"No problem," Franklin told her when she met with him in his office. "If you have misgivings just say so. A very low-level mission," he added, tugging at the gold cuff links engraved with his initials.

It had to be low level since they were meeting in his office on the third floor of the Embassy, and not as she had hoped in the Bubble. While he talked he looked down at his fingernails, at the polished top of his walnut desk, and at one point he consulted the mirror to straighten his wide, polka-dot bowtie, his back toward her as if she hardly existed as a credible human being.

"As I see it, here's something for you to do that's got some tang, some kick," he said, turning to her once again.

He stopped for a moment to let his words sink in, as he looked out of his window toward Mount Lycavettos, where the *nefos*, as the Greeks called the gray cloud of pollution, smeared the sky over Athens.

"The easiest thing in the world. You carry the magazine into Bulgaria, keep it in your possession for a few days. Sometime soon, somebody will come for it." His voice had an edge to it that irritated and intimidated her at the same time.

Unable to frame her concerns, she asked a few desultory questions, wary of appearing hesitant, that he might say, "Well, perhaps you're the wrong person. We'd better not break with tradition by using a woman for this important work." He stretched his neck back, ran his fingers through his elegantly cut hair, picked up a pair of drumsticks on his desk, and began drumming absently on a practice pad. Rumor had it that he had played with a jazz band while at Yale.

"What does this mean for the children? What could happen?"

"Look, Barbara, I'm not going to stand here and tell you horror stories. Not my style. If I thought there was the slightest danger, I wouldn't be offering you this opportunity."

"Dana, I have to smile at your choice of words."

"And I, at your reluctance." He took off his glasses. "To me it seems so easy." He tilted his head, spread his arms in a languid motion, a mocking gesture to signify ease.

She was surprised to see him clown, and it occurred to her that in some circumstances he probably had humor and a certain charm.

He sat down on the corner of his desk across from her, his face level with hers. "I've read some of your stuff, a couple of your articles in the scholarly journals and some recent reports you've put together for the DIA. Not bad at all." He stretched forward and gently picked some lint from her sleeve.

"I stay in touch."

"Barbara, dear, we can't sit here and chat all day, as much as I enjoy your company."

She didn't quite know how to reply to his light brush of sarcasm.

"I'm not just saying that. I really do find you to be an interesting woman. But I have to get back to controlling all of Eastern Europe and of course the Near East, too." He stood up, his legs wide apart, and again, made a broad hand motion, this time more brusque and circular, to imply an encompassing of the globe. He lifted one eyebrow and grinned impishly.

He began putting papers in his briefcase, packing up to leave. Obviously, she had to decide. Oh God. Robert would kill her. She stood.

"O.K. I'll do it."

"Fine." He withdrew the charm. His blue eyes fixed on her. Magnified by the glasses, they reminded her of fish eyes bulging behind the glass walls of an aquarium. "Let me give you some instructions."

At home that evening, Robert asked, "Did you tell Franklin to shove it?"

"He was very professional, to the point." She took a sip from her wine glass. "I told him I'd do it."

Robert closed his eyes and rubbed the lids with his fingertips. "Your decision is absolutely dead wrong. To carry that magazine just for the thrill of playing espionage is madness."

"O.K. Maybe I ought to call Matilda and tell her I want to join the PTA."

"For God's sake, Barbara. Is that crack supposed to be the basis for a productive discussion between us?"

She hated him to be angry with her, even for five minutes. Now separated from him by hundreds of miles, and by an iron curtain to boot, she inched her hand out along the contours of the mattress to the other side of the bed, Robert's side; her palm felt only emptiness, the miniature mounds and hollows.

As she tossed in the rough bedclothes, she still had options. She could decide not to pass the message. But if she did back out, who might be depending on her? Who could get hurt?

In the morning, she felt hung over from lack of sleep. She could not remember her dream, but her chest ached dully as if her heart had been palpitating for hours. After a glance through the window at the icy hills, she put on her heaviest ski clothes and arranged *Paris-Match* on the night table under the *Blue Guide to Bulgaria, Bulgarian Grammar Exercises*, and Kazanzakis' *Zorba the Greek*, in Greek, a casual pile of reading material. Franklin had told her, "Don't carry the magazine around. Leave it on the night table in perfect innocence. There are no glossy magazines in Bulgaria. The maids won't even know what it is." She had leafed through the pages a few times, but she couldn't tell which page of the magazine was coded, or if any page was coded at all. Worse still, she could never ask. The day had begun.

In the dining room, lit pleasantly by the morning sun, a breakfast of thick yogurt, dry bread, and tepid, muddy Turkish coffee cleared her head. Freddy, who had made a loud gagging sound at the sour yogurt, was rolling Bulgarian currency back and forth across the table to Roger. "Mom, where can I spend these stinkies?"

She took in the face of her youngest child. Freddy was dark-haired with gray-blue eyes like his father, in fact, physically, a small replica of him, really a caricature of him the way so many children—adorable, innocent, vulnerable with their unformed features—are absurd copies of one of their parents. Freddy, resilient, bending, light, accommodating; Roger, strong, pondering, heavy, intent. Freddy, the willow. Roger, the oak.

"*Stotinki*," she corrected. "Just put them in your pocket till you need them." It was too complicated to explain to him that the Bulgarian government made them buy thirty dollars worth for every day they stayed to obtain the much needed foreign exchange.

"What a name for money. Cripes. Stinkies." Freddy flipped a few heads and tails with Roger, who had refused to shave the fuzzy yellow hairs off his face. His sideburns were scraggly in the style of the late sixties and early seventies, typical of an American kid living abroad who picked up the "in" thing long after it first appeared in the States. A red pimple swelled on his chin.

Gerda strode into the dining room and joined them at the breakfast table. Her eyes, innocent and docile, gave her face a bovine air. She was shy, and spoke no language but her own. Barbara's college German endeared her to Gerda, who fretted that the authorities had been atrociously rude to her last night as she searched for her passport. When she had finally dug it out of her rucksack, she said to the Bulgarians, in German, of course, which they couldn't understand, "Some joke, as if any sane human being would want to sneak into this hinterland without a passport." Hunched over her yogurt, she confided, "Ich liebe nicht den Bulgarien. Die sind barbaren."

Barbara's Ph.D. dissertation had been on the barbaric German and Austrian occupation of Greece during World War II. She was fully aware of the atrocities that the Bulgarians, allies of the Nazis, and with their permission, had committed against the Greeks in Thrace and Macedonia, how the Bulgarians in fact had acted like barbarians in the last eighteen months of the war, marching fifteen thousand Greeks into Bulgaria for slave labor. So these words of reproach coming from Gerda seemed the greatest of ironies, an incongruity that would be totally lost on the Austrian woman.

An hour later, Barbara and the children, followed by Gerda, went out into the snow and entered a rough-hewn ski shack to take their places in line with others from their group. Skis, poles and boots were lined up against the wall behind the counter, where a man was handing out instructions sheets:

Important to you, cherished visitor to Bulgaria. To rent ski please, we take yellow paper you now fill out.

30

When you bring back ski with pole to it is understood you get back yellow paper. Your passports you had delivered up at hotel desk to be returned only with yellow paper. In cases of lost ski in cases of lost pole to it is understood, you do not get back yellow paper.

At the bottom, in heavy, smudged print, the notice concluded,

The People's Republic of Bulgaria welcomes you.

She read the notice out loud twice to the children, going over it point by point with the boys to be sure they grasped the consequences of losing any part of their equipment.

"You understand what they mean by this?"

"Yeah, we get it," said Roger. Freddy nodded.

Catherine said, "That's scary. Albert says the Bulgarians are almost as bad as the Germans. They can't really keep our passports, can they? I'd feel better if Dad were here. This is really a dangerous place to be."

The snow was thick, a soft, dry powder, its crystals shimmering in the low morning sun. Although the air was cold, she could feel the sun's warmth when she stood full in it. Patches of fir and pine, rooted firmly in granite, cast black shadows against the sides of the mountains. The sky was clear except toward the conical summit, where a mass of storm clouds clustered, staining the snow there a melancholy gray. A few other lodges, smaller than the one they were staying in, clung to the flanks of the mountain, the chimneys spewing dark smoke. The whole operation consisted of two T-bars, a few rope tows, and one chairlift. The chairlift often teetered to a full stop for five minutes or more, leaving the foreign skiers dangling in the frozen void. As the lift stuttered skyward, the upper chairs disappeared into the skyline, as if heading for a Wagnerian apotheosis. She recognized how misplaced the term "resort" really was. Catherine's idea of going to France to ski next year became suddenly enticing.

At the bottom of the mountain, out of sight, lay the dismal capital. At DIA, they turned out reports that documented Sofia's inadequate housing, where two or three generations were crowded together in their allotted space of nine square feet per person; its streets, nearly empty of cars, only 29 percent of all households owned one; its military, pampered and cultivated to prevent another coup attempt like the one in 1965 perpetrated against the pro-Soviet Zhivkov; its "houses of culture" that served as centers to indoctrinate intellectuals as well as "workers"; its Russian friends driven through the streets in black limousines—the Bulgarian *privilegensia* also enjoyed such perks—put up in special hotels and served the best vodka. No, it certainly wasn't Garmisch or St. Moritz, but the company was fine and the kids would have fun. Catherine, chatting happily in French, had already started up the chairlift with Albert, Roger had found the Danes, and Barbara had deposited a sulky Freddy at the ski school. He had resisted the idea of lessons and pestered her to join his brother on the trails, but although he could ski after his own fashion, Robert had insisted he not be left unsupervised on the slopes, where he would struggle to keep up with Roger, a daredevil on skis. She had promised to meet Louisa in the afternoon for a glass of wine.

As she snapped on her skis, the fears of the previous night scattered in the crystalline light of day. Up ahead, Gerda, on her skis, had already pushed off with astounding balletic grace. It was, she was thinking, a magnificent day.

Chapter 3

He was waiting for his colleagues to leave the office at close of business. The bells across the street finally jangled twice to indicate the hour. Now, one by one, the others were buttoning up their coats and departing. When the last person had left, he rose from his desk and raced down the groaning wooden steps to the front door. Through the iced glass, clouding from his breath, he peered left and right to be sure the area was clear. No, no one was returning to retrieve a forgotten briefcase or a pair of gloves. Two steps at a time, he dashed back up the deserted stairwell to his freezing office and sat once again at his desk. Taking a deep breath, he reached under his jacket to his shirt pocket to withdraw the brown envelope, and ripped it open. On the sheets of white paper, stamped with the blue seal of the National Ministry of Defense: his name, Ivan Dimitrov; his rank, Major; and his branch of service, Intelligence, Army of the People's Republic of Bulgaria. His orders: posted as army attaché to Athens, Greece, a three-year assignment. He put the papers down and rubbed his eyes. He read the words again. And again.

On the surface, the very surface, he analyzed, of course the assignment made sense. Although he was born in Bulgaria, he spoke Greek almost fluently, tinged only slightly with a Bulgarian accent, and the English he had learned in Intelligence School in Russia was excellent. They knew he'd never been to Greece, but they figured he'd gained from his mother a rough familiarity with her country. And they trusted him. On the other hand, his superiors had powerful, irrefutable reasons to block his assignment to Greece. What about the relatives he still had there?

Bundled in his hat, coat and gloves in the unheated room, he read his orders for the third time. He and his wife were to leave for Athens in two weeks. He was allowed one week's leave, then he would return to Sofia for a five-day orientation session and be on his way. He would receive compensation immediately for new uniforms and for civilian attire and appropriate clothes for his wife. He could expect compensation for expenses incurred in carrying out his diplomatic duties to maintain a standard of living equal to that of his foreign colleagues who were similarly accredited to Greece. His promotion to Lieutenant Colonel would be effective in a few days. He gloated. What an extraordinary outcome for a skinny kid who decided to make the army a career and spent his first two years doing his obligatory military service in the noncommissioned ranks marooned at an outpost on the Turkish border.

His legs were turning numb. He stood up, shook his feet to regain circulation, and once again ran down the steps. Outside, he stumbled through the yellowing snow along unshoveled streets, past rows of apartment buildings hulked in the gray day. He plowed through Lenin Square, past Party Headquarters, a pale yellow structure, built in the best Italianesque architectural style, with a tower bearing a red star, and the pre-war Parliament building. He chuckled at the lump of snow covering the head of Alexander II, who sat haughtily astride his horse; of course, the Bulgarians adored him—their Russian hero who had chased the Ottoman Turks out of Bulgaria in the last century—and had immortalized him in bronze. He jumped on a trolley. In the distance the gilded domes of the Alexander Nevsky Cathedral, usually glinting even on the dullest days, were drained of color. The trolley stopped a block before his apartment. As he jumped off, he almost slid into a man on crutches, who hobbled precariously in the middle of the rutted street along the trolley tracks. As he entered his own building, from down the hall strains of a melancholy tune played on a mouth organ floated along the corridor. He leapt up the stairs to the fifth floor, grabbing the greasy rail to speed himself along.

At his apartment, he put his shoulder to the door—the damn thing always stuck—and shoved. When it ground open he called, "Hey, Maria, Mareeche, I'm changing out of my uniform. We'll go to the coffee house before we eat. It's a good way to warm up." His apartment was almost as chilly as the office unless you were right on top of the kitchen stove. Without appetite, he smelled the pork, and peered at his wife through the thick cooking smoke that permeated their quarters.

Maria, her eyes smarting, her face and arms red from laboring over the meal, flung out her hands in a gesture of what's-going-on. He put his fingers across his lips. Shhh. She nodded in comprehension and lifted her coat off the hook. "I'm glad you suggested the walk, Ivancho," she said in a staged voice. "Let's head for my aunt's place. She's sick." On the street, empty except for a horse pulling a wobbly wagon, a couple of army trucks, and a black ZIS for ferrying party officials, its black curtains drawn like a hearse, they weaved around the stained snowdrifts, as he announced his new assignment. She listened without comment, but gripped his arm more tightly as they slipped along. From her clothes rose the smell of cooking oil.

On the street, a colleague, who worked in the office on the floor above his, caught sight of him and hollered from down the street, "Hey, Dimitrov, listen to this. I've been told by someone in the ministry that I can expect orders by the end of the week." Approaching was the stout figure of Stefan Mihailov, a loudmouth, from peasant stock. If it hadn't been for the regime, he'd have been a pig farmer like his father. Even in the overcast afternoon, Ivan could make out the loose crinkled skin on his cheeks and chin, the thick pink ears, the full lips and the hairs in his nose. A country of stolid peasants, Ivan thought, and the government offered them first crack at entering the universities and other undeserved privileges.

"So, you aching to leave the capital?"

"Of course, I'd like to go to Russia. Get a ticket or two punched for advancement," Mihailov said.

"Well, anybody would be lucky to get that assignment."

"Get smart, Dimitrov, Moscow is where you want to be headed." He wiped his sleeve across his runny nose. The medals on his green uniform tinkled as he strutted off.

"My God, what a system that rewards imbeciles like him," he muttered, more to himself than to Maria. "Bulgarian socialism." Shit.

The coffee house, a dour, poorly lighted hall, with its square wooden tables surrounded by wobbly, straight chairs, depressed him. Grim, bleary-eyed waiters brought drinks, toast or nuts from the bar to the tables. He guided Maria along the stone floor littered with scatterings of bottle tops, toothpicks, nutshells, and spent cigarettes. Since it was approaching mealtime, only a few old men lingered to keep warm, drinking, smoking, staring into space, or playing *tabla*. The silence was broken occasionally by the click of the dice and the muffled sound of the red and black game pieces as the men slid them across the boards, enjoying the warmth thanks to the government, which gave coffee houses enough wood or kerosene to keep their stoves burning all day and into the evening. He and Maria pulled chairs up to a table in a far corner, took off their gloves and hats, and unbuttoned their coats.

He looked up. On the wall, on every wall, the same picture of Zhivkov. Like a virus, his type spreads across the face of the earth.

As he lighted their cigarettes, he felt the match tremble in his cupped hands. They waited for the waiter to bring their drinks before they spoke. He had ordered *slivova* to chase away his shivers. Maria, calm, patient, ever the scientist, a biologist used to quiet observation and the methodical recording of results, was smiling at him, rubbing her chapped hands slowly, flexing her square fingers, stiff with cold. He looked at his wife, a solid woman, her stubborn black hair pulled sternly back from her face and held in place by a few plastic combs. Her features he found exotic, characteristic of her people, the *Shopi*, who populated the villages of Mount Vitosha, and said to be descended from Mongolian tribesmen who had settled in the area in the eleventh century. Her oval face and dark skin, thin lips, white teeth, straight nose, small, Asian eyes, which crinkled, sparked and ran with tears when she was amused, delighted him. At this moment he wanted to hear her laugh. He attempted a joke, "There were these two bureaucrats from Plovdiv . . . " but his voice caught, and he threw up his hands in despair.

"I'm frozen from this goddamn cold, but under my jacket, I'm sweating like a bull. Can you tell me why they're taking the chance?"

"What chance? What do you mean? Who knows? Take it more in stride, Ivancho. You'll make yourself sick." She was regarding him intently. His face felt hot and itchy, his eyes burned. "We'll never figure out what they're up to. Let's enjoy the dream of going to Greece."

He reminded her that he was the first attaché with Greek blood on both his mother's and father's side to be assigned there. He supposed her uncle Vasili, a real pasha in the Ministry of National Defense, had a hand in it. Who else could have accomplished such a miracle?

Vasili Petrov. Of course, if it weren't for Vasili, he might not have married Maria. He had met her at a wedding, liked her from the first, and continued to see her for months after, because he felt comforted being with her; she calmed him, made him feel everything in the world could be managed with patience and strength to endure. But he had been cautious; God knows, he had to be. A Greek refugee without connections would be better off buried in the grave. Marriage, for him, he understood even as a boy, was the one and only key to acquire for himself powerful connections, to open doors to a meaningful future. When he learned that Vasili Petrov was her uncle, her mother's younger brother, he decided immediately to ask for her. Petrov, an ambitious, temperamental man, disliked the match. That his talented niece, for whom he had a soft spot, would marry a no account Greek, a non-commissioned officer who was making a career of the army, enraged him. Maria had humorously recited the scene.

"I had envisioned an arranged marriage for you, an affair that I would personally manage, the best," he had railed, kissing his fingertips and flinging his right hand in the air, but when she had pleaded, he had given his blessing, and pulled strings for them ever since. Vasili had gotten him his commission in the army, and had protected him throughout his career.

"Thank God for Vasili," she said. "Thanks to him. Of course he must be the one who pulled this off. He knows what a plum assignment this would be for anybody, especially for us."

"Hold it. Has Vasili pulled this off? Maybe he's totally out of the picture, and others are doing this to set me up." He reached his hands across the table for hers. After decades of fighting back fear and practicing deceit, after years of struggling to make a place for himself in a country not his own, he felt like an experimental animal who had run in the same maze forever, now baffled by a new layout, desperate to adjust his behavior to the new situation. In the process, he felt as if he was shrinking.

"Relax, Ivan. We'll live like human beings in Athens. *Ach, Atina*. Think about it, we'll be warm. Remember your mother, how she described the Greek sun? I'll never forget the way she put it: 'The sun rules.'" She leaned over and took a sip of his plum brandy.

"*O helios vasilevi,*" he translated, the Greek words rolling over his tongue sweetly, like the brandy.

She loved him, no doubt of it, but at this moment, slumped over the table, his head in his hands, diminished in his thick winter clothes, he felt like a weakling. He hated for her to see him like this. Bastards. They set me up, *tova e kapan,* they set me up, they set me up; *tova e kapan,* the words beat through his head in time to the pulse in his temples. He wiped the sweat beading on his upper lip. He forced himself to sit up straight.

He called for another drink, put his head back and gulped the brandy. The hot liquid running into his stomach jolted him, warmed his body, sent his mind whirling. He closed his eyes: there the blue arch of Greek sky; there the shimmering Aegean, white yachts under sail; there Mercedes and Cadillacs floating along broad, open boulevards, past tall glass buildings; that's what capitalism means. Yes, and bookstores filled with newspapers and books imported from all over the world; that's what democracy means. His own home, all his, ringed by a garden scented with roses and jasmine, his huge living room filled with people, free, spirited, laughing, telling one marvelous story after the other of traveling through the Western world. Ah, life!

Right off, he'd go search out his own people. He was thinking of his mother, dead these many years. She had fled Greece without anything; no mementos of the family, nothing. So her mind had become like a photo album; there she had held all the portraits of the relatives, the living and the dead. Hearing her descriptions, when he was young, was like turning pages and peering at sepia, blurry, age-tinged pictures. "You look just like my Uncle Vangeli who died in the war in Asia Minor, a green-eyed, handsome *palikari*, a young powerful man, a real hero with a dimple in his chin, cleft by Saint George, the same one who killed the dragon," she said. Maria, he was dreaming, would love them all, and they, her.

"Maria, think. Phenomenal luck. We'll stay in Greece, Mareeche dear, you'll see. We'll find a way to stay there. Never come back to this fucking place." He saw her wince, heard her suck in her breath at the suggestion of defection. She let go of his hand.

"*Za Boga*, Ivan, what are you saying? Quiet." She looked uneasily around the room. The waiter was passing by, delivering drinks to the next table, a cigarette butt hanging from his lips, the ashes dripping into the coffee cup.

He reached into his shirt pocket and handed her the brown envelope, his orders. She took it carefully, as if it were a piece of fragile china that could break in her hand, and placed it unopened on the table.

"I could never stay there."

"You could. Don't be crazy."

"I couldn't abandon my mother and father. The government would take away their jobs. Leave them without a pension as punishment for my defection. They'd die like dogs, Vasili with them." She was speaking low, insistently.

"Jesus, *Isuse Hriste*, Maria, what did you need with a Greek refugee? You could have done a lot better."

She could thank his grandfather for bringing him to Bulgaria. He had spent years seething about the

41

old man. It was not exactly true that his grandfather had actually brought him here. Only indirectly was the idiot responsible—hot-headed, dimwitted Giorgios Dimitriades, the communist. If his grandfather had possessed any sense at all, he wouldn't have gotten involved in this political group or that, but would have kept his nose to the grindstone like thousands of other Greeks, picking his tobacco, and continuing to raise his child in Greece, a free country that had a future.

He had upset Maria, was too quick with her. Let us just get to Greece. There we'll work things out. He couldn't say it, but Christ, weren't her parents old, almost finished? He and Maria had to look out for themselves, for their own future. Thank God they had no children. What a wise choice he made when they had married.

Now he was feeling ecstatic. The chance for defection washed over him as the first view of the sea strikes a man who has lived all his life on the plains—the vast, unending expanse of rolling water and sky, the sting of salt borne on the stiff breeze. God, what infinite possibility. Possibility. They shivered home through the expiring day, through the rain, or was it sleet? They teetered and slipped on the rime covering the snow's surface. Under their boots, the ice crunched.

"I'm scared," she said.

He put his arm around her shoulders.

Sleeping fitfully, they held each other all night. Once they tried to make love, but, nerves unstrung, he failed. Once he thought he heard her crying, but he wasn't sure. Early in the morning, they packed their suitcases. He tied the bulging bags securely with rope and heaved them up on the roof of the rattling bus, where the driver, complaining about the weight, made them secure. They climbed aboard for the short trip up the flanks of Mount Vitosha, for a week's goodbye visit to her mother and father. Maria had brought her workbooks, "Learning English."

Chapter 4

He waited and waited, watching his mother totter in her unwieldy boots down the steep slope away from the ski school, skis hoisted onto her shoulder. In the blinding light, it was hard to gauge how far away she had gone. He waited a few more minutes, and without a word to the instructor clamped on his skis and pushed off toward the chairlift.

"Hey, Freddy, where you going?" Timothy, son of the British Consul General, yelled after him.

"To find my brother, Roger," he hollered, not looking back.

"You're going to catch holy hell, Fred."

No fun at the ski school. O.K., maybe, for kids like Timothy who went to English boarding schools, but not for him. He'd join Roger on the slopes. The trail to the chairlift made a wide bend, and then descended at a steep angle. At first he felt stiff, slid sideways. Then he gathered too much speed and couldn't stop himself from hurtling downhill. After a bit he was managing to gain control by digging his ski edges into the snow, carving a neat series of one, two, three, four . . . eight snowplow turns. Gradually, his body was limbering up, and he bent into the hill, executing ten stem turns, a trick that he had mastered last winter in Yugoslavia.

Now he relaxed into a loose rhythm, floating as wings of snow opened in his wake. Into the rushing wind, he whistled the carol learned in his French class, *"Le divin enfant, jouez haut-bois. . . . le divin enfant, Chantons tous. . ."* On his eyelashes laces of ice formed; dozens of miniature rainbows shimmered before him. He moved through the expanding landscape as if he were flying, the world stretching out on all sides, endless.

The snow, driven by the wind, whirled in small tornadoes. Almost blinded by the white out, he was traveling ahead by dead reckoning, guessing that the starting point for the chairlift lay wherever this trail bottomed out. *"Comme il est beau, le divin enfant."* Wait. Where was he? The trail had flattened, but where was the chairlift? He listened hard for the hum of the generator. All he heard was squabbling from a flock of ravens, circling low over the carcass of an animal, the size of a donkey, bloated and rigid, sprawled in the snow. Above, on fir branches, two buzzards had lighted, one twisting its ugly head to the side as if listening for a distant call; the other spread its wings, preparing to take flight, then jerked its head, then carefully refolded them. The world was quite suddenly quiet—he stopped whistling—except for the cracking of the iced tree branches as they swayed.

He followed the barely visible path, made a detour to put space between him and the dead animal. He tried not to look, but his head turned toward it, to the row of white teeth and the open eye that stayed fixed like a piece of round, black glass in the gray head. In Greece, he knew, when a donkey got useless, they pushed it over a cliff or tethered it someplace to starve to death. The Bulgarians, he figured, probably did the same.

The ground gave way. Huge chunks of snow rolled out from under his skis. Wow! He was tumbling through space, all control gone. The snow piled on him in midair, glued to his eyelashes. He landed flat on his back, his left ski twisted backward under his right leg. Opening and shutting his mouth, frantic for air, he sat dazed, the breath knocked out of his chest. The loose snow continued to cascade from above, a light avalanche powdered him. When his breath returned, he pulled himself up, using his poles as crutches. His left ankle throbbed with pain, kept sliding out from under him.

He pushed forward. How could he stop here? He had to reach the end. To find the place. A place where he felt at home. His face prickled, his lungs burned. It hurt to breathe. At first when the tears trickled down, he fought them back. I shouldn't give in to crying, because if people saw me, I'd be ashamed. I'll whistle. But only a quaver came from his lips, which tasted sour, like blood. Still, there was really no reason why he couldn't cry— there was certainly no one to see him—and he cried out, his voice, unheard he knew by any living thing, drifting off into the white hills, where it faded. The noises he was making were senseless, totally without result, so he hushed. He was nowhere; lost in a land without signs, without markers, without trails, in another foreign place, this place now, the most foreign yet of all the foreign places he had ever been in his whole life. His body was heated by a flash of fury aimed at his parents, who had dragged him since birth to countries not his own. But the anger sank when he realized it was useless. He had to save his strength to keep moving. His sore ankle was puffing in his boot, the pain darting up to his knee, and his legs ached from his heavy equipment. His feet, blistering in several places, felt damp and sticky, probably bleeding.

He lost his balance and fell in the untracked snow. When he pulled himself up, the sky had darkened and the hills beyond turned to purple. The morning had passed into late afternoon.

Home. His grandmother's wooden house, smelling of must, mothballs, and something good like chocolate, where the family went every third summer on home leave: the spread of green lawn, the lobsters and clams, steamed Portuguese style, the watermelon, the sweet corn, the beach, the backyard with the lunch table under the pear tree rooted there some sixty years ago, the same welcoming neighbors he played with visit after visit, the weathered and warped screen door banging shut, yanked by a rusty spring, his grandmother bawling for the hundredth time, "You kids, please don't slam the screen door."

Roger climbed up a sparkling silver diving board as high as the clouds, sprang off against the sky, doing one, two, threefourfivesixseventen flips, perpetually flipping, never landing in the sea below, just Roger rotating ever downward. And his dad, sitting up straight, in the rear seat of a fire-engine red limousine, spinning in circles on the beach, its tires spraying sand, forming a huge dust storm that finally blocked out his father and the car except for the American flag fluttering on the front bumper. His mom and Catherine, standing on a rock in a meadow, a golden light playing all around them, their bodies wavering like luffed sails. They were humming a song he liked, but he could barely hear the melody, only the steady banging of the screen door. Against the skyline, in tall grass, a gray donkey leapt, stumbled, got up, stumbled again, its forelegs buckling, and sprawled on the ground. A mountain cat, face yellow and round like a grapefruit, loped across his path.

A soldier replaced the mountain lion. The man skied toward him, all in a blur: a soldier skiing on barrel staves, using two wooden sticks as poles. Freddy slumped in the snow. He felt strong arms around him, lifting him off the ground. The world went black.

Chapter 5

At the inn, Barbara rested in the lounge on the chair nearest the fire, her legs tingling as they defrosted, still exhilarated by her adventure of the morning. Two hours earlier, she'd been fooled into thinking, given the crawling pace of the chairlift and the shifting, obliterating mists, that she had never climbed to such an altitude. But Mount Vitosha was only some seven thousand feet high, meager compared to the German and French Alps, where she had skied in years gone by. The lift made two stops, in fact, but she had mistakenly expected only one. How could she know that owing to the treacherous visibility up there, no one ever got off as she did at the summit stop? There were no trail maps; the few crude signs in Cyrillic, nailed to trees, had been blurred, many of the letters obliterated. After an almost vertical ascent lasting about ten minutes, the lift stopped for the first time for just one second at a narrow, iced-over platform. The few passengers in front of her stumbled off into the vaporous heights before she realized they had actually exited at a station. As she rode past, she heard a voice yelling something, probably in English, but the message was unintelligible. Another ten minutes carried her to the terminal station. When the lift jerked to a halt, she, the lone passenger, sprang off.

Where in God's name was she? This was no longer earth, she thought, but Saturn, far from the sun, devoid of solid surface, made up entirely of atmosphere. On Saturn, if you descended, the light would fade as you fell. You'd continue to go down through the endless dark, and the pressure would become greater than at the ocean's floor. She hesitated to push off, fearing the failing light, the unbearable pressure. Courage, courage.

The descent, though, surprised her, taking her along a partially groomed trail, blazed with a black diamond, bringing her out of the mist into ever-brightening paths. Speeding through light, she existed in a place where life seemed limitless; she had never felt freer.

Now, this noon she was enjoying the embracing warmth of the fire, the stumps in the open hearth blazing, sending up a display of sparks with the force of a forest fire.

"Drink this delicious wine," said Louisa, "and you will come alive again. Crazy people to go out in such a weather." She threw her hands up in an elaborate gesture.

Barbara sipped from the steaming wine glass. She looked over at Louisa, who wore an après ski outfit, black with an abstract Nordic design traced in yellow and white on the sweater. The opera drifting over the loudspeaker was sung in Russian, by a deep-throated baritone and bass choir, punctuated by the lugubrious tolling of bells. *Boris Godunov*, she guessed.

"Bulgarians make splendid music. They do opera wonderfully. I cannot understand it. Strange, very strange, what a people can do and what they find impossible," Louisa said, her hand in the air beating time to the music. "Look there at him. Of course he does not represent the whole of the Bulgarian people. What you do you think he is capable of?"

The man, wearing large sunglasses, a shabby black suit textured with muted silver stripes, was sitting in perfect indolence, twirling his keys monotonously in his fingers, his gaze fixed on the tips of his pointed black shoes. He was luxuriating in a shaft of sun that beamed through a huge window. The nosepiece of his glasses was outlandish, shaped like some kind of bird, possibly an eagle.

"Capable of? Who is he? What would *you* say he's capable of?"

"Almost anything, I assure you. Such a man does not deserve such a stupendous ray of sun to rest in. He is sitting in a seat meant for the gods. For Apollo himself. *Testa di capra*," Louisa said.

"Louisa, we shouldn't be too critical."

"You don't remember something. I'll tell you, my innocent American friend. They put him on our bus at the airport last night. He is here for one task only. To watch us."

"I don't doubt it. They do that in all the bloc countries. It's smart of you to notice him, though."

"I tell you something else, my innocent friend. They know we are not tourists, that our passports are jokes, and that is why I say he is capable of much. He is not the simple Intourist guide. He is special. For us," Louisa said.

Barbara related how last year there were two Intourist men assigned to watch their ski party in Yugoslavia. But by evening they were all drinking together, and Robert with others of their party got the agents drunk on the vinegary slivovitz they guzzle around Tetovon, right by the Albanian border.

"Those people are clowns," Louisa said. "You are careless. Americans need care with everyone. These people don't care about Italians, you know. I could do anything and they don't pay close attention. They watch first Americans, in the next minute they seek the British, and next the French. Italians, they pass by like we are shadows. You noticed in the passport line, they see I am an Italian citizen, they asked me a few questions, and they let me pass easy. If you came through with many such stamps from the bloc countries in your passport as I have. . ." She ran her index finger across her throat and grimaced. "These poor devils. They have not eyes to see, no, . . . *niente*," and she tapped her index finger to her temple. "These Balkan people, they are all trouble. *Bestia*," she said, forming the *B* as if she were spitting. Then in an unnaturally soft voice, strangled with anger, Louisa told how members of her family had been murdered by the Yugoslavs. After World War II, when the United Nations divided Trieste into two zones, the port of Trieste went to Italy, but the hinterland, a fertile area with large farms, where her father and his brothers had holdings, was handed over to Yugoslavia. "We had magnificent farms on estates with their own chapels and gardens, and oh, you should have seen the houses. The communists came one day, when the family had the bad luck to all be gathered in one place. The brutes seized our land and murdered the men. They put my father's and uncle's heads on pikes, jeering, left them to rot for days, a warning to other landowners to submit."

Dizzy from the wine and sickened by Louisa's story, she was passing beyond mellowness, into a headachy, post-euphoric state. Outside, in the cold, an old charwoman was washing windows with a ragged cloth, warming bare, chapped hands under her armpits after every stroke. Barbara watched the door, waiting for the children. Freddy's ski classes should have ended a half hour ago.

After a few appropriate words to Louisa, she excused herself and went upstairs to her room to take a couple of aspirin. The beds had been made, the towels picked up, the bathroom cleaned. The magazine lay exactly where she had left it. Sitting on the bed, she opened the pages and flipped through: first, an interview with auteur François Truffaut, focusing on his latest film; second, an article written by Madame de Gaulle's former maid, claiming "to tell all." Next she glanced at a review of the new production of Gounod's *Faust* at the Paris Opera, then, a story about France's Olympic ski team. Last was a piece by Prince Michael of Greece, an historian, describing the ins and outs of the sultan's harem, displaying a photograph of the urbane Greek prince. An engraving of a sultan being served by a half-dozen fleshy nude concubines was sure to titillate. She turned to the cover, an innocent photo of a French ski team at practice, the snowcapped tip of Mont Blanc in the background, and then held a few pages, one by one, up to the light. Nothing. With a kind of dread, she shoved the magazine aside; it slid to the floor.

Outside, the skiers were making their way back to their hotels for the midday meal. Freddy should be back in their lodge by now. Picking up the magazine, she repositioned it carefully on the night table with the books, and returned to the lounge. When she did not see the children, she went in search of Louisa to ask if she had seen them drift in.

Louisa was seated at the piano in the far corner of the lounge.

"Be calm. I play you some music. If the children don't come, we will go to the desk." Louisa began to move her fingers randomly up and down the keys, then coaxed out a melody, and sang a scale, the voice and the instrument shaping the first notes of an aria. Barbara picked out the piece immediately, *Vissi d'arte, vissi d'amore* from *Tosca*.

Louisa sang the first few lines softly, noted the expression of pleasure and recognition on her friend's face, and nodded to her to sing along. "*Non feci mai male ad anima viva.*" — I never did harm to a living soul. As she listened to Louisa's dusky soprano, she knew it to be a superbly trained operatic voice; the notes soared above the twang of the ill-tuned piano and vibrated in the air.

When they finished the aria, she thanked Louisa, congratulated her on her marvelous voice. The skiers, who had created a hubbub in the lounge as they passed through to the dining room, had ceased filtering in, and were now seated for the midday meal. The activity in the lounge had altogether stilled. In the sudden almost funereal hush it struck her: Freddy is lost. She hurried to the desk clerk, who was idly smoking at his table where he had stacked stubs of pencils, a ledger and a pile of manila files.

"The ski school, does it finish every day at the same time?"

"Yes, yes, Madame. Same time."

"My boy went to ski lessons. He should have been here more than half an hour ago."

"Don't worry, Madame. Everything O.K. Boys are playful." His face was vacuous like the faces of the stewards on the airplane and he exhaled a succession of smoke rings. The rings floated toward the photograph of Zhivkov tacked on the wall next to a Bulgarian flag.

"Do you have a phone to call the ski school?" "No. No phone to there. Such small distance. Not even kilometer."

"Do you have a vehicle? I need to go there immediately. My son is missing."

"Don't worry. I assure you, Madame," he said, placing his hand on his heart. "We have fine ski patrol. Good men."

"Mom," came Catherine's voice across the hall as she ran through the entrance door into the inn. "Thank God you're O.K. Why did you go all the way to the ski lift terminal? No one goes there. You always go beyond where people aren't supposed to. I yelled at you to get off at the first station. Didn't you hear me? How the heck did you get down?"

"Freddy's not back. I'm going up to the ski school. Where's Roger?" By now her voice was choked from forcing back tears.

The door opened and Roger, his face scraped, went over to her, patting his bruise with a handkerchief stained with blood.

"This place is packed with ice. Boy, did I take a fall."

The clerk sat at his desk, mesmerized by his smoke rings.

She told Roger to go up to the ski school and find Freddy. She turned to Catherine. "We should never have come here. Never. They have no resources if anyone gets hurt. Not a single telephone. I made a terrible decision." She realized she was jabbering, and made an effort to quiet herself. She'd wait with at least a modicum of dignity until Roger came back. Of course, Freddy would be in tow. Of course. Hadn't the kids disappeared before? How many times had she and Robert paced the floor, pressed their faces against windowpanes, looked to lowering hills, across squalling lakes, into tangled woods, only to have them return with a wild tale: "Mom, Dad, we had the neatest time. Guess what happened . . .?"

And she herself was such a wanderer. Even when she was little, she'd stray from her neighborhood along the cobblestones down to the wharves, where she could feel the pulse of the sea, where the ferries departed from New Bedford for Cuttyhunk or Martha's Vineyard or Nantucket, and the fishing trawlers with women's names like *Hope Ann* or *Ernestina* or Portuguese names like *Infanta, Açor,* or *São Miquel* headed for Georges Banks. Even the skiffs, propelled by outboards, putting a few miles across the river to Fairhaven, excited her. Weren't they crossing to another shore? The smells of tar, and gas, and fish, and seaweed, and salt water were intoxicating, the exotic odors of another world. Her parents drove down to the docks in the car -"My God, can't you stay put in the neighborhood? Why do you roam down here to these stinking piers?" Frightened not at all by the fishermen swearing and drinking—sometimes fights broke out—she remained there till day's end, adoring the excitement of it all. And summers at the family camp in Vermont, she'd paddle the canoe into the evening hours, traveling freely along the inky water, returning home in the dark to the barely contained hysteria of her parents, until one night her father splintered her paddles on a rock.

Roger came back without Freddy. His bruise had turned blue in the cold. "Mom, I just came back to tell you I'm on my way to find the ski patrol."

The desk clerk motioned to the man who had been sitting in the shaft of sun wearing the absurd sunglasses. "Eh, Svetlozar. Come here." The man shambled over; he and the clerk spoke in Bulgarian. She picked out a few phrases—"*ima vreme*," —plenty of time—enraged her.

The man took off his glasses and turned to Barbara. "I am Svetlozar, guide from Intourist here to help. Do not worry about your son. Intourist inspector will come by in car sometime later. I tell him, and we drive to ski patrol house to report your son." He spoke English with a thick accent.

"Look here. We can't wait till sometime later. The child is already late by almost an hour," she said, her voice rising. "You don't seem to see how serious this is. Jesus Christ Almighty. What a place." She was stumbling toward the door, but Catherine held her by the arm and Louisa brought her a bowl of soup from the dining room.

"There is an Italian proverb," said Louisa: "*con moneta e ceppi seechi, si puo accendere il fuoco sull'acqua.* In English, goes something like this: with money and dry twigs you can light a fire on the water." She reached into her purse and handed Svetlozar two fistsful of levs and stotinkies.

"Get help," she ordered. "Now." Her soprano had plummeted to the mezzo range.

He pocketed the money in one snappy sleight of hand. Before he could get on his way, a policeman entered, looked confusedly around the tourist lodge as if he had been dropped into a big city and couldn't find his way. After viewing all the startling luxury, the lounge, the bar, the entrance to the dining room, the outsized, plush, purple couches, the great window, where the sun was now failing, he headed for the desk to confer with the desk clerk. The clerk beckoned to Barbara, his hands fluttering in the air like bats.

Chapter 6

The village was raw, unhealed, like grief: a dozen or so two-story stone houses topped by red tile roofs huddled together, seeking comfort from each other; a tavern, palely lit by a bulb or two against the descending night; a crumbling church, its doors gone and its window frames blank, the gold cross on the dome askew; the road, two ruts sunk in the mud. A bony hound, eyes glinting, barked once, and slunk behind the houses, whining like a child. Chickens straggled across the sweep of the headlights.

The duty sergeant stopped the jeep in the middle of the road and Barbara and he got out. They climbed the flight of stairs to a wooden porch in the traditional style of village houses. The sergeant entered through the narrow door without knocking, motioning her to follow. The room was a like a cave with candle light flickering on the low ceiling. From logs of burning pine came the pungent smell of resin. In front of a fireplace she saw Freddy, buried in a pile of wool blankets, the firelight playing over his face. A doctor, a stethoscope around his neck, one hand on Freddy's wrist, was looking at his watch.

Running to her son, she placed her hands on his face, noting his eyes, bright and clear, felt his cool head, ran her hands under the blankets to touch his arms, his hands, his fingers, his chest, his stomach, his thighs, his legs, his feet. To ward off evil spirits, someone had pinned a blue bead to his shirt.

"Mom, I want to go home," Freddy whispered, grabbing her hand.

His lips and nose were badly chapped, blood had coagulated in the cracks, his voice choked and she knew that for the first time in years he was going to cry. She held him in her arms, rocking him like a baby, murmuring thanks to him, to fate, to the kind, newly reborn world.

She asked the doctor what languages he spoke. He smiled, shrugged his shoulders, "*Bien, bien, gut,*" pointing to Freddy.

"Can you walk? Does anything hurt?"

"What do you think, Mom? Everything hurts. My ankle is killing me." He tried to push the heavy blankets off and stand up, but fell back. He reached up and pulled her head down close to his mouth. In her ear, he said, "These people, that army officer over there especially, were so nice to me. I know they're communists, but still, thank them."

"What army officer? How on earth did you meet an army officer?" She peered into the shadows at the back of the room, where a few people were clustered, apparently around a table.

A man advanced from the dimness.

"How do you do, Madame. I am Ivan Dimitrov, Colonel, Bulgarian Army."

She was surprised to hear him speak such clear English, although his accent was thick.

"Oh, good. You speak English, Colonel. Did you talk with the doctor?"

"The doctor says Freddy is sick from the exposure. Nearly frostbite. Only damage, sprained ankle, bad blisters on feet and exhaustion." He moved to the boy's side and stroked his shoulder. "The doctor does not want Freddy to go out until morning, his ankle should have cold compresses all night, and you are welcome to spend the night here right with us in the in-laws' house next to your son." The sergeant would return in the morning to drive them back to the hotel.

She agreed.

"Mom, that's the army guy I mean. He's the one who carried me for miles over the snow, like Dad would. He slipped and fell lots, but somehow he never let me touch ground." Freddy's voice was hoarse. "Thank him."

The Colonel explained how he had come across Freddy half-frozen lying in the snow.

A woman, carrying two mugs of tea smelling of wild chamomile, and a white dish heaped with pieces of bread, cheese and dried fruit, offered them to Freddy and Barbara.

"My wife, Maria," said the Colonel. "Unfortunately she speaks only little English. But she is trying to learn. If you speak German, she understands but can speak very little." He explained that Maria was a biologist and that Bulgarian scientists learned German in school.

"We," the wife said to her in English, hesitating to find the next word, "talk. You, me."

The wife was a confident woman, with an arresting face, her features marked by an oriental cast, something around the eyes, the nose.

61

"You are nice to show us this hospitality. My son wants me to thank you for everything you've done for him. We are both extremely grateful."

The doctor pointed to the black, steaming tea and thick bread and to Freddy and signaled her to feed him; he gulped the tea down, lay back on his blankets, and took her hand again.

The wife's mother, toothless, earnest, her face slightly purpled as if she had been frostbitten every day of her life, laid a supper of thick peasant soup, hard boiled eggs, bread, and wine from a barrel, extending a ritualized hospitality to the strangers. The table, the old, low *sofra*, was set with an immaculate white, embroidered tablecloth, probably from the old woman's dowry, and three smoking candles smelling of rancid tallow. On the wall hung the *iconostasis*, the icon of some Orthodox saint set in tarnished silver. They sat on the traditional three-legged stools. Barbara asked about the customs of people in this part of Bulgaria.

The Colonel translated back and forth for all of them. His wife's parents, he explained, had worked the unyielding land on the side of the mountain for all their lives until the ski resort had opened a few years ago. Now they had a better living, she taken on in the kitchen, he as handyman. Or at least they didn't have to work so hard for what they got. The father, deaf from an air raid in 1943 when the Allies bombed Sofia, watched everyone's lips raptly, even hers although he didn't know a word of English.

The parents, she noticed, had aged like olive trees, bent and gnarled. Their prewar lot: the perilous birthings at the mercy of unclean and superstitious midwives, or worse still, the birthings in the fields followed by an immediate return to work, a barbarity that caused hysteria; the swaddling of infants that produced skin ulcers; the colds that turned into pneumonia and death; the Balkan wars and the two world wars from which men returned without a hand, minus a foot, face scars from shrapnel twisting their features until they were no less than monsters. Malaria and droughts in the summer, cloying mud in the spring thaw, frostbite in the winter. The contrast to her own parents, straight and svelte, probably very close in age to these wasted people, jarred her.

The Colonel then related how he had carried Freddy here, gone for the village doctor and ordered the local policeman to go to the hotel to report finding an American boy and to arrange for transportation to fetch the parents. Freddy, half asleep, half waking, chimed in from his spot by the fire, "And when Colonel Dimitrov came, I couldn't believe it was really somebody to help me. I thought he was part of my dream. Like the wild cat."

"He is a very brave fellow, your little boy. I would choose him to play on my soccer team, anytime."

She was studying the Bulgarian officer as he talked. His fluent English, accented, had a pronounced Slavic intonation, the language of a man who had probably not been much exposed to an English speaking society. Stone-faced, he was like an expressionless Indian character you'd see in a crude cowboy movie. His smile was tentative; his lips turned slightly up, but his deep-set green eyes remained serious, so if he bore any real expression at all, it was conflicting. His teeth flashed with gold fillings and caps. His chin was cleft, lending to his face a note of strength, and also, she thought, making him quite attractive. He had a habit of pushing his fingers through his black wiry hair, trying to tame it. People from the bloc, especially the Russians, were apt to serve anywhere in any capacity. A cook at the Russian Embassy in Washington, she knew for a fact, showed up in Paris once as a political officer, and she'd heard the story of a wife, acting at one time as a secretary in London, who turned up later as another man's non-working wife in Bonn. Maybe he had served abroad, where English was the *lingua franca* among foreign diplomats.

She avoided asking him any personal questions.

Maria pointed to herself and then to her husband. "Athens."

"We are assigned to Athens. I am to go as military attaché to the Bulgarian Embassy," he explained.

She started. Bulgarian Intelligence, then, for sure, since he's been assigned as an attaché. She was finding it hard to breathe. No ventilation. No doubt the burning pine logs had eaten up all the oxygen. She took a deep breath and asked for a glass of cold water. "You'll enjoy life there, it's truly a wonderful place to live," she managed.

The Greeks and Bulgarians had slaughtered each other for centuries, she well knew, in their struggle to claim lands, particularly Macedonia, that they both believed belonged to them. The descent of the Iron Curtain between them had simply put another spike in their thorny history, but had not changed the basic narrative. What would be the couple's vision of life in Greece? Blinded by Russian propaganda, they were sure to have a negative, distorted view.

"I have no doubt that we will be pleased living in Athens," he responded.

"Freddy told me your husband is in the American Embassy there."

"Yes."

"Ask her," Maria said, "what she does during the day, if she works at the American Embassy with her husband? What's her profession?"

She understood enough Bulgarian to catch the gist of the wife's questions.

He faced Barbara and asked her what the climate was like in Athens, the Peloponnese and Central Greece, and gave those answers to his wife. For the slightest moment Maria seemed not to understand and was bewildered that her husband had not pursued her questions, but she quickly recovered and lowered her eyes, embarrassed at her indiscretion.

Barbara caught the ruse. She felt sorry for the gracious woman; her questions had not after all been so indiscreet that her husband had to conceal them. "Maria, you're a scientist. What an accomplishment. In the United States we've few woman scientists. I'm an historian. I study the history of this part of the world."

The Colonel raised his glass in a toast to friendship and hospitality, first in Bulgarian then in English, obviously a traditional welcome to strangers. She knew he was watching her attentively, but with solemn neutrality, betraying no overt curiosity. His green eyes, shaded by the thick lashes, were flecked by the candlelight. His eyes asked no questions, they didn't insinuate, they didn't menace, they didn't reveal, but she suspected they were calculating, at times brooding, under the deep brow.

Since Americans possessed no such ritual toasts, she returned his sentiment by expressing her gratitude and that of her husband for his saving their child and promising to find a way in some small measure to repay their enormous debt to him. She tried not to make her curiosity obvious, catching glimpses of him as best she could, but she had seen enough. Almost. When she arrived back in Athens, she would, in a report, describe him as alert, guarded, intelligent, with a dash of charm, obviously capable of acts of kindness, smart enough to be dangerous. Still, there was another quality, something quicksilver, something she could not define— a defensiveness, a characteristic of the hunted.

After dinner, she lay on the mattress they had placed on the floor by the fire for Freddy and her.

"I want to go home," he said. "I want Dad."

"We'll be going home in a few days."

"No, I mean really home. To the States. When I was lost in the snow I heard the screen . . . "

"What do you mean?" She paused. What did he mean? "Grandma's screen door?" Her question had come too late. He had fallen into a deep sleep. From his throat came the rattle of a light snore. Of course she knew exactly what screen door, the one with its rusted spring shrilling its own unique welcome. His calling up that image of her mother's back door pierced her. She knew that he had been petrified, could have frozen to death on an icy ledge alone in a foreign country, while she — transported, selfish — was having the time of her life, skiing on a mountaintop in Bulgaria. Her guilt filled her with self-revulsion.

The other two children back at the lodge under Louisa's shrewd and watchful eyes would be well supervised. For the first time since noon she remembered the magazine. Certainly no one would touch the pile of books on the night table. Although Catherine could read Greek, Kazantzakis' colloquial dialogue in *Zorba* would discourage her; nor did she have the mature traveler's curiosity about Bulgaria to glance at the pictures of monasteries and museums in the guidebook, or at the book on Bulgarian grammar. As for *Paris-Match,* well, there was a danger. Catherine loved to read French and she devoured *Elle.* Would she pick it up, leaf through it and toss it aside carelessly?

The end of the first full day in Bulgaria; it seemed to have endured a lifetime. Freddy was safe, thank God. In eight hours or so they would be reinstalled in the lodge. Her story, when she got back to Athens, would be incredible; what a position to be in, lodged in the home of a Bulgarian intelligence officer. How many American officials had slept in the house of a Bulgarian army officer? They met members of the bloc at cocktail parties or formal dinners, they elicited what they could, they reported every conversation if it included anything but pleasantries, and sometimes they even reported the pleasantries. They had to have permission to lunch with them, had to report every one-on-one meeting with them. They invited them to their homes for intimate gatherings only if they suspected that they wanted to defect, and then the gatherings were strategically planned with exactly the right CIA agents in attendance. Franklin, in his wildest leap of imagination, could never have envisioned this scene.

She moved closer to Freddy, whose body was comfortably warm, his breathing still calm, rhythmic, heavy. Freddy was back, alive, safe. Dimitrov had earned some real capital, although, she realized, he wouldn't have used that expression. No matter how either of them might have expressed it, she had fallen forever in debt to this Bulgarian officer with the still face. She began to think about the concept of gratitude. What did it entail? What and exactly how much did you owe to the person who saved your son's life? All types of measurements became redundant against the enormity of this debt. And even beyond the matter of definition loomed the awesome questions, the imponderables: what play of luck, what act of God put the Bulgarian officer on the path toward Freddy at that exact moment? A randomness? How did that fit the concept of gratitude?

Kyrie Eleison. She ought to go to a dark, gold-glittering, incense-drenched Orthodox church to kiss the icons, light dozens of beeswax candles and make the sign of the cross, even though she hadn't attended her own church in over twenty years because she didn't believe: *sto onoma tou patera kai tou yiou . . .kyrie eleison . God have mercy.* She remembered that when she was a girl, just introduced to Latin in school, caught up in the fascination of learning a foreign language, she had invented words. One that she still recalled, she'd coined from the Latin *merces*; it expressed thanks. She whispered her old word, like a benediction, in the stilled room.

Chapter 7

The next morning, they drove to the lodge together in a jeep, he sitting up front with the driver, the boy buried under blankets next to his mother in the back. The jeep climbed up the mountain on a narrow road, careening along the curves, jostling the mother and the boy, who had buried his head in her lap. For the moment, Ivan preferred this arrangement: to talk to the woman without facing her, although depending on the angle of the sun, he could glimpse her form reflected in the windshield.

In the intimacy of the jeep—Freddy asleep, the driver unable to understand English—he could finally approach her. But how? Last evening when he introduced himself, he couldn't decide whether to kiss her hand in the European way, or shake it in the British way. All he knew about Americans was the propaganda the Russians taught at Intelligence School: Americans were greedy, materialistic, devious, competitive, aggressive, and all the rest. In class they had shown pictures and maps of population centers—aerial photos and movies of New York, incredible silver skyscrapers with needles atop their roofs and canyons of streets crammed with automobiles, trucks, buses; road maps of Los Angeles, the network of roads from the city center sprawling for kilometer after kilometer toward the suburbs, or the mountains or the ocean or the desert; black and white sketches of Washington and its suburbs, or the strategic military centers circled in red. But they never taught what American women were like. The broad categories— imperialist, aggressive, degenerate and so forth—had never seemed more absurd.

First he'd try a few pleasantries.

"Do you like our country?"

"I've only been here a few days. But your country seems lovely."

"Yes, very picturesque. The countryside is splendid. How many days will you spend here?"

The jeep swerved to the right, skidded on a patch of ice, barely missing the stand of beech trees that descended to the side of the road. In the morning light slatting through the trees, the woman's face flashed across the windshield. She did not belong in this battered jeep, he thought.

"Not long, just a few more days."

"Maria and I look forward to seeing you in Athens. No doubt we can find you easily at your embassy."

He caught her slight hesitation and vague answer.

"Easily. Our names and my husband's telephone number are listed in *Corps diplomatique d'Athènes*, the official handbook the Greek government will issue you when you arrive on station."

He ordered the driver, a huge man who grasped the wheel with grease-stained hands, to slow down. Their voices were almost drowned by the muffler's roar and the wind's whine as it blew through the shredded canvas that enclosed the jeep.

"We must have a reunion." He made an effort to smile, and swiveled in his seat to pat the boy, who was still smothered under his blankets.

"By all means. We'll meet often at the cocktail parties, dinners, national day celebrations. There's no end to them. Many are boring."

They were passing a wayside tavern; he told the driver to stop. The brakes squealed, metal grinding against metal, fumes of burning rubber came up from the floor boards. "Do you want a hot tea for the boy? Might help him to be warm. And maybe something for you?"

No, she didn't want a thing. She pulled the blankets back from the boy's face; he moaned that his leg was cold from the compresses; she seemed anxious to move on. Ivan calculated that at their present pace they'd arrive at the lodge in a half hour. Too fast. Much too fast.

In the tavern he bought sunflower seeds, taking his time getting out the coins. He asked for the toilet and ambled back to where the waiter pointed, and when he had killed as much time as he could, he strolled out to the jeep. He looked up at the cloudless sky, where a striped kite was mounting, tugging at its string, struggling to be free of it, when suddenly, caught in one of the powerful down drafts that swirled around the mountain, the paper bird dove helplessly toward earth.

He stepped up into the jeep. She was sitting back against her seat, her head in profile, squinting at the landscape, absently patting her son's head. Now, he judged was the time.

"I speak Greek, you know."

"No, I didn't know. How's that?" Her eyes rested on him now.

He had done that just right. Just right. He motioned the driver to get going, and turned in his seat to face her.

She was giving him her full attention now, sitting straight up. She placed her hands on the back of the driver's seat: they looked soft, smooth, ivory, her fingers tapered and manicured, her thin wrist decorated by a narrow gold bracelet. He noticed these details for the first time; last evening he had been so fixed on how he was presenting himself that he hadn't taken a good look at her, had missed the delicacy of her face, an amazing fragility that he had never seen in Bulgarian women. Yet the face wasn't weak; each feature was pronounced—he noted her defined chin, finely but fully drawn, her lips slightly painted, dainty, vulnerable. Her expression seemed bland, yet was it? Her teeth were perfectly straight and white, her skin unblemished, her clothes, although she'd slept in them, unwrinkled, her boots were of fine tan leather. Her hair, all silken and brushed, framed her face as if someone had spent time cutting it and arranging it just so. She had an easy smile and the untroubled slate-gray eyes of someone who had never faced cruelty and hunger, never been eaten by rage. A tingle started in his scalp, ran across his shoulders and down his spine. She reeked of luxury, like a well-cared-for English horse, impeccably groomed. Unmistakably, he concluded, she reeked of the West.

She moved uneasily in her seat, straightened her jacket around her, moistened her lips, signs, he realized, of discomfort, feeling herself under his scrutiny. Better return to my story before she loses patience with me. He tried to smile again.

72

How much had she read about recent Greek history? Anyone that had read anything about it knew that after the population exchanges at the end of World War I, there were no Greeks left in Bulgaria. She probably was aware that the only Greeks living in Bulgaria today were Greek communists who had fled Greece toward the end of the civil war in the late 1940s, or children who were kidnapped by communists from northern Greece during the same period and carried over the border to be indoctrinated, the plan being to send the youths back to Greece with the mission of subverting capitalism.

"I am Greek." He handed her and the driver the tiny white paper cones of sunflower seeds. He cracked a nut open with his teeth, spat the shells on the floor, and waited.

After a moment she spoke. "That puts you in a real minority."

"I'm from the people that came here at the end of the Greek civil war. My grandfather, a communist who fought with ELAS, took my mother and escaped into Bulgaria in 1949. My grandmother had been killed earlier by government troops when they raided our village in Thrace."

She sat back in her seat and began again to stroke Freddy's forehead, as if she were considering, he feared, disengaging from the conversation, as if they had already exchanged too much. But no.

Her eyes widened with curiosity. "I am amazed you're being posted to Greece."

The driver had sped up again. "Slow down," he ordered.

73

"You are thinking that the Bulgarians can't trust me because I'm really Greek, and the Greeks can't trust me because I grew up in Bulgaria." He laughed when he said this to make a mockery of the truth, to bring the riddle out in the open where the light could get at it, to dispel the shadows that were probably gathering around him as she began to contemplate who he actually was. What he didn't say, couldn't possibly make a joke about, was that if the Greeks couldn't trust him, then the Americans might not trust him either. He was watching her carefully, calculating how far he needed to go to enlist her sympathy.

"Of course, my mother was no communist; she was only a girl, fleeing along with her father. He had come to Greece in 1922 with a million Greek refugees from Asia Minor, when the Turks put fire to Smyrna. He barely escaped and only with his life from the massacre at the hands of the Turks. This is complicated, but you seem to know something about our history."

She reminded him that she was an historian of modern Greece, that every student of Greece knew about the holocaust in Asia Minor. "Tell me more of your family's story." Her face seemed attentive.

He spat out a mouthful of shells on the floor and angrily told the driver to slow down on the curves, that the Americans in the back seat were getting carsick. The driver, annoyed, tugged his moth-eaten fur hat lower over his ears.

He told her how in 1922, when his grandfather, Giorgios Dimitriades, arrived in Greece, he had been settled by the refugee commission in northern Greece to work in Xanthi in the tobacco fields. When the German occupation began in 1941, he joined the Greek resistance, and when the Germans withdrew in 1944, he immediately joined the leftist guerrillas, who were fighting against the nationalist forces "to make a communist state, you know, a heaven on earth, in Greece." With the last several words he allowed himself a hint of sarcasm. In 1947, in keeping with the Truman Doctrine, the Americans were supporting the nationalists, as she no doubt knew, and then and there the tide turned against the left. By that time, Giorgios Dimitriades had too many murders to his account, had slit too many villagers' throats with the tops of tin cans. Should he have told her that hideous fact? Surely as an historian of the Greek civil war period, she'd know all the horrors.

"My Pappou—Grandfather—found it wise to take his daughter, my mother, over the border to the communist paradise." He made a clucking sound with his tongue. "He never reached Bulgaria. He died on the way of an old stomach wound, or tetanus, or a knife stab, as the victim of a grudge, depending on which of his Greek cronies told the story. My mother survived the odyssey. She arrived in Bulgaria pregnant from a boy she had been with on the hike across the mountains."

He noted that her eyes remained fixed on him, so he continued. The boy, Ioannis, tubercular, did not survive, either. They stuffed his dead body in a crevice to hide it from wild birds and animals and walked on; it was this ultimate indecency that tormented the refugees, an agony that tore at them for the rest of their lives—that they could not bury their dead, especially their parents and children, in that impenetrable frozen earth,

He withheld a crucial detail, the recurring dream that had ruined his sleep from the time he was an adolescent.

He was marching with his mother and the boy, Ioannis (always, he thought of him as the boy, Ioannis, never as his father), across the snow-covered crags, their feet raw with chilblains, dripping spots of blood on the snow. Chasing them from behind were the Greek nationalists, pounding them with rifle butts, trying to shove them over the sides of the mountains, and in front the Bulgarians, *vavari,* pointing guns in their faces, every once in a while pulling the trigger to decapitate one of them. Often at four o'clock in the morning, he'd wake, suffering from a sharp gnawing in the pit of his stomach from an imagined hunger, a hunger that could not be fed.

He had never told Maria about the dream, or given her the reason for his waking in the middle of the night a sweating mess. A man could not easily relate such a weakness to anyone, not his wife, not a relative, no one. After his mother died, and he understood what it meant to suffer loss, he wondered for the first time if she had ever grieved for Ioannis. Probably not; grieving would have been too much of a luxury for her, she who had one pair of shoes, which she stuffed with paper in the winter against the snow, and no coat, only one black wool shawl to stop the bitter wind. Only he had grieved for that Ioannis, he, an undefended boy, whose mother spoke Bulgarian with such a Greek accent she could barely be understood. If it hadn't been for the support of the Greek community, he and his mother would have starved to death.

Who could you tell such a story to? Not the American woman, not anyone.

As it was, he suspected he had told the American woman too much, continuing, probably, way beyond his purpose. "I was given" — he decided to bring the story to an end — "the Bulgarian, Ivan, for Ioannis, after my dead father, and for a family name, they gave me my mother's, Dimitriadis, which in Bulgarian translates as Dimitrov."

The boy, his head in his mother's lap, began to stir. "Where are we? I don't know where we are."

"We are on our way to the lodge," his mother answered. "Do you want some sunflower seeds?" The boy sat up and taking the paper cone he began chewing on the nuts, leaning against her shoulder and swinging his good leg in a spurt of energy. She tilted her head down until her lips rested on his forehead, her brown hair tumbling across her face, like silk.

The jeep slowed to a crawl. The driver cursed and told him that the radiator had overheated again.

"Overheated? Shit, Zhelev, that's bad news, it's freezing out here. Those two passengers will freeze to death."

The driver got out, spat twice into his palms, and with his burly arms yanked up the hood as if he wanted to rip it loose from the chassis.

"Sorry about this Cadillac," Ivan said, pointing at the jeep. "Russian-made vehicle. Never any spare parts. Our world halts every second because of no spare parts. Heaven is where spare nuts and bolts, washers and gaskets, radiator caps and mufflers float through the sky instead of angels."

"In Athens we suffer from that problem, too."

He was delighted to see her expression change, the corners of her lips turn up. He jumped out to help the driver, who had poured water into the radiator from a goatskin container. They took turns trying to screw the bent and dented radiator cap back on, then together in a combined forceful effort they yanked the protesting hood closed.

The jeep, brought back to life, rattled on its way again. She was growing chilled and pulled a corner of the boy's blanket to cover her chest. " I find the story fascinating. I've done a lot of research on the Greek refugees." She asked to hear the rest.

"When I was nineteen, just beginning my service in the army, my mother married a Bulgarian, a good man, a violinist with the Bulgarian Symphony, a marriage that in official government eyes, made her and me bona fide Bulgarian citizens. A miserable childhood, but as I said, the Greek community stuck together, helped each other, unbelievable what one person did for the sake of the other. Yet, we pay a big price back in Greece because of Pappou's politics. The Greek government counts us as trouble, forever made rotten by communist ideology. As you know, they refused to repatriate us until a few years ago. Even now we. . . ."

The jeep was speeding up again, the driver bearing down, afraid if he slowed, the motor would overheat, and so Ivan let him drive as he wanted. The trip was over anyway; the American woman was now the keeper of his story. What she chose to do with it was a serious matter. "Be courteous and good to strangers, but do not trust them till they are once again upon their way," went a Bulgarian proverb he had heard all his life. He would add, "And even then beware; no one can ever know the motives of another person, not even those closest to us, let alone a perfect stranger's."

The lodge swung into view. He wrapped Freddy tightly in his blankets and, following the American woman, carried him through the lounge up the stairs to his room, and laid him on one of the beds. The boy thanked him and sprang from the bed, energetic now, and hobbling on his bound ankle into the corridor, he called, "Roger, hey Roger, where are you? I'm back."

She was standing in the middle of the bedroom. A swinging light bulb, set into motion by the boy's activity was inscribing dim circles across her body. How with the meager hips, the long, slight legs, the thin shoulders, all like bird bones, had she borne three children, and nursed them with those small breasts? Thank God for Bulgarian women with their broad pelvises, wide hips, muscular legs, women you could mount, ride, without breaking their bones. Still, she must have her own kind of durability, a kind of pale strength he knew nothing about. What would she feel like if he touched her? The light revealed rings under her eyes, and fine lines drawn around her mouth like parentheses. She looked a bit older now than he had noted before, but so well kempt that in fact she seemed ageless. The tingling came back again, traveled from his head to his back and stopped at the bottom of his spine. No, he didn't want her, that was not it, he was sure he didn't want her. It was something else, something akin to wanting, some other sensation that he couldn't explain.

She frowned slightly when she realized he was staring at her. "Are you leaving, Colonel?" In fact she was dismissing him, not in annoyance, he thought, but in a businesslike way, as if they had finished part of a transaction. When he held out his hand and felt her fingers slide across his palm, all of his senses seemed to rush to his right hand.

"I will be back again tomorrow to see if I can be of service. Yes, *avrio*," he repeated in Greek. He put on his cap and turned to leave.

"*Nai, avrio*," she smiled. "I am so full of gratitude. I can't ever thank you enough." Her voice had a softness to it, an evenness, something he liked, something he couldn't exactly express.

He took in her words, marking them well, and glanced back over his shoulder to fathom her expression. He could trust her. Yes, he could definitely trust her. To the list of three people he could trust in the whole world— Maria and Vasili, and a fellow officer, Rusinov—would he be crazy to add her as the fourth? Her? Through much of the night, he heard her speak of gratitude, as he lay awake, and even in his dreams.

Chapter 8

After depositing the Americans at their lodge, he drove to his office in Sofia. Carefully but quickly he wrote a report on his contact with the American woman and child and delivered it to his superior. By dawn, the Americans had become the focus of gossip throughout the village, and no doubt the story had gurgled down the side of the mountain, cutting through the neighboring villages like a babbling stream. Of course he had to account for having them stay with his in-laws and delivering them back to the inn.

Now, summoned, he was hurrying down the corridor to report to Bereznyi. Rusinov was waiting for him in the outer office. As liaison officers, they spoke only Russian, as laid down clearly in the regulations. "Your report, Ivan," his friend Bogdan Rusinov began in Russian, "amazes me. You've walked into something fantastic. Of course, General Bereznyi was wild to read your account of such a high-level American contact. He's studied it thoroughly, and wants to coordinate with you ways to follow up."

All intelligence activities concerning the West were "coordinated with" the Russian Liaison Intelligence Bureau. Although the correct phrase would be "directed by," all Bulgarians had attuned themselves to "coordinated with," a disgusting euphemism, Ivan thought. Zhivkov, himself, relished saying that the Soviet Union and Bulgaria would "act as a single body, breathing with the same lungs and nourished by the same bloodstream."

Rusinov, a rotund, extroverted man, was not smiling. He led Ivan over to the far corner of the room by the windows, where he signaled him with a nod of the head and a wink to look out across the city. When they were both facing the window, Rusinov whispered in Bulgarian, "Watch it, my friend, he's not in the least sold on you. Suspicious of the Greek blood. He's furious with my office, claims we didn't fill him in on your assignment to Greece. In fact, we did send it over there for approval, just one of those bureaucratic tangles. He chooses to have a tantrum over it. Another way to teach us a lesson. Exercising control, I call it. He's a tyrant. I've got no idea what to expect from him."

He had known Rusinov since school days, although Rusinov, a pudgy and good-humored boy, had been two classes ahead of him. They had grown up together in a village not far from Sofia, where his mother worked in the orange canning factory. He had never forgotten how the Rusinov family had always been kind to him and his mother, defending them against the petty meanness displayed by a few of the neighbors. Sometimes the meanness was worse than petty. One haunting boyhood incident—to this day the stench lingered in his nostrils— flashed through his mind. A neighbor, a fanatical patriot whose father had fought with the prewar irredentist terrorists, the IMRO, emptied the stinking contents of his outhouse into his wagon, hauled it in broad daylight over to the Dimitrov's place, cursing the Greeks, *gadni*

Gartsi. Like a maniac, he flung shovels of excrement against their house, where it stuck like glue. Ivan's mother, gagging, too sick to cry, tried to clean the mud-brick walls, but after hours of futile labor—Ivan running back and forth to the village well drawing buckets of water—having used up the few rags she owned and fouled the broom, a useless, brittle thing made from twigs, exhausted, she almost collapsed. A few hesitant neighbors lent a hand, but soon backed away from the smell. It was the Rusinovs, charging up from their fields, mother, father and three oldest sons, including Bogdan, who worked till evening scraping the mess off the house. Later the family rubbed walnut leaves against the walls to disguise the smell.

Rusinov and he, both of them in Intelligence, had become even closer friends through their military service, and since Bogdan Rusinov was known as a comer, having a brother in the National Ministry of Defense and an in-law on the Politburo, the relationship had served Ivan well. More than once, Rusinov had put in a good word for him and was actually, the key person to recommend him for Intelligence School in Moscow.

Rusinov moved toward the door that led to the inner office. "He's waiting."

General Boris Bereznyi, head of the Russian Liaison Intelligence Bureau in Bulgaria, sat at a desk scanning papers in a file, an empty ivory cigarette holder clenched in his mouth, causing his chin to jut. Bereznyi did not bother to acknowledge Ivan's entrance, the work at hand apparently more important. Ivan like everyone else in the Bulgarian army often the target of Russian arrogance usually bowed under the insult. But now, tense over what

Rusinov had relayed to him, he clenched his fists until his nails bit into his palms to restrain his fury.

The General looked up. Ivan snapped to attention, saluted and gave his name, "Ivan Dimitrov, *tavarisch.*" Bereznyi, a square man, his complexion pinkish as if he shaved too close, his blond hair glossed with gray, held his blue eyes in a permanent squint. His teeth were stained with nicotine. He nodded at Ivan as he inserted a cigarette into his holder.

An enlisted man brought in three cups of coffee on a copper tray and set it on a small table, propped up by a stack of ledgers piled under a broken leg. The windows, scratched and too dirty to see through, were barred. For a moment the Russian studied his coffee. "A valuable contact, very valuable, Dimitrov."

"*Da, tavarisch.*"

"We will have to exploit this for all its worth." Bereznyi returned to the file, rifled through the papers, pulling out a sheet to read with special care, bending his head like a man inspecting a rare gem. "Ha," the Russian said, and waved the paper back and forth in the air like a banner. "Look what's here. I didn't expect to find this bit of information, *tavarisch.* Your mother, she's Greek. One of the refugees from 1949."

He was still standing at attention. To steady himself, he shifted to an at-ease position. He had assumed the Russian had been reading the report he had filed earlier this afternoon on the American woman; instead, the bastard was burrowing through his file.

"Here, Ivan," said Rusinov, dragging a chair toward him, "have a seat."

"*Was*. My mother *was*. She's been dead for five years." He remained standing, ignoring Rusinov's gesture.

The Russian smiled at Rusinov; he seemed somehow feline. "That part of his record, Rusinov, about his mother's death, is not entered. I'm impressed to see how you keep your personnel records right up to the minute," he said in a hoarse whisper, as he slapped Ivan's file shut.

Rusinov took a sip of his coffee, got up and squinted out the window at the night sky. When he turned back toward the room, he was frowning and biting his lower lip. Rusinov was too confident to be unnerved by the Russian's sarcastic rebuke about the omission in the file. What the two of them sensed, and so dared not look at each other, was the aura of menace that Bereznyi was creating.

"Now then, Dimitrov, what a lucky coincidence you happened to be assigned to Athens. Perfect timing, isn't it? These American parents, they owe you plenty, don't they? I noticed in your report, you said the mother was standoffish, not offering you the kind of gratitude you deserve. Surely your quick and intelligent reaction saved her boy's life. But the father'll be different, I can assure you."

"Perhaps, sir. It's hard to tell."

"To the contrary. Not hard at all. You've been to Intelligence School—that's where you polished your impeccable Russian, my compliments— you should be able to predict as well as I. Tell me why the father will be more effusive. Base your answer on what you learned in Moscow."

"Well, imperialist that he is, he's bound to be cocky, so he'll have confidence, and maybe in this case confidence will breed gratitude, I mean allow the natural emotion of a father to well up."

The Russian pursed his lips and nodded in agreement. "Would you tell the Americans you were Greek? Would you ever gain anything by admitting that?"

"No, Sir. That would be entirely the wrong thing to do."

He banged his fist on the table. "You're lying, Dimitrov. You're a fucking liar. You know they'd be thrilled to hear you're a Greek. The Americans are crazy for the Greeks. They've got them licking their imperialist hands like puppies. Your correct answer to me, Dimitrov, should be, *Nyet, tavarisch,* I'm not Greek, Sir, I'm Bulgarian, Sir. Get that, Sophocles?"

Rusinov strolled back to the window and resumed peering out at the empty night, his hands stuffed deep in his pockets, his shoulders hunched against the attack that the General had launched on Ivan.

"Rusinov, we need a history lesson. Tell your friend Dimitrov about Basil the Bulgar Slayer, so he'll grasp why Greeks are not loved here."

Rusinov turned. "Sir, you'll note in his file that Ivan was born in Bulgaria and went through school here. He learned about Basil, like the rest of us, from the time he was five years old."

"I said tell him."

Rusinov faced him, and spoke in a breathless monotone as if he were a pupil reciting in the classroom: "In 1014, the Greek Byzantine Emperor, Basil II, tried to reconquer Bulgarian territory, and annihilated the Bulgarian army at Balathista. For good measure, he blinded 1,400 Bulgarian soldiers. He left every 10th soldier with sight so that he could lead nine soldiers home. When our Emperor Samuel saw the returning soldiers, he died of shock."

"That was a spell-binding recitation, Rusinov. Maybe you should have been an historian." The General hunched forward over the desk. "Your wife, Dimitrov, a lovely woman. She has a good job in the Ministry of Agriculture as a scientist. And her uncle, the big shot in the ministry. What's his name?"

He stood still, did not wet his lips, did not shift his gaze, did not alter his breathing pattern. "Vasili Petrov."

"Lucky you have those important in-laws. *Svatove*, as they say in Bulgarian. A lovely Bulgarian family?"

Ivan said nothing.

"Well, don't you agree you have a lovely family?"

"Yes, Sir. Of course."

"A man with a nice family like yours doesn't take chances. You get my point? So if you have any insane ideas about defection, she can just stay here. You can go to Greece alone. Wait. As a matter of fact, I know the perfect woman you can take with you as your wife." The Russian chuckled at some private vision; the cigarette holder warbled in his teeth. "She's just finishing up as the head of the Bulgarian trade mission in Belgrade. A real beauty."

The Russian picked up his coffee cup, made a face as if he had tasted sour milk and hurled it across the room. Rusinov spun around as it smashed at his feet, the coffee grounds spattering his boots. "Colonel, get us something more interesting than this Turkish mud you drink here. It looks like sewer water."

Ivan lowered himself deliberately into the chair, his back straight. He crossed his legs, clasped his hands lightly in his lap, to keep them from running through his hair. He held his eyes steady on the General, feeling the wave of fury ebbing and in its place the old self-protective instinct reasserting. For moments of danger, he had learned to keep his body still, his tone of voice low and even, his expression bland, his lips slightly parted to ease any tenseness around his mouth. Throughout his military career he had trained himself in front of a mirror like a movie actor so that every body gesture, every vocal inflection would convey exactly what the part demanded. From studying close-ups in the movies he realized how a raised eyebrow, a quivering nostril, the flick of a tongue—such nuances—gave the stamp of truth to a performance. He controlled his blood pressure, the tint of his complexion, the glint in his eyes, by pretending the situation was a fantasy, that he was acting in front of a camera, the lines he heard were written by a screen writer, and that his own words were likewise part of a fiction.

Rusinov opened the door and called to the enlisted man to bring three glasses of vodka. A moment later, the corporal shuttled in with a bottle, glasses, and a dish of walnuts.

"*Nazdrovya*," said the Russian, who was seated under a photo of Zhivkov. The other two raised their glasses in the toast.

"Let's talk about defection, Sophocles. It might not be as easy as you think. First, you're no real prize, no Nureyev or Baryshnikov to be trotted out and paraded around the world like a real catch. Second, you can't go over to their side and continue to help them in any way. Your only value to the Americans is to act as their agent, by keeping in the middle of things so that you can carry information to them about the Soviet Union. Defection, you must understand by now, would take you right out of the picture."

Bereznyi stood and leaned over the desk, addressing his remarks directly to Ivan. "They don't give a shit about Bulgaria; it's a non-place for anyone except the Greeks, who are like turtles, always peering into their own shells. The Americans would want to know what Russian Intelligence Service does here, who the operatives are, what kind of technology and weapons we've installed in Bulgaria, what we've concocted at the Bulgarian military bases, how we've designed the Bulgarian order of battle, what's on the borders, you know, the standard information."

Bereznyi, his face red from the vodka, slumped back in his chair to relax, raising the glass to his nose like a Frenchman sniffing fine brandy. By Christ, Ivan thought, the bastard was growing expansive, enjoying himself, a man chatting cordially over drinks with trusted friends before taking the midday meal.

"What's your opinion, Rusinov?" asked Bereznyi. Ivan watched Rusinov. Sure, Bogdan Rusinov was a faithful friend, still, he would be forced to look out for his own neck if it came to any real confrontation with the Russians.

"There are a few things to consider here, Sir. If the parents really are grateful to him for saving the boy, Dimitrov will have a chance to cultivate them in whatever way is helpful for our side. If on the other hand—don't forget he's a good contact for them, as well—they try to cultivate him, he will find himself in a touchy position, unless he can work out an exchange. It's always uncomfortable to be pressured by the other side, even dangerous. The best situation would be an even exchange, and in that case, Sir, you will have to select out from the items you just mentioned which ones exactly Ivan can trade."

The Russian trained his eyes on Rusinov, squinting so tightly that they appeared closed. "What's the latest on the American Embassy in Athens?"

"Our understanding is that this particular Embassy is always staffed with smart people—experienced CIA chiefs and some highly trained military attachés, one army officer who has trained his whole career as a Greek-area specialist. He feeds the CIA and DIA. Right now they have a political appointee for an Ambassador, not one of those State Department professionals. However, the station chief is a real professional. They won't fall for soft intelligence, sir."

Thank God, Rusinov had coolly by-passed the defection issue. He, too, was capable of delivering a superb performance.

Ivan watched the Russian take a small pad from his tunic pocket, scribble some notes with his left hand, his arm bent around in a 90-degree angle in the manner of left-handed people, read them over, scratch something out, and then write more. After filling two pages, he put the pad back in his breast pocket.

"Let's look at the situation this way," he began, his manner professional now, his delivery calm. "I know that Bulgarian Intelligence has been careful in their selection of you, Dimitrov, and that right now we need someone to cultivate the pro-communist elements in the Greek army —we know there are very few—and that you have exactly the right profile for that task. You haven't been briefed on your mission yet. But that's it, cultivating pro-communists in the Greek military. So here's what we'll do. You take your wife along. You'll need as much stability as you can get. She's a good Bulgarian, and as an only daughter, as noted here—he flipped through the file —she'd never defect. As a second mission, though, you'll work out an arrangement to trade information with the Americans. I'll set up a series of specific briefings before you depart so you'll know what to do."

His eyes suddenly opened as he articulated his game plan, his own grand strategy. "You've just been launched on a new career, Sophocles. Consider yourself a front-line spy." He laughed congenially, as if he wanted to invite Ivan into a circle of comradeship he had just this moment created, as if the hard part were over and now they could be colleagues.

"Rusinov, quit stargazing out the window. This calls for a celebration." Bereznyi held his glass up to make another toast, but all three glasses were empty. He raised the bottle and with one eye shut, measured how much remained. With scrupulous care, he poured the contents into his own glass, which overflowed. The vodka sloshed on the floor. He hoisted his brimming glass. "*Nazdrovya*," and then in a stage whisper, he rasped, "a Greek, brought up to be a Bulgarian. God, you must be cursed." Ivan and Rusnov raised their empty glasses, and with a ring of enthusiasm they, too, said, "*Nazdrovya*."

The General put on his coat and scooped up some files to take along in his briefcase. "Make sure you use your new rank. She won't pay much attention to Major, but Colonel she'll find more impressive. Thirty years old. You must be the youngest officer with that rank in any army," he said civilly, giving a low, admiring whistle. "And he can start now, Rusinov, by being solicitous of the American woman. Assign him the means to keep in touch with her, you know, a vehicle to drive to the lodge to see how she's getting along, and some kind of phone communication so she can reach him if she needs anything. And, Rusinov, get me some bios on that group of diplomat families staying at the ski resort. That might yield something interesting."

Chapter 9

In the dining room, the younger children wiggled on benches at a long table, giggling and toying with their silverware. The youngest ones, wearing thick, colorful knitted sweaters, slithered on and off the benches, a peril to the stability of the tablecloth and glasses. At another table sat three couples in their late teens, including Catherine and Albert, with their backs to the children and the parents. The adults were settling themselves at a third table in anticipation of the folk dance performance arranged by the inn.

From the kitchen seeped the aroma of herbs—basil, oregano, marjoram, garlic, sage, thyme—perfumed plants that had so delighted Robert and her, when in the course of their living in Greece, they roamed the sere hills and untamed mountains of the Balkans. Laid with red-striped tablecloths, the tables were heaped with traditional Bulgarian food: ceramic bowls filled with delicious *shopska* salad; terra-cotta glazed platters of *pechneno sirene*, a white cheese, butter and paprika heated in rolled paper; painted dishes of *kebabcheta*, a grilled meat roll; plates of *sarmi*, stuffed grape leaves; and an assortment of other food that Barbara couldn't name. She had expected such a spread; Bulgaria had been designated the breadbasket of the bloc and hence the Bulgarians enjoyed one of the best diets among the satellite countries.

She was enjoying a symphony of languages at her table: French, German, Italian, Spanish, Dutch, Swedish, Danish, English, even Walloon, each beating in its own cadence, pitched to its own key, rising and falling with its own intonation; the French-speakers dropped an octave when they switched to English; the Italian-speakers broke their legato when they changed to the gutteral German; almost all of them moved into English lightly.

The group poured red or white wine for each other from copper beakers waiting for the rest of their company to be seated. By now, the end of the second day, their ever-faithful Intourist guide Svetlozar, had lost his pariah status; when he had taken off his outlandish sunglasses, he had become one of the group. He was being invited exuberantly by the Danish and Dutch women, both plain and robust, to take a place between them. He wore the sheepish smile of someone who had just learned that he was loved.

Behind the bar a woman was washing glasses and crying, streams of tears running down her face. Barbara noticed that every few minutes she gathered herself up, took the corner of a towel, dipped it in water and ran the damp cloth over her face. Then she returned to her work again, with renewed industry, as if her life and well-being depended on keeping at her task. After a time, her shoulders started to shake, and again the tears fell.

All the while, Barbara watched for Louisa. When she caught sight of her entering the dining room, she pointed to the seat she had saved for her.

"You looked like death earlier. Are you and Freddy better after your naps?"

"We're fine. Freddy didn't take a nap. But I passed right out."

Finally, the whole party was complete except for Gerda, who'd sent word she wasn't feeling well and would come later. Everyone started to eat.

"Louisa, I'm disturbed by that woman. See her behind the bar?"

"I know who. Everyone's been talking. The police have taken her son. That happens every day here. Everyone's afraid. They spend their happiest hours of the day spying on each other, then become miserable when one of their own is arrested."

"That woman is falling to pieces. It's awful to look at. I can't bear it."

"Of course you can bear it. You must, since you can't do a thing about it. By the way," Louisa added, "I finished my book today. Have you noticed there are no foreign magazines here? What a miserable country this is. Nothing to read, not a single newsstand."

"No, they don't circulate foreign magazines or newspapers. I miss the *Herald Tribune, Le Figaro, The Times*. It's weird to have no sense of what's going on in the world, this terrible disconnection. They have no convertible currency to import scholarly journals, either. Like living before Gutenberg, isn't it?"

"Do you have anything I could read tomorrow morning? Something light before I begin my next book? A magazine would be perfect. Besides English, I read French. In fact, I love to read French, a very elegant language. I would really enjoy a French magazine," Louisa said, taking a sip of wine, her dark eyes fixed on her over the rim of the glass.

"No, sorry. I don't have a thing," she said, and stopped eating. She couldn't swallow. No. It was absolutely impossible. She stared at Louisa. Absolutely impossible to imagine Louisa in the courier scheme. Louisa's appearance was the product of self- indulgence; she was hardly someone who'd risk her neck for a mission. She was so perfectly well-turned out, without blemish, the designers of Milan having accomplished a spectacular job in fashioning her white after ski outfit. True, I have never tried to picture the other courier, never fantasized if it would be a man or a woman, she thought. Certainly not an opera singer. Would Louisa possess the kind of guts it took? But then her own part was rather dangerous, too, and how much spunk would she have if tested?

She continued to scrutinize her new friend, seeking a clue, searching for coarser features, ungainly posture, a stain, some telltale mark of a rougher sensibility.

"Not to worry," Louisa said, "my concern is just the earlier part of the morning tomorrow. I am very occupied from before noon until late afternoon." She explained that she had an appointment to meet the director of the National Opera and some of the singers. She was looking forward to touring the opera house as they had promised her. She had sung last year with a Bulgarian colleague of theirs, "a defector," she whispered, who now made his home in Paris, and she was bringing them greetings from him.

Over where the crying woman had stood, a spidery, dark-skinned man with the coal-black eyes of a gypsy now worked. Where had the poor woman gone? Barbara shuddered, and tried to fix her attention on the party. As they finished dessert, eight men in costumes, wearing brown cummerbunds and fur hats, trouped into the room playing flutes, string instruments, drum and bagpipes. A young man draped in a bearskin, only the lower part of his face showing under the pelt, shuffled across the floor, more like a Quasimodo than a bear, chased by a hefty woman in a full red skirt and an embroidered blouse. In what seemed to be a serious tussle, the "maiden" wrestled the "bear" down, and with brightly colored ribbons tied his arms and legs together and proceeded to taunt him with crude facial expressions and menacing hand motions. The bear, struggling to free himself, was writhing on the floor when a group of twenty dancers bounded into the room to music so frenzied, it seemed to be driving the wild action of the pantomime. The performers circled around the contorting bear and the feisty maiden, the men whistling and hooting, the women smiling and laughing. One by one they peeled off toward the bear, loosening the cords until, smiling triumphantly, he stood up free, the bearskin heaped at his feet.

Many of the children were laughing; others were staring mutely at the little drama, as if they were witnessing something sinister. At the end Roger, ever concerned about the plight of animals, came over to ask her, "What were those Bulgarians supposed to be doing to that bear?" She said the meaning was probably lost in the mist of folklore, and he should regard the performance as nothing more than a fairy tale, that many fairy tales were morbid. But Roger pulled up a seat next to her, where he sat glumly for a while, unable to perk up.

The musicians faced the children's table holding out their instruments and naming them in Bulgarian for the children to repeat: first the strings—*gadulka* ; then the flutes—*kaval* ; and last the bagpipes—*gayda*. A few youngsters were invited to try the bagpipe, their puffed, blood red faces causing hilarity among the others.

And here to her astonishment was the Bulgarian officer, entering the hall. He moved through the room, light on his feet, with the nimble stride of an athlete. She hadn't noticed before how agile he was, but she did remember the dark unmanageable hair, that softened his face, made him less severe. It flashed through her mind how fascinated she'd been by his story, how she had felt an unexpected attraction to him. Her emotional reaction at the time had so overwhelmed her that she had dismissed him from the lodge rudely, only to be disgusted with herself an hour later for her rash, ridiculous behavior. Had she actually been attracted to him? Or just emotional over his plight, as if they were in league, both in search of the same treasure. She had made a pact with herself not to think about that particular issue. Just let it be. He was searching through the guests until he spied her, and headed toward her table, carrying a crutch. She introduced him to Louisa, who waved to the waiter to bring another chair. The waiter placed the chair between her and Louisa.

The music struck up again, and the dancers joined hands to do a *horo*.

"I came to see how Freddy is and to bring this crutch from the doctor. Ah, I see he is fine." He was watching Freddy, who was rolling on the floor, his sweater pulled over his head, obviously mimicking the bear to the delight of the other children who had tied him in napkins. One of the girls joined him in the parody, making arabesques around the squirming Freddy.

"Do I remember the doctor say he should keep his leg up high?" Dimitrov remarked with the slightest trace of a smile. Really, it was his lips that smiled while his eyes, as always, remained expressionless.

She grimaced and shrugged her shoulders in helplessness. The dancing continued, this time the dancers donning masks and ringing bells "to drive away the evil spirits," Dimitrov explained. He helped himself to a dessert of *banitsa* with syrup, and coffee. Louisa struck up an animated conversation with him, unfazed by the din coming from the performers, who had moved into a showy number, whistling, hooting, leaping, and slapping their knees to the booming rhythm of the drums.

Freddy caught sight of Dimitrov and hobbled toward him. "Colonel Dimitrov, hey, here's my brother, Roger. Remember you said you'd take us to the place where some Russians fought the Germans in World War II, and there's still cartridges and stuff we can dig up there. Can we go tomorrow?"

"Tomorrow the doctor will come to look at your leg and to put on a clean bandage. According to his advice, and of course your mother's, if all is well, we can go maybe the next day."

"No, I don't think he should be off so soon, hopping around on that injured leg," she said, astonished at the invitation, at his personal desire to extend his friendship, especially at his liberty to mix so freely with them. Sure their conversation in the jeep had fascinated her—she had always wanted to interview Greek refugees—but she was

99

wary, put on guard by the inflection in his voice when he described his communist grandfather, his undisguised disdain, as if he meant to send her a message. You hardly needed to listen carefully for the innuendo; it was definitely there.

"Don't worry, Madame, I watch out for him. It is no trouble for me, you have my assurance."

She had expected exactly that exasperating answer, such a common mode of behavior in this part of the world. She was annoyed by the impossibility of refusing any gesture of hospitality without the offer being thrust back at you more insistently, often with other extravagances added to the original offer, and always with the assurance that the gesture included no inconvenience to the host, when in fact the inconvenience was to the guest, hence the guest's refusal in the first place.

The boys looked mutinous. When Roger started grumbling, she put them off with "We'll see."

The dancers had left and the musicians were packing up.

"Good night, Madame. I'll come by tomorrow to see what you need. Also, I have told the desk clerk how to reach me if you need me for anything." He searched her face as if he needed to memorize her features.

Louisa extended her hand. "I look forward to seeing you, Colonel, in Athens at our Embassy after you and your wife have taken up residence." She injected a purr as if to give warmth to her voice, keeping the tone friendly, but at the same time formal. He inclined his head to take in her words, and nodded politely. But he kept staring at Barbara.

When Dimitrov turned his back to leave, Louisa winked at her and chuckled. "My dear, I had to extend to him a welcome; we were on the same side in World War II, don't forget." Her hands moved gracefully through the air like agents of choreography. "*Dio mio,* what a strange, strange world it is. I have a feeling about that man. He is quite handsome, that marvelous marked chin, those cold, green eyes hiding like watchful birds nesting under those lashes; they reveal nothing. If eyes mirror the soul, his eyes conceal that he even has a soul. He is like a person in a play, searching for his soul."

"I certainly agree. He has me completely baffled."

"Because his face is without expression, somber, somehow alien, he has about him a deepness which in truth he probably does not have." She patted Barbara on the cheek. "Good night. *Domani.*"

"Oh yes, tomorrow." Louisa stopped at the piano on her way out and played a few bars, again from *Tosca—perche, perche, Signor, ah perche me ne rimuneri cosi,* "why, why, Lord, do you repay me thus?" It was then that Barbara remembered the heads of Louisa's father and uncles, their gruesome display on the pikes. She wondered if Louisa, as a young woman in Trieste, then not yet twenty years old, had actually seen the heads, blackening and shriveling like mushrooms under the savage sun, or if she had only heard the reports from relatives. Never mind, it came to the same thing; the stories that relatives pass down fuse with our own vision.

Gerda, who had just come in, waved, called over a hearty "*Guten Abend,*" and arranged a couple of desserts in front of her. She had bought a Bulgarian head-scarf and tied it Balkan style around the back of her head; from one ear dangled a huge, golden gypsy earring. Svetlozar's tablemates had left; he scooted along the bench to sit next to Gerda. Barbara waved back. Most of the guests had retired to their rooms. She watched Catherine and her friends saunter into the lounge to play Scrabble on Albert's French game board. Catherine and Albert were holding hands, singing a Bruce Springsteen song to each other.

She gathered Freddy and Roger to go upstairs. The boys would pester her to go with Dimitrov to hunt war artifacts. She was dismayed by the turn her thoughts were taking. Earlier, she'd been overcome by sentiments of pure gratitude, and now, she was beginning to feel the burden of that gratitude, as if it carried terms she couldn't fulfill, an enormous price she might not be able to pay. She caught herself: no; an enormous price she would have *difficulty* paying. Conscience dictated that she would have to pay it. To allow the boys to wander off with a Bulgarian officer was, on the face of it, probably unwise. Odd. If the Bulgarian could form a relationship with them right in front of his own authorities, he must have permission from superiors. She sensed a kind of entrapment: Dimitrov had put her in a terrible position, that of denying his first request. And what a battle she'd face with the boys when she refused.

The boys were not totally innocent in this matter, especially Roger; they enjoyed the adventure of going off with members of the bloc. Two years ago, at a party on the island of Mykonos held for members of the diplomatic corps accredited to Greece, Roger and a few other American boys had gone down to the beach with some junior officers from the Russian Embassy, after Barbara and Robert had gone to bed. The Russians had brought some beer with them and "shared" it with the boys. The next day Roger told his parents that the Russians had asked him questions about Robert, Robert's colleagues, the layout and details of the Embassy building itself; Roger had felt so clever because he had "given them all kinds of crazy answers." Robert was furious that Roger had so little judgment as to drink with the Russians.

She watched the boys go in their room. Freddy, balanced shakily on his bed, plunked his baseball cap on his head and rakishly adjusted the brim to the level of his eyes. He did a windup, then took a wide stretch for the pitch. He fell, sprawled across the mattress as his injured leg gave way. She lived again the wonder of his birth, grew amazed at his being; his safe return struck her as a reenactment of the birth, part of the miracle.

"Go to sleep. Don't horse around all night. You'll want to be fresh for tomorrow," she said.

" What a blast that would be, to go off digging with that Bulgarian officer," he said.

She shut their door and proceeded to her own room. She needed to know the Bulgarian officer better, if only to feel more comfortable about the children. Yes, that was the reason, the only reason—to feel more comfortable about the children.

And what about Louisa? Part of the scheme? Louisa working with Franklin? Inconceivable.

Chapter 10

The next morning, she sent the boys downstairs to breakfast, while she relaxed in her room, lolling by the window, where the mountain in the background loomed above her. Flocks of white pigeons were wheeling, breaking, weaving, and reforming like a fugue against the low winter sun. The angle of the sun, the long black patches it created on the snow, gave the landscape an El Greco lift. She had passed up coffee for mountain tea, made from the leaves of plants gathered in the local hills. The tea, tepid and mildly bitter, sent out a pungent, medicinal aroma. The people in the Balkans claimed that certain teas offered healing properties for everything from melancholy to dysentery, gangrene, gonorrhea, cracked nipples, urine retention, flatulence, hysteria and nose bleeds. Good, she decided, she'd be prepared to face anything today.

She was writing out the exercises in her Bulgarian grammar book when she heard a tap on the door.

"Barbara, it's me. Louisa."

She unlatched the door.

"I'm sorry, it's so early to visit." Louisa closed the door quietly behind her.

"I didn't know your schedule for the day. Maybe you would go out this morning and still be gone when I had to leave for the opera house. Someone from the opera company is coming for me in a few minutes."

In her patent heels, black gabardine suit, white blouse and multicolored silk tie held in place by a gold stickpin, Louisa was obviously bound for the city.

"I have no schedule today except to entertain Freddy. God help me," said Barbara. "I'm glad you've come. Would you like some of this tea?"

Louisa wrinkled her nose. "That tea smells sickening. So Freddy is better?"

"He seems to be. But of course he can't go skiing and he's begging to. I said 'God help me' because there are no amusements here for kids."

"No, *cara* Louisa. However, there are amusements for adults here. Gossip is not my habit, but I tell you the following not for gossip. That fool Svetlozar. He stayed in Gerda's room last night. The maid claims she saw a mess on the sheets this morning"—she wrinkled her nose again exactly as she had done earlier in reference to the tea — "and when she saw Svetlozar's sunglasses left on the sink in Gerda's bathroom, she comprehended and told the management. These idiot peasants, all of them— Bulgarians, Austrians—a peasant remains a peasant, it is a matter of eternity."

"Poor Gerda. How misguided. She's pathetic, you know. Nothing else."

"Poor Gerda," Louisa's voice fell to a mezzo tremolo worthy of Carmen. "She could bring trouble. The Bulgarian officials might start paying more attention to us. We don't need trouble, especially today. That's why I tell you the gossip about your poor *maledetta* Gerda. There is an Italian saying, *Melio soli che male accompagnati,* better to be alone than to be in a bad company. It seems that there is no such saying in German for Gerda to heed."

"Let's just hope it all passes. I don't think she could handle a bad situation competently, never mind gracefully."

Louisa went to the mirror to retie her scarf. The arrangement she concocted was intricate, involving a couple of elaborate wraps around her neck, a loose knot, and a final insertion of the gold pin.

She pivoted on her heel. "Barbara," she paused, and fingered her scarf, "I've come for some reading material."

"You've misunderstood me, Louisa. Remember, last night I told you I had nothing to read." The light filtering into the room switched from bright to dull, dull to bright, as clouds floated over the sun. She turned from the window to study Louisa, whose face was set, her mouth drawn down like the masks worn in Greek tragedies.

"That Prince Michael of Greece. Do you know anything about him?" Louisa asked. "You were in Greece when his cousin, King Constantine, the blockhead, who knew only how to sail, attempted a counter-coup against the junta, and was driven out of the country. The whole occasion was like an operetta."

Of course, she said, she remembered the king's counter-coup against the military dictatorship in 1967, a key moment in the survival of that regime and ultimately the downfall of the monarchy. And she'd heard of Prince Michael as a writer, a good one at that.

"Michael, the historian, one of the brighter members of that whole dreary Glücksberg dynasty, now living in Paris. I so enjoy reading about him, Barbara."

"Yes. Prince Michael," she said, scrutinizing Louisa and sipping the tea, now cold, rancid. She stood and strode to the night table and removed the magazine from under Kazantzakis. "Here. I'm thrilled to be rid of it. It's been like the Hope diamond without the sparkle."

Louisa reached for the magazine casually, as if she had come by to borrow a pair of gloves on a cold day. "Oh, yes, one thing, Barbara. You know Bulgarians are not allowed free association. Do you think it wise to let the boys go out with a Bulgarian intelligence officer?"

"I have an intuition—at this point only an intuition—that the boys would be safe with him. They are precious to him. He needs to make friends with them."

"Yes, but still his motives, how do you say in English, are ulterior." Louisa rolled the magazine under her arm, opened the door, blew a kiss and left.

At midmorning, she and Freddy went down to the lounge to play *tavli,* while they waited for the doctor. Freddy, twirling the crutch, was walking rather well without it.

"Mom, roll the dice."

She looked distractedly at the red and black board and the dice. She had assumed that once she had passed the magazine, she could take deep breaths, exhale, and sink down in her chair to stare off into space, clicking her blue worry beads, so to speak, thrilled with her own bravado for a job well done, her mind clear to concentrate on Bulgarian grammar— perhaps have a few conversation sessions with a staff member at the hotel. The damn magazine. A superstitious person might believe it had brought her bad luck, a string of misfortunes including Freddy's disappearance, his injured leg, and the added burden of getting involved with Dimitrov. God knows where that might take her.

Freddy sat bent over the *tavli* board, blowing on his hands and making a spitting sound over the dice before he rolled them. He snapped his fingers and yelled "yippee" each time he got doubles. She smiled at his vigor and enthusiasm, which indicated that he had no idea his opponent found it impossible to keep her mind on the game. His hands, their thin, long, adolescent fingers, were smeared with inked tattoos.

"Mom, come on, it's your turn."

She picked up the dice and threw them. Across the lounge the oafish Svetlozar was sitting at the bar drinking a cup of coffee and chewing on a toothpick. She could not warm up to him the way the others had; he represented too neatly the closed world he inhabited, his small eyes under the hooded lids were too shrewd, he became too personal, had insinuated himself into the group, in her view, like an unwanted in-law at a family party. Even Louisa, despite mocking him in the beginning, was friendly; in fact, she seemed at times to be positively ingratiating toward him: "Where did you get those marvelous sunglasses? You give to Vitosha the aura of the Riviera." Once, telling him a joke, much to Barbara's amazement she slipped totally out of character to rub his shoulder in the manner of a common flirt. The man rewarded her with a grin, obviously captivated. Her servant for the asking. No request would be excessive.

"Mom, you got a five and a two. Move your pieces."

Her mind was fluttering all over the place like a bird locked in a barn. She was entering the post-magazine period; she could not forget the magazine entirely, nor could she keep her mind on anything else. It was as if she had an empty area in her brain, a hole that was filling with forebodings.

"Mom, you moved onto my space. Watch out."

A blast of cold wind came into the lounge when the door flew open. Gerda entered, dripping snow, wearing a gray Bavarian hat enlivened with a pert green partridge feather, her chubby cheeks scarlet from skiing. Without a glance around the room, she waddled in her thick ski pants directly to the bar to join Svetlozar.

The two sat together talking. Gerda inched closer to him, her eyebrows bunched as she listened intently. Svetlozar spoke a brand of German he had picked up from the tourists, barely adequate to convey the most simple information, yet he had Gerda fascinated. How, Barbara wondered, did those two communicate?

"I'm already in my third column," said Freddy, a squeak of triumph in his voice, "and you're still in your first."

Gerda rose and headed purposefully for the steps. When she saw Barbara, she changed direction and hurried toward her. "*Ach du lieber Gott*," she began. Then she sat down and whispered, "Louisa, *die Polizei.* . . ."

Gerda's cheeks were flaming, fuzzy bits of stray, yellow hair poked out from under her Bavarian hat, while incongruously from an ear hung a gypsy earring. She put her hand on Gerda's arm to calm her. Svetlozar, Gerda related, had just told her that a little earlier Louisa had been waiting out front for a car—probably to go to the city judging by the way she was dressed. When the car drove up Svetlozar recognized the driver and the man beside him, but of course Louisa didn't. They were from the State Security Police. One man stayed at the wheel, the other jumped out of the car. That man pushed, the driver pulled. So Louisa disappeared into the car in a blink. The car seemed not to have even stopped—just cruised by and snatched her. He couldn't tell Gerda anything more or he'd get in trouble.

"What can we do to help Louisa? We must help her; she belongs to our group. *Ah Gott. Die Polizei. Die Bulgarische Polizei*," said Gerda, whose feather bobbed up and down as she shook.

"Easy, Gerda, easy."

"We have trouble with the secret police, the Stasi, in the East. They are bad, those German communists. We in the West know about them, but the Bulgarians are worse. Still, you find good and bad all over. Look at Svetlozar, what a *Schatz* he is. He gave us information, so put himself in danger."

Gerda pulled gracelessly at her wet ski pants, waved to Svetlozar and headed up the stairs to change to dry clothes.

"Mom, are you going to play, or what?" Freddy insisted.

She called to the waiter to bring a crème caramel to appease him and headed for the desk.

She recalled some details of the Bulgarian police organization. From her DIA days, and from the reports she had read through the years, she remembered that the Bulgarian Ministry of Internal Affairs had under its control units of the elite State Security Police. DIA didn't have enough information to deduce their exact functions, but concluded, that among other duties, the

SSP took care of relations with foreigners, and Bulgarians abroad. Just two years ago, an exiled writer, who spoke out against the regime, had been murdered in London, stabbed with a poisoned umbrella tip, or according to another source, poisoned with a pellet shot from an umbrella, most probably by the SSP, much to the horror of the international community. A zealous bunch of patriots, brutal in the extreme, they were suspected of having made at least two other assassination attempts on émigrés.

What had Louisa done with the magazine? Did her arrest have anything to do with passing it? No answers came to her. There was one thing she could do, one person who might have contacts in the right place. She waited several minutes, tossing a hundred what-ifs around in her head. Against her better judgment, she made her decision. "Get in touch with Colonel Ivan Dimitrov, immediately," she told the desk clerk.

Waiting for Dimitrov gave her too much time to avoid mulling over what she'd done. She could hear Robert's voice counseling prudence. *Louisa is a casual friend, someone you just met, her problems are not yours. Watch out, Barbara, or you'll jeopardize your own safety and the children's.* Robert had a raft of Greek proverbs he could pull from his mental store chest and hurl at listeners. One was particularly apt. If she remembered correctly it went: "Only a fool tests the depth of the water with both feet." Well, she'd plunged in with both feet. She looked for Freddy and saw him at the bar, his belly on the stool, spinning himself round and round like a top. She was beginning to worry that the magazine would somehow come back to her, as if she exerted some gravitational pull that would keep drawing it toward her.

An hour later, just as Dimitrov came, the doctor arrived, too, not the same person they had seen at Dimitrov's in-laws, but a woman instead, large-boned and unsmiling, wrestling with a big black bag. When she unbuckled it, potent fumes of alcohol, ether and antiseptics escaped. The satchel was crammed with menacing instruments from a dark, medieval age, suggesting that the physician was more apt to harm than heal. In limited English, the doctor managed some questions, but mostly she wanted to see the ankle and rotate Freddy's foot.

"Sprained ?" asked Barbara, unconvinced that doctors could make such positive diagnosis without the aid of X-rays.

"No. Foot fine." She bound the ankle in a fresh bandage and pointed to the crutch. "Use always," she said in a husky, authoritative voice. "I come. Tomorrow."

Dimitrov entered into a short conversation with the doctor. Barbara understood the doctor to say "*da*."

When she left, Barbara asked Freddy to wait for her because she wanted to have a word with Dimitrov. Freddy wobbled into the bar to twirl himself around on the barstools again.

Barbara motioned Dimitrov over to a corner of the lounge. "I think a terrible mistake has been made. Louisa Borromeo has been taken by your people."

"How do you know such a thing? We do not take foreigners just like that."

"Things like this get around."

"She is with the Italian Embassy?"

"Italian, yes."

"Then you should report it immediately to her Embassy, if you think she has disappeared."

"But you know very well that official channels are slow. If I reported this to her Embassy, there would be a *démarche*, and she'd be caught in the middle of an international uproar. Direct, personal contacts are best. Can you help? You're in Intelligence, aren't you?"

"I am not connected to the police in any way."

"Who says this is police?" His face told her nothing.

"Well, who do you think has taken her?"

"I do not know. But since she's a foreigner, I guess she's with the security police."

"Maybe she's just gone off on business. She's an opera singer, isn't she? Internationally known she told me last evening."

She looked down at the floor. "Please," she said, "Ivan."

His face flushed at the use of his first name. He seemed embarrassed or touched or shocked, as he shifted about, running his fingers through his mussed hair. She stared at him, taken aback at seeing his face for the first time register such expression, his brows raised, his lips parted.

"I will do what I can. By the way, the doctor said Freddy could go on the excursion with me tomorrow. It is up to you completely, of course. I will be in touch with you later today about your friend Louisa. Goodbye."

He put on his baggy, khaki military overcoat and cap and hurried out the door. Why in the world would he cash in any chips for her? Of course, he wouldn't. Not just for her. Before returning to Freddy, she sat down a moment to puzzle it all out. If he pulled off Louisa's release, it could only mean one thing. He's acting under Russian guidance. She stood up abruptly, and in her excitement ran her hands down her sides.

Look what I've brought you from Sofia, Dana Franklin. You cunning s.o.b. Guess what? Like it or not, I'm at the very center of this high-level operation. You'll have to deal me in. Dimitrov is working directly for the Russians.

Chapter 11

He went immediately to call Bogdan Rusinov about the jailing of the Italian woman. Within a few hours, Rusinov directed him to go pick her up.

"Ivan, the jeep assigned to you by Bereznyi," Rusinov said, "use it to take care of the Italian woman. See the importance he gives to your cultivating the American?"

Never mind that the muffler had completely blown, and the noise was exasperating, he reveled in the marvelous novelty of having a vehicle for his own use. Buoyed by the sensation of motion, he maneuvered the jeep skillfully on the icy curves, down the steep declines, speeding toward his destination; he had total control of his destiny. God, how free you feel at the wheel.

He steered toward the city, his mind centered on the new "possibility," as he called it to himself. Defection. On the day he had received his orders, and every hour since, the thought was spinning through his brain—a comet in the night sky. Defection.

Wherever he was he plotted the various aspects of this possibility— while he was skiing in the mountains, brushing up on his English or Greek, trapping animals in the fields, strolling through the village, out shooting birds in the woods. The mornings, the afternoons, the nights, blended into each other. Possibility. Most of the time, he didn't notice if it was light or dark, snowing or sunny, it was all the same. He picked at his food, awoke too early in the morning, and stumbled around all day as if in a dream.

Since their conversation in the coffee house less than a week ago, he hadn't dared to mention the possibility to Maria again, but she knew what was eating him. For the first time in their marriage she was pretending. She acted as if he were simply absent-minded. "Ivancho, I've called you three times, why don't you answer?" Or "Ivancho, you left the door open and the snow is blowing in." Or "Ivan, you left the dog tied outside last night and the poor thing is half dead with cold." He tried to mask his preoccupation; he made light conversation; hummed as he got dressed; told a joke to his mother-in-law; busied himself in his in-laws' house white-washing the walls and puttying the windowpanes; made love at night. Maria responded to his touch with a quickness that was new. Just feeling his fingertips run lightly over the planes of her face, along the indentations of her throat, caused her to thrust herself against him, nibbling at his skin. Through her excitement, he had discovered new power in himself, which, unconnected as it was, heightened this obsession for possibility. Yet, even in his self-indulgent state he perceived in her high-strung passion an act of desperation, the only way left for her to communicate with him. Poor Maria. He would make everything up to her in their new life.

In his lucid moments, he loathed himself for his self-indulgence. He had harbored that flaw since he was a little boy. Ilcho, his stepfather, had accused him often of being self-centered, but his mother always ran to his defense. "No, no. He's not really self-indulgent—he has lots to think about. An ill-fated boy. He has his future to plot. He belongs to no country. Nowhere. Fate has fixed him with the evil eye, the *kakomati*." But Ilcho, a gentle soul, who had meant the criticism for Ivan's own good, had been right, and Ivan had known it all along, although he had hid in the cloak of his mother's protection and love, and never troubled himself to change.

He pulled into Makedonja Street, took a right on Graf Ignatiev and drove past the stadium until he came to the SSP building, where two soldiers, holding Kalashnikov rifles, presented arms when he arrived at the gates. Inside, he identified himself to the duty sergeant, who directed him down the corridor to the commandant's office. A guard swung open a door to the commandant's waiting room, revealing Louisa, sitting by herself, perched tentatively like a captive bird on the edge of a straight wooden chair, curled forward, her feet resting on the front rung.

"Thank God," she said in a flat voice when she saw him.

She looked weary, morose. Her dark hair fell over her face, and she flipped it back with a furious toss of the head; a silk scarf hung askew from her neck; the animated expression he had noticed last night was gone, the melodious voice had thickened.

"A long while ago they said you were coming for me. Where in hell have you been?" Her eyes were damp with anger or crying, he couldn't tell. Beyond the tears he saw the flare of fury, the stubborn resilience, and was surprised when he felt a tug of kinship toward her, an admiration for her defiance. He looked quickly to the floor.

"I came as fast as I could."

There was nothing else in the room but a ragged brownish rug, three lop-sided wooden chairs holding overfilled ashtrays, and two photos on the wall, one of Zhivkov and the other of the Bulgarian national soccer team. The gray walls were swollen and flaking in the corners from dampness; on the floor some slime, like snail trails. The place, which smelled of mildew, seemed all the more dismal in contrast to her desolate glamour.

The commandant, Marko Danevski, opened the door from his office. "Well, well, Dimitrov," he said in a hearty voice, as if it were absolutely customary for the three of them to meet in this building. He nodded politely to Louisa, then made a slight inclination toward her from the midsection of his short, paunchy body. "As I told you before, we have made an unfortunate error, dear lady, for which we will make formal apologies to you and your Embassy. I used to speak some Italian, but that was long ago, and now I wouldn't even dare," he told her in perfect English. "We should not have brought you here. A mistaken identity, after all." Danevski shrugged and raised his eyebrows. "I understand you are staying at an inn close to Dimitrov's in-laws. Good. You are already friends. Dimitrov, you'll drive her back, is that right?"

He had been in Danevski's presence once before, many years ago, an occasion of bitter humiliation, one of those catastrophes that memory refuses to release. He prayed that Danevski, the son of a bitch, wouldn't remember, although sons of bitches like him never forgot names and faces; any details they didn't have in their minds, they kept in their files. Their job was to remember, it was why they had been born. To recognize and to organize files that documented if an individual had a police record, if the individual drank too much, if the individual had certain impolitic allegiances (to the church, for instance), if the individual was a smart-ass dissident at seventeen, making unrealistic demands at the lyceum for up-to-date textbooks or microscopes, if the individual's father was in the wrong party right after the war, if the individual loved his wife too deeply, if the individual was too keen on his children, if the individual had ever taken a lover. Any vulnerability, any deviance attracted him.

The sickening scene that Danevski had witnessed was one that Ivan had tried to blot out over time. They had arrested a young woman. Elena, they called her, daughter of Greek refugees, whose brother had tried to defect, had in fact raced across no man's land and miraculously reached to within meters of the Greek line when he was picked up by searchlights. From the Bulgarian watchtower, the border guards blasted the hunched, zigzagging figure with machine guns. In the morning they delivered the riddled body to his parents in a bloody canvas sack, dumped in their house after everyone had left for work, like the carcass of a goat. When Elena, the younger sister, came home, she saw the sticky crimson pools on the floor, ripped open the sack, and became hysterical. Heedlessly, she ran to the central police station, where she screamed, "Idiot communists, filthy Slavic pigs, heartless barbarians." They locked her up for failing to report foreknowledge of a defection and for causing civil unrest. Members of the Greek community, impotent, seething at the idea of a young girl locked in a jail cell, by chance met Ivan on the street and swept him along with them to the station to plead for her freedom.

Each man was allowed to step forward for one minute to present his plea before Commissar of Police Danevski, who in those days was in charge of the central police station—nothing like the exalted position he held now. The women huddled together by the door, like an ancient chorus, muffling their sobs in their hands. Ivan hung back to hide among the woman.

"You, there, *esi vre, ela.* Aren't you coming forward?" the men urged in Greek.

He stayed rooted among the women, his mouth shut.

"Do you intend to speak, *phile*?" they yelled.

He turned his back and bolted from the group of incredulous men and moaning women. To this day he was haunted by the eyes, wide—unblinking, accusatory. Yes, it could be seen as an arch betrayal. But he preferred to call his behavior a "denial," to signify an act less damning, more pragmatic. The Greek community had put a curse on him for that act of cowardice— how ludicrous, a medieval superstitious notion, and this the second half of the twentieth century. Think of it. But in truth, the whole idea of their anathema lay on him like a foreshadowing, and every time he sensed himself in danger, the memory of that curse, which he usually kept suppressed, rose to the surface and left him anxious and downcast for days. His mother, denounced by the Greeks for her son's action, was ostracized, and suffered from her exclusion so profoundly that he feared it hastened her death. Toward the end, she would cry out to her people, agonized, "*i dhiki mou,*" her thin sob resounding in the shabby room, her cry eating at his heart. For him it meant a complete rupture from the Greeks of Sofia. He had, quite simply, saved himself: never to end up shot in the back in no man's land, or locked in a jail cell, or whimpering for the release of his daughter. The girl, after four solitary days in the cell, without representation, without seeing her family, and God knows what else, hung herself.

"Excuse us a moment, Madame, while I fill out your release papers," said Danevski, like a benign post office bureaucrat accomplishing the most perfunctory task. He asked Dimitrov to come into his office. He slammed the door behind him.

"What in hell's going on? I've been dying to get my hands on her. Why in God's name should I let her go? I picked her up on good grounds. Then, 'Release her immediately to Ivan Dimitrov,' Rusinov tells me on the telephone."

"I can't tell you a thing. I'm just doing what they told me — 'Go pick her up,' they said. Better argue with Rusinov. Not me."

"An Italian opera singer, the bitch is carrying on all over the place with opera singers here and in Rumania, Hungary. Other places, too. Many of her contacts have defected—causing a lot of embarrassment. She's mixed up in an international safe-conduct organization for ballet dancers, musicians, those kinds of deviants." Danevski explained that this morning he'd taken for questioning a few suspects from the opera. The information that he'd managed to get from them tied her in, so naturally he'd brought her in for investigation. "She's hot. Only Bereznyi, he's like a bloody tsar, could have the power to order her release."

Ivan raised his palms upward.

"Screw Bereznyi, anyway, and take the bitch home." Danevski handed him her"effects," as he called them— a pocketbook filled with the usual woman's junk, an English trench coat with LB initialed on the lining, a French magazine stuck in one deep pocket, a rain hat in the other, and a beige and black plaid wool scarf. The scent of lilacs or some other perfume rose from the coat.

"By the way, did you . . .?" Ivan pointed at the door to the waiting room, where Louisa was sitting.

"No. Can't you tell by looking at her? Rusinov called before we even began the interrogation."

He gathered up her things. You're probably lying, he thought. You'd lie on the heads of your own children. Scum. He stepped back into the other room and guided Louisa, who was unsteady, out to the street. She turned and spat at the building. " *Va al diavolo.*"Her trench coat belted tightly, her scarf tied under her collar, she stumbled along the ice in flimsy high heels as they made their way to the jeep. She bumped against him and went down on one knee. He lifted her gently, held her under the arm, the improbable whiff of lilacs in winter rousing his senses. Again, he felt the tingle start in the back of his head and make its way across his back and down his spine, the same sensation he had experienced with the American woman. Now he understood. No, he didn't desire the opera singer any more than he wanted the other woman. He now understood exactly his craving.

"I'm filthy. What a hellhole. You people have taken a page from Dante's *Inferno.*"

She might somehow fit into his scheme of possibility, and so he was disappointed that all the way back to the lodge she made it impossible to talk to her, singing one aria after another, or sometimes just a line or two, or only a fragment; he recognized most of the melodies. Strange to hear arias that he had heard performed only in Russian at the opera house in Sofia, or Moscow, sung now in Italian, and a few, in French or German. He felt foolish that he had never envisioned them sung in any language but Russian. Each aria she chose was an explosion of vengeance, will, outrage. *"Frappez-moi donc, ou laissez-moi passer."*

She sang, sitting upright in the seat next to him, her eyes on the splattered windshield, but he knew she didn't see a thing. Once when the jeep skidded on its bald tires and even he felt his heart pound, her voice never broke, but rang at the same pace, the same pitch, with such concentration and awesome emotional power that he knew she was not singing in an effort to ignore him, but to empty out the anguish.

Chapter 12

She rapped lightly on the door. When no one answered, she knocked harder. A voice called out weakly, "Barbara?"

"Yes."

After a moment Louisa opened the door a crack, beckoned her in and climbed back into bed, pulling the cover up under her chin. The curtains were drawn, but here and there they sagged, letting in pale shreds of the late afternoon sun. Louisa's face, scrubbed clean of all make-up, was haggard; her eyes, dark olives, usually flashing with some superior knowledge, were half shut under puffed eyelids. Her hair, loose, straggling to her shoulders, was held off her face with a scarlet headband. She was so reduced, the cocksure Triestina. True, whenever Barbara had seen her, she had been dressed in full regalia. This pitiable sight was due to her ordeal in detention, surely, but Barbara also took into account her present lack of finery, an Ariadne, tattered and abandoned on the island of Naxos. Louisa lay rigid against the pillow, her tongue flicking across her parched lips, like a hospital patient too weak to take water. "Oh, God, they've hurt her," thought Barbara.

"Louisa, are you all right? What can I do?" She touched her hands, which were dry and unnaturally cool, almost like wood.

"*Jesumaria,* I look worse than I am. Just traumatized. Nothing else. Could you get me some warm broth, my dear Barbara? Anything warm." The beautiful voice was ragged.

"Louisa, should we send for a doctor?" In an automatic gesture she put her palm to Louisa's forehead to test for fever, but her head was peculiarly cool, almost clammy.

"No, I am just in shock. They shoved me in a freezing cell. More like a refrigerator. Without my coat. Water on the floor. Nothing to sit on. They took my shoes."

How would she herself have stood up to Louisa's ordeal? As she descended to the kitchen she was thinking only of herself, her own lack of exposure to such dangers, her lack of hardening. Once, as a child, she had been thrown from her horse. She had sat dazed and aching on the gravel; her father ran to her, hurled her, as she quivered with fear, back into the saddle, instructing her that whenever she fell, she was to climb right back on the horse, because if she didn't remount immediately, she would always be afraid. Such was her genteel schooling, not tough enough to get through the hell Louisa must have experienced, a child witnessing human heads displayed on pikes.

She returned with lukewarm soup and a corner of stale bread left from breakfast, an orange, and a glass of red syrupy wine called *Mavrud,* from Plovdiv, which the cook assured her was "a wine drunk by the ancients, delicious."

"Sorry, it's all they had at this hour. The variety in this place is truly astounding," she said, placing the tray on Louisa's bed.

Louisa's lips twitched in an effort to smile. "My voice. Can you hear how thick it is? Oh, God, the dampness there. And I sang all the way back in the jeep. What a stupidity." She was whispering now to spare it, stroking her neck with her hand.

"You shouldn't put your throat at risk. What a precious gift you expose to danger."

Louisa dipped the bread in the soup, her hand unsteady. "Your remark, Barbara, bears great irony."

For a moment, she pondered, and then she, too, caught the irony. She opened her mouth to defend herself against the implication that she was exposing her children to danger, and decided to let the comment pass.

Would Louisa reveal other details about her ordeal? Franklin had placed Barbara's mission on a need-to-know-basis, meaning she had no right under any circumstances to probe into the magazine's fate or the particulars of Louisa's arrest, and certainly not Louisa's role in the whole courier affair. Though consumed with curiosity, she felt obliged to skirt around the edge of the incident; what she couldn't gauge was where exactly the barrier lay, how closely she could waltz around its perimeter before she approached the sensitive core. She decided to move in as far as she dared.

"Did Ivan get you released?"

"I don't know. It was mysterious. 'Just a moment, you imbeciles,' I said. 'Do you know who I am? You are forbidden to arrest the wife of an Italian diplomat.'

The brute in charge doubled over, howling, as if I had told a joke. One moment they rejoiced to get me in their clutches. And later, they let me free, just like that. What role Ivan played, I have no idea. I only know that he came for me. You, Barbara, are a dear to bring me this food." She spoke slowly, as if it pained her to talk.

"Now we're both indebted to Ivan. I myself owe him so much, probably beyond my ability to pay," Barbara said.

"Oh, my dear, what a thing to say. You exaggerate." Louisa finished the soup, put her head back on the pillow and shut her eyes.

"I mean it. He saved Freddy."

"He acted correctly. But another would have done the same. He just happened along at that moment."

"Another person might have come along, say, one of those superstitious old peasant ladies. She'd make the sign of the cross, spit over her shoulder three times and trudge home to light a candle at the *iconostasis*, thinking she'd seen an evil snow spirit."

"O, yes, there is something to what you say."

"And, Louisa, think, even if someone hurried to report spotting Freddy sprawled in the snow, where in the world do you go to 'report,' in this country, and who responds to the report? Telephones aren't the handiest commodities. If you reported it to the *Obshtina*, just imagine. Those primitive village police don't have telephones or vehicles. They'd sit and wait until the duty driver came by at God knows what hour."

Louisa opened her eyes and propped herself on one elbow. Her shaky hands lifted the orange from the plate and began to peel it. "I'm not sure what you mean by indebted. How far can you carry that notion of yours before it becomes dangerous? Before you become too involved with him?"

"You are also indebted to him," Barbara said tentatively, not wanting to excite Louisa, who now seemed more relaxed.

The afternoon light had dimmed, leaving the room in deep shadow. For a moment she lay there in silence, then broke apart the orange and offered a piece to Barbara. The large diamond on her antique gold ring sparkled even in the gloom.

"These oranges have an exquisite aroma," she said, her voice toneless. "Such was the perfume of oranges we grew on our farm in Trieste. We grew so many. Baskets full. Hundreds of baskets. Too many oranges some seasons to harvest them all for market. We opened our fields to the peasants. Come, *contadini*, we called to them, gather what is left on the ground, dear people. Take it all. We invited them in a spirit of gratitude to help them out a little; they were ragged, some of them hungry, and, as you say, we were indebted to them for all their hard work on our land. And what was the consequence? Years later they come and slit our throats. You see, they looked on our gratitude as an act of charity, and they were bitter to take our charity."

"What lesson should I draw from that story? I'm sure there's a moral." She didn't mean to sound sarcastic, but thinking of the disparity of wealth in that area in years past, she had really spoken ironically, and she was sorry she'd said it. The smell of oranges wafted through the room.

"Dear Barbara, don't make a joke. Just be careful to whom you express gratitude, lest they become bitter."

There was a knock at the door. Barbara pulled it ajar and saw a tall, lean man with a narrow head, a trim mustache and sallow skin.

"I am Todor Danov, Intourist guide."

"Where's Svetlozar?"

"He's gone. I am in his place." He sidled forward, pushing at the door, one foot on the threshold. She held the door handle firmly.

"But he was here this morning, just a few hours ago."

"I'm sorry, Madame. I know nothing. There is Colonel Dimitrov downstairs to see you ladies."

She thanked him and slammed the door.

"So they took him," she said to Louisa. "What a price to pay for tumbling around in the hay with Gerda. Poor slob."

"What did you expect? You Americans, if you will forgive me, are hopelessly naive. You are without a history. You are people who live totally in the present. To comprehend complexities, one must possess a long, savage history. You had, I think,one revolution and one civil war on your soil. Such puny events in the grand scheme. Six months after the two world wars, you forget all about them." Her voice was barely audible.

Barbara went to the window and pulled aside the curtains. In the west, the sun, about to sink, had flared to gold; as she let her eyes wander over the amber hills, she said, "By the way, it was Svet who told Gerda that the police grabbed you. He saw it happen right outside of the hotel. Gerda then reported it to me."

"*Gran Dio*, then that's why they took him away."

"No. Impossible. I'm the only one who knew that Svet told Gerda."

"Do you have any idea who told Ivan I was detained?"

Barbara turned back toward Louisa. "I did." She felt uneasy. Were they breaking the need-to-know rule, entering that danger zone?

Her eyes wide open now, Louisa glanced at her affectionately. "I thought so all along. You Americans are naive, certainly. But most of the time your hearts are in the right place. Still, you shouldn't have involved yourself. An extremely dangerous act."

"Well, I appreciate your compliment, at least about our good hearts, but Ivan is the one I turned to for clout."

Finally Louisa was able to smile, not broadly, but enough to show she was regaining her equilibrium. She sipped the thick wine and sputtered, "This is the most hideous drink I ever swallowed. It tastes like sap from a wild tree."

Barbara tasted the wine and agreed.

"Be kind enough to go down, Barbara. I cannot. I am a wreck. Present to the Bulgarian Colonel my warmest greetings. That will suffice. Do not thank him for a thing, I beg you. Whatever he did for me, he did for a reason that has nothing to do with me. Do you agree with my opinion?"

"I agree with a lot of what you just said. Stay in bed, and when I come back, I'll bring us some supper and tell you some vivid chapters of American history. Valley Forge will make you eat your words about American history. The *Risorgimento* really pales in the light of that fascinating episode."

"Then if you are going to recite that dull American history, you had better bring some wine to speed us through the evening," she teased. "Mind you, Barbara, treat the Colonel skillfully. He will be useful when he gets to Athens," she said.

And that, thought Barbara, is the enormous difference between us. You want to exploit him and I want to repay him.

Ivan was waiting for her in the lounge seated by the fireplace, smoking an acrid cigarette and drinking coffee. As she approached, she noted he was leafing through a French paperback that a member of the group had left on the table. He studied the picture on the cover, then the binding and flipped through the pages.

"Do you read French?" she asked.

"No, unfortunately. Do you know this book?"

She glanced down to see the title. "Yes, *Bonjour Tristesse*, Françoise Sagan. It's well known in the West. It's already about twenty-five years old. You've heard of it?"

"No. We do not import books. The cover suggests much."

The picture in neon colors on the cover was lurid. In the foreground, a young woman clothed in see-through lingerie, a thin bra strap hanging loose from her shoulder, a cigarette dangling from puffed, crimson lips. Over one eye hung a lank strand of blond hair. In the background was a shadowy image of a suave older man dressed in a business suit, who, one had the impression, was a figment of her dreams.

"Believe me," she said, "the cover implies more than is written."

"Do Greeks import books like this?"

"Of course." She wondered what it would be like to lack Western literature, to be so isolated from a world that had so much to communicate.

"Then I will learn French and read as much as I can. How is Madame Borromeo?"

"I think she'll be fine tomorrow. She needs a day to recover."

"They can be brutes, those police. But in this case, they probably, I say probably, did not touch her. It is only that the whole incident scared her. I am happy to have arrived there in time." He seemed to feel more comfortable with her. He smiled slightly, picked the book up again and ran his fingers over the cover and flipped through the pages.

She couldn't ask him how he had managed to release Louisa; why he'd bother to help her; why she had been taken in the first place. These answers she could only guess; she sensed she had the right answer for the first question, but was not sure about the others.

She ordered a cup of mountain tea. The waiter said he didn't have any tea, she'd have to wait until the morning. Coffee, yes. Tea, no.

She told Ivan that Louisa sent him warm greetings, and that she, herself, was once again grateful to him, this time for stepping in to help Louisa, an act that went way beyond any normal favor.

"Madame, I ask a favor of you," he said, emphasizing the "you." The slight smile had faded. His face once again assumed its stiff expression.

She moved to the edge of her chair. Here comes the big payback, she thought, and gritted her teeth.

"Of course."

"Will you and your husband have dinner with Maria and me the day after I arrive in Athens? I can tell you the exact date," he said, taking a calendar out of his pocket. She thought his hands trembled slightly. His voice registered a slight tremor, mixed curiously with a degree of persistence, as if he were asking for some enormous courtesy he was unworthy of, but was nonetheless struggling to attain. His face remained impassive.

"Call my husband's office when you arrive," she said, sitting back in her chair, relieved at the meager request.

He leaned closer toward her. His front tooth, capped in gold, glinted.

"No. I know what will happen. By then your trip to Bulgaria will be a far memory and you will have no time for me." He shook his head.

"No, not at all. We, that is my husband and I . . ."

He interrupted. "What I have to talk about is not unimportant. He will find it significant. I will not speak with anyone else, you understand, no one but you both. I am not trusting of others. For all our sakes, please arrange it." His tone had turned strident.

"Since you feel so strongly, I promise to discuss it with him as soon as I get home."

He was fingering the French novel distractedly, tapping it lightly against the table. His green eyes were focused on her.

"Go one step further. Make me a promise that. . ."

"Oh, you have my promise."

Chapter 13

Freddy was waiting just inside the door for Ivan. He admired himself in the reflecting glass door: the Bulgarian army fatigue cap, stuffed with newspaper to keep it from sliding over his ears, and the army backpack, spotted with grease, things Ivan had given him for the day's expedition. Slung over his shoulder, a dripping canteen dampened the side of his jacket. Roger, broad shouldered, husky, passed by on his way to the mid-day meal.

"He isn't coming for another hour," Roger said.

"Where's your equipment?"

"Wear it in to eat?" Roger put his index finger to his head and swirled it round to make the crazy sign.

"I did."

"You would. Cool it, Fred. I can't see anything exciting about digging around in the mud. Like little kids in a sandbox. Plain boring."

"You don't think Mom will change her mind?"

"Nope. Once she saw how good your ankle was this morning, and she told Ivan you could go, why would she change her mind?

"Too good to be true, going out to a real battlefield, digging for stuff. Just like Schliemann excavating at Troy. We're studying him."

Roger smirked.

When Ivan finally arrived, Freddy stepped out of the building to observe the conversation between Ivan and his mother from a distance. If she actually ruined the day by crabbing and changing her mind "the boys can't go" he couldn't stand to hear it. Immediately, he felt sorry he'd thought of her as a crab, because she wasn't and he loved her. He remembered how, when he came home from school and she was out, the house was empty and sad. The discussion appeared to him from the other side of the glass door like a pantomime, his mother talking a lot with her hands, just like a Greek, probably giving Ivan instructions: don't let them take off their jackets when they're sweaty; don't let Freddy out of your sight; don't keep them out on these slick roads after dark. Blah, blah. blah. Ivan shook his head a few times, pointed to his watch, shook his head again, and finally waved to Roger and him to climb into the vehicle.

Over rocks and stumps, across the open fields, under the winter-bare chestnut trees, the quarter-ton truck thumped, jostling them as they sat in the cab. The vehicle, which Ivan had borrowed for the day while the jeep went to the motor pool for repairs, left the road, and was bumping along a gravel track. Wedged between Roger and Ivan, Freddy strained to look out the windows from the low-slung seat, whose springs were protruding and pinching his bottom. As the truck rattled along, he watched the leafless treetops fingering the sky, a cloud bending to lay an arm on the shoulder of a hill. Roger puffed on a cigarette that Ivan had given him, dangling the butt from the corner of his mouth, letting the smoke run up the side of his face to his eye, copying Ivan. Freddy felt his eyes tear, choked from the smoke, and was ready to throw up from the motion of the truck, which swayed like a rowboat.

Ivan said the fields were beautiful in summertime, but in winter everything was ugly. They were heading toward the river valley where conditions were warmer, not frozen like up on Vitosha, so they'd be able to dig at least to a depth where they'd be sure to discover things. In the middle of a field, Ivan put his foot on the brakes. "Here, this is a good place," he said, and jumped out, spitting his cigarette in the mud. Freddy watched Roger do the same. Ivan went in back to the truck bed and hauled out some shovels, rakes and a metal detector.

"This is where the worst happened, right here," Ivan said, and handed Roger binoculars, as he traced a wide arc with his hand across the broad, mucky fields.

"The worst of what?" Freddy asked.

"He already told you, dummy," said Roger.

"Where a small force of Germans who were left behind and the Russians fought," said Ivan, opening a plastic case and spreading a yellowing, tattered map across the hood of the truck." Look here on the map you can see the line clearly." Freddy couldn't follow it on the map at all, but nodded his head like Roger.

"Were Americans fighting here, too?" Freddy asked.

Roger spat in the dirt and rubbed it with the toe of his boot as Ivan had done.

"No, just the Russians chasing out the Germans. The Nazis had thousands of troops here in Bulgaria at the beginning of World War II. They used Bulgaria as a place to make their invasion of Greece and Yugoslavia," Ivan explained.

Ivan described how the Bulgarians joined the Germans, enticed by the gift of the Dobrudja, land the Germans took from Rumania to give to Bulgaria as bait. Toward the end of the war, the Russians entered Bulgaria, in the wake of the departing Germans, and gradually established the communist system.

"That's life, eh, whether it is war or peace. It is the nature of man for one to take from the other by force if that is the only way he can get it," said Ivan, handing Roger a shovel and Freddy a rake.

"Yeah," said Roger, "mainly in war, though. They can't just take anything from you in peacetime."

"Wrong my young friend. You must be strong in every way so no one takes from you. Every minute, you have to watch, how do you say, calculate," Ivan said, tapping his head with his finger. "And be as we say superhuman, in Greek *iperanthropos.*" He raised his arm and made a tight fist. "Hey, Freddy, feel this."

He reached up and squeezed Ivan's muscle, which bulged under his jacket.

"Wow. That's bigger than my Dad's." He didn't say that his father had taught him the opposite, that you get nowhere with "brawn and swagger, only with education and brain power."

"Then your father better build his muscles so no one takes from him," said Ivan.

"The Greeks were not on the same side with the Germans in World War II. How come the Bulgarians were?" he asked.

"Shut up," muttered Roger, poking Freddy in the ribs with his elbow. "Ivan's going to think we're a couple of jerks."

"No. The Bulgarians were on the German side in World War I, too. They are always thinking the Germans are going to get Macedonia for them. Bulgarians are crazy for Macedonia."

Ivan moved out ahead, concentrating on the metal detector that he swung in front of him.

"If you don't quit poking me, I'll tell Mom you were smoking. You're always mean to me when there's an older guy around." Freddy spoke in a half whisper so Ivan wouldn't hear him. He was never mean to Roger. When his friends came to their house, he was always happy when Roger sat and talked with them.

The metal detector peeped, and Ivan called to Roger to bring the shovel. "Start digging here." Roger's broad shoulders bent over the shovel, cracking through a layer of ice as thin as bat wings. He turned over only bits of rock. "Some more," said Ivan." Dig in deeper." Roger leaned into the shovel with all his strength, heard the blade scrape on metal.

"I can't get under it. The ground's too hard."

Ivan took the shovel and put his foot on the blade. With a couple of strokes he turned over a piece of metal.

"Looks like a part of a mortar shell. O.K. to pick it up, Roger, it is not live."

Roger picked up the shell, and he and Freddy turned it over and over in their hands. It was nothing but a twisted piece of iron, covered with mud and stuck with rocks. Still, unearthed, there was a mystery about it,

Freddy remembered, like a thing they had dredged up from the lake at Ioannina last summer when his father had pulled up his fishing line, figuring from the violent tug he'd caught a big fish. Instead, an ordinary small, wooden crate, holding several tiny plastic dolls broke the surface. At first they couldn't make out what was in the crate, and when it dawned on them, the sight of the dolls, dripping with slimy green weeds, had given them all the creeps, these human-like creatures hauled up from the deep. His father had said, "Grotesque."

"What year was that mortar shell from?" asked Freddy, taking a swig from his canteen.

"1944. Thirty-five years ago. Before you were born. Put it in your knapsack, Roger. Take it home, if you want.

"Better show it to Mom first, Rog."

"Who asked you?" Roger reached over his shoulder and dropped the shell into his knapsack.

"Freddy, use the rake to take off the top of the dirt. Maybe you will turn over a bullet or two. Who knows what? Everything is buried here. No one comes to dig. They think it is just junk. And besides they think the place is cursed, because of the people who died here. They are not archaeologists like us. If my life had been different, I would have become an archaeologist. Still my dream, you know." Then in a low voice, in a hoarse whisper Freddy heard him say, "My dream."

Pulling on the rake, his arms aching, Freddy turned up a black disk, the size of a quarter. Ivan got out a canteen, poured water over it and shined it on his pant-leg until they could see it was a copper coin, its markings rubbed off. Ivan handed it back to him; he dropped it

139

into his knapsack; he could show it at school when he got back to Athens.

Ivan demonstrated how to dig a trench and search within it, making the hunt more methodical. "Like professional archaeologists," he said. They dug for an hour or so finding a few bullet casings, and Ivan unearthed a metal belt buckle, which he couldn't identify as belonging to the Russians or the Germans. He gave it to Freddy.

Roger, who had crossed the trench to stake out his own digging area, hit something hard with the tip of his shovel. Ivan looked down at it. "Looks like just a rock all rolled in mud, but it has a real shape," Ivan said, going over to Roger; he wiggled the thing loose in its bed of dirt. After a few minutes of careful work, Ivan's hands cradled a dome-like object with three holes packed with pebbles. Freddy moved closer for a better look. From his pocket Ivan pulled a knife and gently chipped away at the muck; he then poked his knife into the holes, unpacking the pebbles with his fingers to reveal an ivory- colored form: eye sockets, a nose hole, some crooked teeth in the upper jaw, the lower jawbone ripped away. Unmistakably a human skull. Around the teeth, some mud was still encrusted, and as it crumbled away, a few white worms dropped to the earth, wiggling blindly.

Ivan, excited, shouted a few words in Bulgarian, and then remembering Freddy and Roger, he said in English, "Well, did we or did we not make a big discovery? What a prize. Hello, my fine fellow. Welcome to this big, wide world."

Freddy couldn't manage a word. He looked across the trench at Roger who was staring at the skull, his hands pressed across his open mouth.

"Rog, Rog," he called, "are you O.K?"

Ivan held the skull out at arm's length, talking to it, really teasing it, as if it were a live person, some guy he'd run into as he was walking through the fields. Roger leapt across the trench to stand by Ivan and Freddy.

"I've never seen a skull before. Never thought I'd ever dig one up," Roger said, his face streaked with dirt.

"Holy God," Freddy said. He whistled, but his lips were dry and the sound came out hollow. Something hot and burning came up in his throat.

He and Roger knelt close to examine it, as Ivan threw the equipment back into the truck and struggled to secure the truck's gate with a frayed rope. At one point Freddy grabbed a stick to poke the bone, with the tip of it, but Roger knocked the stick out of his hand.

"Leave it alone," Roger said, low and commanding, in a tone that reminded Freddy of his father's.

On the way back, Ivan tried to teach the boys some Bulgarian rhymes but Freddy was barely able to repeat the words, sickened by the head that Ivan had placed on the floor, calling it "baby," as he wrapped it protectively in a greasy rag he'd found in the truck. On a sharp curve Ivan said, "Hey, Roger, hold that thing between your feet so it does not roll around on the floor and break."

Roger, his eyes shut, couldn't open his mouth. For that matter, neither could Freddy, who stared sidelong at Ivan, scared Ivan would tell him to pick it up, hold it in his lap.

"Hey, you two guys look sick. The truck ride or the skull?"

Neither boy answered.

"This was supposed to be a fine day, an adventure for us to remember. Not a funeral."

Ivan told them a few comical stories about the peasants in the villages, their superstitions and some of their stubborn ways. Then he took up again the Bulgarian ditties with their catchy rhymes and rhythms. By the time they neared the lodge, Roger and Freddy could recite a few lines by heart in Bulgarian, especially those with dirty words. . . *vchera starshina ta rech.* . . which they translated into English, and then into Greek. Freddy howled at the smutty words while they jumped from one hilarious synonym to another in three languages.

"Hide those lines from your mother," Ivan said, winking.

Freddy was thinking that Roger was having such a good time, and admired Ivan so much, probably he'd tell him anything he wanted to know. He elbowed Roger. Roger frowned at him, perplexed, and pinched Freddy's thigh. Hadn't Mom told them in one of her hour-long lectures before they went off not to get too chummy with the Bulgarian, to just be polite and have a good time, but not discuss the Embassy or anyone there?

By the time they returned to the lodge, he had rolled down the window and was leaning out, singing the Bulgarian verses on top of his lungs, while Roger, sitting in the middle, was acting like a grownup, discussing with Ivan the details of World War II. When the truck came to a halt in front of the lodge, he climbed down and loped into the lounge, his face like a coal miner's just risen from the pits, covered with grime, his eyes, two white circles. Mom was waiting for them. Before she could ask how the trip went, he burst out, "Ivan's really cool. He knows so much history. He dug with us, and you should've seen what we discovered. An honest-to-God skull." He fished in his backpack and drew out the coin and belt buckle to show her.

She smiled and searched for Roger. "We left him there overnight to dig, he was having such a ball."

She frowned.

"No. Just kidding, Mom."

Roger trudged into the lounge, distracted, but when he saw his mother, he waved and said in a dreamy voice, still absorbed in the novelty of the day, "Great. It was really great. I've decided to become an archaeologist."

"Yeah. We're going to see Ivan in Athens. He's going to find out about taking us on a dig to find valuable Greek antiquities," said Freddy.

His mother's eyebrows shot up.

"Did he tell you when or try to arrange a place to meet you?"

They looked out of the windows at Ivan, who waved at them from the wheel of the truck before he drove off.

"He said he'd call me and Rog as soon as he gets there."

Chapter 14

In late afternoon, the Balkan Airlines flight from Sofia, bucking a headwind, made a shuddering landing at the Athens airport. From the stultifying cabin, she and the children stepped out squinting in the brilliance of a halcyon day, the gentle time in midwinter, recorded even in ancient times, when for a week or so the capital luxuriates in sunlight, the air so tepid that it hardly moves through the gilded pines.

The taxi, a black Mercedes, windows shut against the Greek winter peril—a draft— was piloted by a maniac whose life was protected from the hazards of the road by a clutter of icons and amulets glued to the dashboard and pinned to the cloth above the windshield. For extra protection, blue beads swung from the mirror. She expected that Freddy and Roger would laugh at his language as he swore at the world—"*malaka, panayia mou, sta arxithia mou, as to diavolo, Christe eleison,*" an impossible mix of filth and religious entreaties. Tires squealing on the heated asphalt, the Mercedes raced down Syngrou, onto Vassiliou Konstantinou Avenue, where the Parthenon swung into view sited far above the huge billboard with the letters advertising the household helper "HOOVER" in gargantuan letters. From her perspective, the venerated ruin looked gray and squat, oddly monolithic. On the summit of the Acropolis streamed the Greek flag, its blue field the exact color of the sky.

"I'm glad to be home," said Catherine.

"This is not our home," said Freddy, with enough petulance in his voice to unnerve Barbara. The return to the thundering city excited her—the vitality of the street culture, the careening cars, the shouted bickering as every Greek stood up for himself —*xereis pios eime ego*—stood in contrast to the stagnant, muffled cities in the bloc, like Sofia. What made Freddy so parochial? Why did he insist that home was in the States? Freddy, who usually swung with the wind, was unyielding on this one point. He rolled down his window. The driver ran his hand along his damp neck and pulled his jacket collar up. "Close it, *agori mou*, we'll get a draft, catch cold and die," and with a stretch of his long arm, he reached back and rolled up Freddy's window.

The taxi stopped repeatedly and then lurched forward in raging traffic, the tumult of a large city. She recalled that only 2 percent of Bulgarians lived in Sofia, while 30 percent of Greeks lived in Athens, figures that accounted for some difference between the capitals. But even if Sofia were ten times more populated, it would still be stagnant. In the morning before they boarded the plane, they had been taken on a tour of Sofia, and members of their group had commented on the sullen silence that gave the city the air of a necropolis.

Now they passed the Olympic Stadium on the right, the Venizelos statue on the left, and the Truman statue and the American Embassy on the left, drove up through Ambelokipi—she loved to count the landmarks—

and swerved into the less polluted, elegant suburb of Psychiko, home to most of the diplomatic corps. When the taxi turned onto their street, they rolled past the crumbling palace of the late Queen Frederika, mother of ex-King Constantine—the monarchy had been abolished by plebiscite in 1974—forlorn in its abandonment. How ironic, she mused, that the former Queen's residence, a pre-war structure, cringed, unassuming, truly humble, in contrast to the elaborate neighboring mansions and sumptuous formal gardens conjured up by Greece's post-World War II plutocracy.

They pulled up in front of their large two-story home, barely visible behind the whitewashed wall and obscuring hedges. Even from curbside, it struck her as more inviting, more gracious, safer than ever before. How oddly different even the most familiar things looked after an absence. But aren't we travelers? Changed beings? Haven't our nostrils inhaled the dust of foreign cities, our hands touched other surfaces, our eyes engaged the eyes of other people— how can anything ever look the same again? She leaned forward to pay the driver.

"Bulgaria's not that bad, but I'm glad to be home, Mom," said Roger, scrambling out to help with the luggage.

They nodded to the corpulent guard who sat in a small shack by their gate, a precaution the Greek government took to keep the top American diplomats safe from terrorists, although the lax ways of Greek security did absolutely nothing to reassure the Americans.

"This isn't our *home*," said Freddy, this time shrilly.

"Cripes, Freddy. You're all hung up on where your home is," said Catherine. "You're lucky to have such a nice home at all. What's the difference where it is? Some people don't have any home at all. The poor people in Beirut . . ."

But Freddy, clutching his pile of *Asterix* comics, was darting up the steps on his gangly legs, favoring his bad ankle. The dog raced out to greet them, spinning wildly, legs sliding out from under on the slick marble porch.

Barbara stepped into the front hall, and with a kiss on both cheeks, greeted Ourania, who stood in her gray uniform and half-moon white apron. A refugee of Greek descent from southern Albania, she had escaped four years ago with her immediate family over the border into northern Greece, fleeing conditions intolerable for all Albanians, but especially for the Greek minority. Ourania told unimaginable stories about their madman dictator, Enver Hoxha. If the stories were true, he had built thousands of pillboxes throughout the countryside—not for protection along the borders—many of them connected by tunnels packed with ammunition. Hoxha was improbably allied, not with the Soviet Union, but China.

Picking up the phone, she dialed the Embassy.

"We're back, Robbie."

"Everything O.K.? The children? You?"

"We're glowing from our luxurious outdoor sauna baths. Wow. That St. Moritz is quite the place. Oh, and the *literati* there. I finally met Henry James."

"Did things work out right?"

"Not really. But I've got stories to keep you roaring, so to speak."

"I bet. I'll jump in the car right now. Tell the kids to stay put. God, I'm relieved you're back."

"I love you. Hurry."

She called out to Ourania to have dinner ready by 6:30 because Mr. Robert was coming home early.

After dinner, when the children left to go about their evening activities, Robert poured himself a snifter of Metaxas brandy and they moved into their upstairs sitting room, her favorite place in the house, an oasis she could call home, apart from the formal rooms where they entertained to fulfill their diplomatic responsibilities. Still, the downstairs was all lightness in the Greek way, the living room all white, a globe full of air and sun. But up here, in one corner—her work space—her beloved typewriter she'd had since college and a bookcase crammed with books she used for research, files of papers. In another corner, their phonograph and record collection. These things marked out the hearth, a place she couldn't live without. Yet it was enough— all she wanted of home. On her desk Ourania had put a cut glass vase of salmon-colored roses.

Along one wall was Robert's bench, smelling faintly of formaldehyde, where he kept specimens of bats, in their liquid containers; dozens of others were pinned to a board on the wall. On the bench was scattered his correspondence from bat-lovers around the world; on the floor were stacked piles of newsletters from bat societies and thick black notebooks scribbled with data on sightings, habitats, eating, nesting, mating habits. As a world-renowned authority on Chiroptera, he was invited to international seminars to give papers on his sub-specialty, bats of the Balkans. Displayed on a shelf were fencing trophies he had won from dozens of competitions, and a picture of himself in college in the en garde position holding his foil.

He bent down to kiss her. "Lots to tell?"

"Lots. I don't know where to begin."

"No matter. You'll spill it all out over the course of the week. No need to tell it all now, except for the magazine. That part I should know right away in case something comes up with your soul mate, Dana Franklin. And who is this Ivan the boys seem so taken with? The story the kids told at the table, all speaking at once, was garbled. One thing I heard clearly: Catherine thinks the Bulgarian officer is weird. She said when he smiled it looked like his face split in two. Lips curled happily, eyes cold. What a Catherinesque observation."

"Weird, no, not weird at all. A total mischaracterization. She missed the point entirely."

He sat down on the edge of the ottoman where she had propped her feet, and rubbed her ankle with affection. His eyes were a darker gray than hers, clear and tinged with blue, set strikingly against his thick black hair, and now that he was up close, she noticed his eyes were slightly puffed, and the age lines around them spread when he smiled. Although they'd met in graduate school, she couldn't recall that younger face anymore. On the table nearby was their wedding picture, token of a distant era. The wiry, innocent couple beamed at the camera; to her, they looked like complete strangers, so much had she and Robert grown together, and changed together. She loved his face now, at this stage in their lives, distinguished, ambassadorial, so perfect for the part. That day would come: Mr. Ambassador.

She had loved two men. Robert was the second. As an undergraduate, she had fallen for a premed student; a Southerner from Louisiana, he so different from her culturally, they could have come from different countries, and so he fascinated her. Whatever Irish blood had coursed in his family's veins must have been canceled out by a stronger strain— he didn't look Irish at all with his full features, dark complexion and tightly curled hair. He claimed for himself "Negro blood," for which there was some very distant genealogical evidence, but his family who insisted on their Irish roots (with a trace of French from his paternal great-grandfather), refused to discuss the possibility of miscegenation, and claimed he looked French "like those people from around the Mediterranean." He was gracious, unlike her own clipped, taciturn Yankee people, and he charmed her with his looks, his accent, and elaborate, often hilarious, sometimes tragic tales of Southern life. After medical school, he planned to head for the Delta to work among impoverished blacks. He was too rooted for her: rooted in his career, rooted in his patrimony. After a passionate affair, lasting through the last three years of college, too sexual for most young people to handle in the generation of the 1950s, especially for women from "good families," who typically remained virgins, she broke it off. She was stronger for having passed through the intimacy, had looked on the affair as an act of liberation; he was wounded badly, barely able to cope because of his "habit of fixedness," as she called it. Months later, after the biting loneliness—the most frightening emotion she'd ever experienced—had worn off she met Robert and recognized in him a fascination with the world -

at- large, which matched her own. She loved him for his quirky hobbies—his interest in bats, his status as a world-class fencing champion. And he was certainly not a pusillanimous bureaucrat, as Franklin had once intimated. Rather, he was a clever foreign-service officer who knew how to bend the system to his own ambitions. Ironically, it was when she was feeling her happiest with Robert, that she thought of her first love still, realizing how wrong he would have been for her, making her moments with Robert all the sweeter.

She pushed back in the easy chair, closed her eyes, and took several deep breaths, as if it were possible to draw into her body the exquisite warmth of the day, the safety of her home, her husband's affection.

"You know what's going through my head?" she asked.

"No, my love, I rarely know what's going through your head."

" 'Home is the sailor, home from the sea, And the hunter home from the hill.'"

"I think it's Robert Louis Stevenson, but I can't remember the title," Robert said. Without getting up, he bent forward on the ottoman, kissed her on the thigh and buried his head in her lap. "I hope you've gotten most of that out of your system." His voice, deep in her skirt, was muffled.

"Most of what? Stevenson? Why, is he subversive? A security risk?"He sat up. "You, yourself, are some rootless sailor home from the sea."

"Rootless, yes, but also rabid. Ravenous. Roiled. Raving. But with it all— ravishing." She laughed, stood up, performed a few steps she'd picked up from the

Bulgarian folk dances and spun in the direction of their bedroom.

Afterward, when they turned the lights on, he said, "I'll have to agree. Ravishing." Naked, he lay on his back, stretching, his eyes still half shut. He stayed like that, every now and then emitting soft, purring noises, before he rearranged his pillows against the headboard and slipped under the blanket. "Now, first, tell me about Freddy, then about the mission."

But when she began to relate the details of Freddy's disappearance, she realized all the episodes of the past week were seamlessly connected, that there was no way to break the story into segments and introduce Robert gradually, tomorrow or the next day, to her deepening entanglement with Ivan, especially the parts when she pleaded for Louisa's release, and when she decided to let the boys go off with him to dig. These decisions were bound to strike him as examples of appalling judgment if not presented with utmost care. So she narrated every detail, precisely, chronologically, event after event, including the last harrowing moment, when Roger lost his ski poles, and she was unable to redeem the passports. She suspected someone had snatched the poles to make things difficult for them, then decided she was developing paranoia. Only intervention from Ivan, at the last minute, had saved her from getting snarled in a Kafkaesque situation. "It was only Ivan who could get back that official yellow paper to redeem our passports so we could leave the country."

Robert looked at her, his eyes narrowed in concentration, an expression she had learned to interpret from the first days of their marriage: he was taking the subject with the utmost seriousness, and she expected him as usual to give an immediate analysis and instructions on how to proceed. So she spoke quickly, deliberately, to make her standpoint clear.

"Naturally, I feel a profound sense of gratitude for his saving Freddy. That dominates all of my considerations."

"Considerations? What are you considering?" Irritated, he got up, put on his pajamas, frowning in concentration.

"There's plenty to think about," she said.

"Good. I'm glad you're thinking. Contrary to Shakespeare, thinking is never dangerous. Remember, 'He thinks too much: such men are dangerous.' ? That's all wrong. It's actions that hurt."

"But actions are life, they give life meaning. If we don't act, we come to the end of our lives and don't know the meaning."

"Don't be ridiculous. Let's talk pragmatically and leave the Existentialism for another time, please." He uttered his remarks with his head turned away from her.

"Don't talk like that. Dimitrov will be arriving on station within days."

"Great. He'll be a fine addition to the diplomatic community."

"You're being horrid. You should be as grateful as I am."

"I am. But I go no further."

"Is that the way you look at it? But there's something else."

"What else?"

She was silent for a moment. Then they agreed not to bicker, to put the situation in perspective. Surely, they both agreed, Louisa's release, given that she was the wife of an Italian diplomat, could only have been handled at the highest level—orders from the Russians. They had released her as a favor to Barbara. Dimitrov could only have formed such a close relationship with Barbara with the encouragement of the Russians, the most apparent reason being that it gave the Russians, through Dimitrov, a direct contact to the American Embassy. And Franklin would undoubtedly find this an exciting opportunity to set up an information exchange through Dimitrov. "As for your Bulgarian officer," Robert said, starting on one of his perorations, "he's Greek. He might want to defect, something I definitely don't want to be associated with." He reminded her of an incident a few years before when the agency had used the Athens aiport to spirit a defector out to Rhein-Main Airforce Base in Germany. The Greeks were incensed over the undercover shenanigans on Greek territory. It caused a real problem in Greek-American relations, took months to repair. "I needn't tell you that a State Department officer couldn't risk such a scandal. Worse still if a capricious wife was directly involved. And if the Russians understand your sense of gratitude to that character Dimitrov—and, mind you, I'm not suggesting they do—it makes their work even easier," he said, his voice lightly sarcastic.

"Don't be clever," she said. "We haven't touched on what I'm considering. If you have any sensitivity, you might give some thought to how I intend to proceed."

"Are you ready for us to discuss that? It could spoil what has been a delicious homecoming. Delicious."

She got off the bed, pulled a robe around her and opened the French doors to step out on the balcony. From a nearby tree came the hoot of an owl, followed by the answer from another.

"I missed Greece," she said. She was standing in the light of a three-quarter moon, her back to him, facing east where the mountains that form a bowl around Athens were now invisible. Still, she sensed their looming presence and searched for their silhouettes in the darkness. Inhaling, she tried, from habit, to catch a trace of jasmine that hung voluptuously on summer air like an aphrodisiac, but of course, now in winter, only a few hardy plants bloomed, quite scentless.

She came back in and shut the doors, but kept her eyes angled at the moon, shining through the glass.

"Franklin will have to deal me in."

"Obviously. Or better, let's demand that he cut you out."

She whirled round, her face flushed. "Cut me out? Damn it, this is exactly what I wanted. Remember? The whole reason I carried that bloody magazine. What am I supposed to do? Sit on the sidelines my whole life?" His eyes had taken on that steely glint, betraying a temper barely held in check. Yet, it would take a bit more for him to storm, she knew from years of experience. The exhilaration she had felt earlier in the day was gone. Marriage, it seemed to her, with all the affection, companionship, deep sharing of experiences, was nonetheless, at times, a form of tyranny.

"Barbara, sit down. Listen. This guy's a menace, he can only survive by lies and betrayal; think of him as viewing the world like a bat, he sees everything from

155

an upside- down position. From what you tell me he's already begun a campaign to ingratiate himself with the boys. Too much is at stake for us to argue."

"All right. Let's discuss it calmly." She got into her nightgown as he talked.

"The story you just told is pretty transparent. But there's more information I want to tell you, so we can think this business out together. What you quoted from Louisa about the Italians not being important was not altogether correct."

"I'm listening."

"Here are some facts you don't know, but they're uppermost in Franklin's mind. There's a suspicion, just one suspicion along with dozens of other suspicions, that the Bulgarians, as agents of the Russians, are supporting the Red Brigade. Aldo Moros's death in Rome last year at the hands of the Brigades is an example of how powerful and successful these terrorists are. Some of Franklin's people suspect that there are Turkish terrorists too, who may also be supported by the Bulgarians. I read a CIA report recently that mentioned the Vatican as a possible target. Big stuff here. Big enough to rivet Franklin, who wants to nail the group that killed his predecessor—the Greek November 17 terrorists."

"Does anyone know if the Bulgarians are involved in November 17?"

"Someone may know. I don't. Franklin is holding the information close to his chest. My gut feeling is that if they are not linked now, eventually they may be if the terrorists continue to thrive. But then, who knows. At this point there is a general consensus that the Greek terrorists are supported by a force outside of Greece.

Louisa, she told him, had stuck scrupulously to the need-to-know classification, so of course she had never mentioned what happened at the SSP or whether she was able to pass the magazine. "How does Louisa fit into all this, and what do you suppose was in that magazine?" she asked.

"I've got enough sense not to ask what was in that magazine; Franklin's not about to tell. But Louisa's opera career and her husband's position offer her lots of mobility—Italy, Greece, Bulgaria, the whole Eastern Bloc is her domain. Doesn't take much to grasp how valuable she is."

He added that he had spoken to the Ambassador while she was gone.

Her mind turned to Paige Gardner— not new money and not old money, just plain oil money, he had supported the President's campaign and was now reaping the reward as a political appointee. A tall, gregarious Texan who walked with a pronounced limp, dependent on a cane for every step. Although little was actually known about him on station, a tangle of rumors were rife about his disability: he'd contracted polio when he was a kid after a swimming meet; he'd ridden in rodeos, took a bad spill; he'd been in the battle of Normandy, stepped on a mine.

He owned a fabulous assortment of canes from all over the world, enough to use a different one every day of the week. In addition, he boasted a special collection he slyly called his *"canea arcana erotica,"* which he shared with a coterie of men ("improper for women," he claimed). According to a chosen few who had the privilege of viewing them, the canes were fashioned into sensational shapes too explicit for women's eyes.

"He's hung up on his predecessor, as all ambassadors are," Robert had once said. Gardner knew that the Ambassador before him, a career type, had no balls. "Gardner is obsessed that people on station might say the same thing about him; that makes him overzealous. We're O.K. as far as Gardner is concerned, probably on his preferred list, since we appear to him, thanks to you, to be as irresponsible as he himself is. Says he's not going to report to the State Department our 'harmless dalliance with Franklin,' as he put it."

"Great. He won't report I worked with Dana. End of problem."

"No. He won't. But I probably will. Don't think I'm going to hide the fact that you and I played games with the agency, only to have the information turn up in a distorted way in Washington to ruin my career months after he's gone back to drilling his oil wells."

She slid under the covers. Her frolic in Bulgaria seemed like child's play compared to the opportunities that lay open to her now. She reached out for him and he came to her quickly. For just a flash, she thought she picked up a faint scent of jasmine.

When the phone rang, they were still in each other's arms, satisfied, depleted, just beginning to haggle again about how much of a role she ought to play when Dimitrov came to Athens.

"Don't forget you haven't any training. You're a DIA analyst, not an operator, so keep out of it altogether, my love. The risk factor is too high."

She grew uncomfortable under his fixed gaze: a slight squint, a half-frown, pursed lips. It took him a while but finally he said, "Is there something more elusive, more profound, a sentiment you yourself haven't figured out yet?"

" No, for God's sake, no. Can't a person be motivated to act simply out of conscience?"

The phone shrilled.

"I demand only one thing," she said.

"Oh, Christ almighty."

"That you never forget the debt we owe him. We must treat him as an individual."

"An individual? What the hell does that mean? He's individual all right. The man's a vagrant, he doesn't belong anyplace. He's anathema."

She winced. He said this too brutally, as if the fault lay in Ivan's character, not in his circumstance. "Everyone ultimately belongs someplace. He definitely does not belong in Bulgaria."

"I thought you went off on a lark, purely for the excitement, you said, of carrying out a mission, or some such thing. Now you're all tied up emotionally in the whole thing, especially him."

"I did just go off on a lark. But now the adventure has been personified. There's a specific human being involved, and toward him there's good to be done."

After the fourth ring, Robert reached over and picked up the phone. "Yes, of course I'll come by. Sure. Your house, eleven tomorrow morning. See you then."

"Dana Franklin?" she asked, when he hung up.

"He's never before contacted me like this to see me on a Saturday. Whatever it is, it can't wait till Monday. First that bloody magazine and now the Bulgarian is ruining our lives," he said.

Chapter 15

She was typing her observations from notes she had scribbled during the trip to Bulgaria when, at noon precisely, the phone rang.

She picked up the receiver.

"Barbara, can you take a walk over here? If you want, we can discuss some of the options."

"This is an odd approach, Rob."

"Any approach to you would have to be somewhat . . . oblique, my little sailor. If you don't like the approach and don't want to sail right over, frankly that would be balm for my nerves."

Never mind. I'll be right there."

She hurried across the porch, squinting at the Pendelian marble floor that glared in the sun. She forgot to brush her hair and change her messy shoes. She fumbled with the heavy catch on the iron gate and left her house, flabbergasted. Why would Robert call without coming home first to go over Franklin's proposals with her? Wouldn't he want to sort them out, to warn her of the dangers of each with an eye, the sneaky devil, to talking her out of all of them?

Franklin's house was just a few blocks away. She hurried through streets lined with eucalyptus trees, now pruned for winter, and oleander bushes, ready to bloom in the next month or so in the first heat of spring. In a neighbor's garden an almond tree had blossomed. She thought of lines from Kazantzakis's haiku: " I said to the almond tree, speak to me of God and the almond tree bloomed." The halcyon days lingered. The god Apollo was at work heating the earth. The sky was perfect, a clear blue, no, not blue, but cerulean, a better word than blue. She mouthed the word again. Cerulean. Not Greek. Had to be Latin. It was the kind of Greek day when the head spun with songs learned in the cradle. The aroma of freshly baked bread floated on the warm breeze; of course, the bread man, a centaur, a man's head and body with bicycle legs. She shook her head in delight. Pedaling more slowly today than usual, the bread man rounded the corner, dipping precariously on his rickety bike, white hair flowing like a mane, bones as thin as the bicycle frame. Long, crusty loaves stood tall, golden, in a wooden box attached, somehow, over the rear wheel. *"Psomi,"* he trumpeted his ware, the *"mi"* rising on the hot air currents. Housemaids, wiping their hands on their aprons, rushed out of doors to take their loaves and to savor, for a few seconds, the sovereign sun.

She didn't want to be any place other than Greece, not standing in the Piazza San Marco, not under the rose window at Notre Dame, not on the banks of the Thames. When she was a youngster, wherever she was, she wanted to be in a different place. If on Nantucket, she longed for New York. Once in New York, she yearned for the Grand Tetons. As an adolescent, she was hounded by the obsession that her life would end before she'd seen the world. And still today she wanted to travel more, but in the last few years, Greece made her content.

As she neared Franklin's house, she was possessed by a childish urge to skip—the Greek sun did that to you—but when his garden came into view, she sobered at once, thinking of her imminent meeting with Franklin and Robert. She entered his yard at a sedate saunter. A manservant in a white jacket opened the door. "Please, madame," he said, in an accent that she guessed was Middle Eastern, and led her from the tessellated reception hall into the spacious living room, where Robert and Franklin were chatting, referring to some reports spread out over the coffee table.

Franklin came forward to take her hand. He could have been any professional—doctor, lawyer, professor— at leisure on this fine Saturday, entertaining friends. He wore a blue button-down oxford shirt, with the sleeves rolled, khaki pants and tasseled loafers. His wire glasses, shoved up on his forehead, rested in the thicket of his auburn hair. Oddly enough, slumped on the couch, Robert looked comfortable, almost at home, his legs stretched full out.

"Welcome back. I see you're all tan from the slopes. Did you have a pleasant trip?" Franklin asked, accenting the "pleasant" to assure that she caught his ironic humor.

"Divine. I met some fascinating host-nationals. We discussed the latest books, the newest movies, news events, this season's Italian and French fashions," she said, falling in with his banter.

Franklin threw his head back and laughed. "I know. Rob's been giving me the rundown."

"I don't know what I'd do without him to talk for me," she said, without bitterness, but Robert caught the note of chiding and shifted in his chair, his eyes narrowing to make a good-natured grimace.

"I say we have some lunch," said Franklin. He tapped a buzzer under the coffee table with his foot. A servant, his eyes suavely averted, brought in sandwiches and drinks on a tray. As they ate, Franklin and Robert discussed the present political situation in Greece and the possible danger—a slide into chaos— if the two political leaders around whom the whole country rallied were to become disabled. The conservative prime minister, Constantine Karamanlis, was already in his early seventies, and the leader of the opposition party, socialist Andreas Papandreou, an outspoken critic of the United States, was rumored to be a drinker and sickly, and a demagogue to boot. Since the fall of the military junta and the return of democracy in 1974, American foreign policy had been mainly concerned with toning down anti-Americanism in Greece, holding the equilibrium between Greece and Turkey, and maintaining stability in a country whose history was burdened with military coups. According to her analysis, American foreign policy— tolerant toward the junta and in many instances supportive—had built a legacy of anti-Americanism that could smolder for decades. In fact, she believed, the terrorist group November 17 had already fired the first volley of what would be an increasingly violent reaction to American presence in the country, to its military bases, educational institutions, and even commercial activites.

When Kissinger was Secretary of State, Robert had made a name for himself in Washington as an expert on Greece. In 1974, the fateful year when the Greek junta ousted Archbishop Makarios, president of Cyprus, and threatened to declare Cyprus' union with Greece, and invade the island, Robert was a senior political officer in Athens. With his easy fluency in Greek, the State Department had rated him a native speaker, the highest category. Due to his genuine interest in the culture, he had fostered close relationships with the chiefs of the Greek army and navy. When Undersecretary of State Joe Sisco, under Henry Kissinger's direction, flew to Athens on a shuttle diplomacy mission to keep the Greeks and Turks from going to war over Cyprus, Robert served as the perfect conduit for Sisco between the Greek army and navy chiefs in the negotiation, an assignment that had won him a commendation. Dana Franklin, like everyone else, knew Robert's prestige in the State Department and probably had been playing to it all morning, she thought, while Robert resisted. A battle of the titans.

When they had finished lunch, and the man had removed the tray, Franklin pulled his glasses down and turned his fish eyes on her. Apparently, the affability had gone out of the room on the lunch tray.

"You realize the magazine never reached its destination," he said.

"No, I didn't. I'm sorry."

"No fault of yours, be assured. The mission was iffy from the start, had a very slim chance of success, but since there was no other way, it was worth the try. You'd be surprised how many attempts that seem doomed actually succeed."

"Then you knew there was a possibility that Louisa. . . . "

"We're talking about national interests here, not individual relationships. Let's not make a big personal deal out of this." He scowled at her. "They were bound to watch Louisa," he explained. "They were on to her for her role in defections, that's why we had to have someone else carry the magazine through passport control. They had probably been notified over there the moment she applied for a visa here in Athens at the Bulgarian Embassy, made a note of her arrival, counterchecked her registration at the lodge, and then waited for the right moment to snatch her."

"Actually, the SSP probably would have finally noticed the magazine when she was detained if your knight in armor hadn't shown up to distract them," he said. "You might be curious to know that the magazine carried a blueprint to establish a code with an administrator at the opera house, a guy who has actually penetrated a terrorist organization. The code was for his use to report back to us on those terrorists. Since the SSP didn't grab the magazine, we know it never aroused their suspicion. Still, we've got to find another means to exchange information with the guy at the opera."

"You can count me out of a quick return to Bulgaria for a ski trip," she said, trying to laugh casually, but the sound from her throat, she realized, sounded more like a nervous tic. "And, yes, of course I wondered what was in that magazine."

"Robert tells me you have a new Bulgarian friend."

"You're being facetious, Dana. Hardly a friend. Something else."

"Well, what?" His voice had taken on a coaxing quality.

"An acquaintance, I suppose, made through happenstance. In your parlance, a contact."

"What can you tell me about him?"

"Quite a bit, actually." And she described what had happened in Bulgaria and her impressions of Dimitrov and his wife, told him nearly everything, but kept to herself her gratitude and anything else she might feel toward Dimitrov.

Franklin asked her to be more specific about the wife, when exactly she would stand by her husband's side and when she might be apt to put a brake on him. In trying to answer his question, she became aware of how little she had grasped of Maria's personality, of their relationship.

"What do you think of his running these messages through to Bulgaria for us once he comes to Athens?"

"How's he supposed to do that?"

"That's for him to figure out. He sounds like a desperate man, a person who'd try very hard. I'm just curious to know what you think of the plan."

"I've no idea. I'd have to ask what's—"

"—in it for him?" Franklin interrupted.

"Exactly."

"I'll ask you another question, Barbara, and then we'll know the answer to 'what's in it for him.' What does he want?"

"I'm not altogether sure."

"You have suspicions, though."

She was silent. She didn't look directly at Robert, but from the corner of her eye saw him sit up straight and lean forward in her direction, his elbows resting on his knees.

Franklin suggested that since Dimitrov was being led by the Russians to ingratiate himself with her, he must want information.

Now she caught the men exchanging glances, Robert's making a begrudging signal to Franklin to proceed. But the beeper that Franklin was wearing on his belt, a newfangled contraption that the CIA agents and military attachés had been issued, sounded. He excused himself and left the room.

"Is there some sort of conspiracy between you two guys? Have I missed something? Why didn't you come home to discuss this privately with me first for God's sake?" The Socratic dialogue that Franklin was conducting with her had put her on edge.

"Now, don't call it a conspiracy, we were trying to make a feasible plan, and include you in the planning."

In his white shoes, the servant moved purposefully over the gleaming wood floor, his crepe soles making a sucking noise. Scattered about were handsome rugs, hand-loomed in Ouranoupolis near Mount Athos, the holy mountain in northeastern Greece, inhabited by monks and forbidden to all females, including hens, sows and heifers. He asked if they "desired" anything. They "desired" a fruit drink, *portokalatha* would be fine.

"This morning Franklin briefed me on the problems of communicating with some Bulgarians. It has to do, I suspect, with terrorists, as he just said. He's being very guarded, too guarded to please me, and he asked me if you. . . ."

167

The man returned with two frosted glasses of orangeade, slices of lemon and sprigs of parsley floating on the surface, placed them on the coffee table, each glass on its individual silver tray, and went over to open the window. A light breeze played with the voile curtains, whose hooks snapped nervously against the window frame. Three or four torpid black flies, fooled by the heat of the last few days, had been coaxed into birth and flown in, attaching themselves to the white curtains, where they remained inert. When the servant left the room, Robert resumed.

"He asked me if you might be willing . . ."

Franklin came back in and took his place next to Robert on the couch. He repeated the question he had posed before he left the room.

"Yes, I assume he'd like information," she said.

"Anything else?"

She didn't answer.

"Defection. Isn't that a strong possibility?" he said, almost whispering, leaning forward, his eyes widening to take her in.

"We didn't get that buddy-buddy for him to inquire, thank God. There, I'd have been out of my depth. He did infer very cryptically that he wasn't a fan of the communist system."

"Yes, defection. A disturbing subject. Disquieting. We don't get into much more affecting stuff than that," he murmured. "Defection gets sticky, too personal, wives, kids, parents, their security, all that stuff.

"What is my role in all of this, Dana?" Her voice had grown impatient, annoyed.

"Frankly, I'm mapping it out as I go along. First I wanted to talk to Robert, see how he might feel about dragging his family into this—he is my colleague, after all— and then I wanted to debrief you, get a clearer picture of the Bulgarian officer. Now we're at step three, exploring what role you're likely to play, Barbara."

"Don't kid me, either of you. Robert has already heard your options and has told you which of them he's willing to have me do."

The doorbell rang. The servant hovered at the edge of the living room and signaled to Franklin, who walked quickly toward him. They spoke in hushed tones in what sounded to her like Hebrew, and stepped out of the room together. The house was as busy as a bus station.

Robert cleared his throat. "Mossad," he said, jutting his chin to where the servant had been standing. He explained in an undertone that the Israeli agent was here to learn about November17—the Israelis were chary of the organization because the hit men might have trained in an Arab country. "In his spare time he acts as a bodyguard and general factotum for Franklin."

Robert stood, flexed his knees and thrust out his arms in a pretext of exercise, but she guessed he felt tense, by now thoroughly put out with her, fuming that she was about to drag them into disaster. He made his way around some chairs, stood at the windows, then stepped over to examine on one wall, the series of oil paintings, views of Israel that the Franklins had purchased when they were posted there, and on the opposite wall, four exquisite watercolors by the superb Greek painter Hadjikiriakos-Ghikas, depicting scenes from Nikos Kazantzakis' *Odyssey,* a modern-day version of the ancient tale. From there, he strolled to the bookcase and became engrossed, inspecting several of the titles from the extensive collection on Greece. He glanced at a set of drums standing in a corner— a couple of snares and a trap. Finally he sat down heavily on the couch.

"I'm telling you something right now, Barbara. This whole business is as dangerous as hell, so from now on take the lead from me." He was speaking quickly, softly. "If I understood him correctly this morning before you came, you can, as you put it, be cut in, and, I'm pretty certain, be kept out of trouble. I told him this morning, I'd work along with you. That's a good compromise, for you and me. One that puts me at ease."

Before she could respond, Franklin returned, his expression businesslike. To ease the atmosphere, he made a feeble half-smile and picked up the conversation as if he had never left the room.

"No denying, Barbara, you could be very useful. And I could keep you safe. I want you to continue to keep your lines open to the Bulgarian. Bringing Robert along makes it a natural relationship—it will be a foursome with his wife, Maria, isn't it? The objective is to get those messages to Bulgaria. And, hell, we'll load him with plenty of information to give to the Russians. Enough to choke on. So far so good, eh? But, before we go any further . . ."

"Isn't there a real problem?" she asked.

He rubbed his hands together and a pleased look crossed his face, actually delighted. She suspected that he was pleased that his Socratic method had worked, that he had subtly moved her onto his track.

"An exchange of information would be quid pro quo," she said. "However, by arranging for him to convey those messages to Bulgaria, you are pushing the assignment to another level altogether. So therefore he will want something more from you, and you're going to have to hold out to him the promise of delivery, or those messages of yours will end up in Russian hands."

"Right. Now we are back to the subject we were discussing a few minutes ago."

What I don't know yet," he persisted, "is if you can depend on him to yearn for that something else, a possibility so . . . extreme. . . . so final. Defection?"

Robert frowned. "Hang on. I hadn't bargained for this. This will be putting her in too deep. This is not what we decided this morning, Dana, when I told you about the Bulgarian officer she met. Earlier, you described the operation as our cultivating a friendship with him and his wife, just to keep lines open for you to communicate with him and to exchange some information. Now, out of the blue, you bring up his getting messages to Bulgaria. And terrorists. You want to turn him into a counterspy. Now defection. This is entirely out of my line. It's gotten too damn complicated—and dangerous." The veins in his throat knotted with anger. "Barbara and I cannot play with defectors. They get desperate. I cannot have her involved with desperadoes. We've got three kids, for Christ's sake. And what about my position back in Washington?"

In his private talk with Franklin earlier, Robert had thought he'd gotten away cheap, she realized. Now she understood why Robert hadn't come home to discuss the options. He had hoped to buy her off with a small piece of action—a simple exchange of information at practically no risk. But Franklin had just double-crossed him by upping the stakes, offering defection for running messages. Her eyes locked with Franklin's; she nodded her head slightly, once.

Suddenly, enormous raindrops tapped against the windows. The curtains tugged at their rods and hooks. Nearby, some shutters torn loose by the wind banged against the house. The sun had abruptly vanished. The air turned cold and damp, gusted in through the open window, ballooning out the curtains as if they were sails. The halcyon days were over.

Chapter 16

The whack of the plane's wheels on the ground, the terrific swaying and stuttering of the whole cabin, shook him out of his daydreams. He had landed. Greece. Ivan focused his eyes downward, descending the gangway to the bottom rung, where he paused before he stepped on the ground. On land, he halted again. He placed both feet side by side on Greek soil, and pressed them into the ground as if through his shoes, through the tarmac, he might feel the earth.

A few people shoved him forcefully from behind.

"*Pame*, who's slowing us down?" shouted a woman, pushing ahead, carrying numerous plastic bags stuffed to the breaking point.

"*Siopi*," ordered a priest, in angry disapproval of the complaining passengers. "He's an army officer, can't you see?"

His mother's beloved language swept around him, a tide of Greek. He heard the words but dazed, he wasn't conscious of their meaning. Before entering the terminal, he swung round for his first glimpse of the Aegean, his first glimpse of any sea for that matter, and saw in the distance the water, bright, flat, strewn with dozens of boats of all sizes— like a panoramic picture he'd seen taken from a Russian spaceship, a sight so strange, and in a way, alienating. Here, too, as in the picture, the sea swept out so far that he saw the earth curve.

"Ivan, watch out," Maria whispered, as if she could feel the pounding of his heart through his winter clothes. He found himself inside the terminal, Maria tugging at his sleeve, where they were greeted by the first secretary of the Bulgarian Embassy, Petar Pechlov, and his wife, Katerina. They were guided through the control point, thanks to the magic of the diplomatic passport, and due not at all to the self-important Pechlov, who spoke to the officials in atrocious Greek. Pechlov's wife, a lumpy, red-nosed woman in a stretched, white sweater coat, pockets stuffed with handkerchiefs, spoke only as an echo of her husband. The four of them crowded into the Embassy vehicle, driven by a chauffeur, introduced by Pechlov as Stoyan.

Pechlov, as verbose as he was pompous, filled every corner of the small car with his hearty voice; he pointed out all the sights along the way, thrusting a pudgy index finger across Ivan's line of vision. He offered an interminable stream of facts: the Parthenon was damaged when the Venetians blew up a Turkish powder magazine on the site in 1687; the Olympic Stadium held 80,000 people; it took one and a half hours to reach Psychiko from the airport because of traffic. "Look at this," he boomed, "and look at that." Ivan craned his head for a view of the city, but finally gave up in frustration, trusting that he and Maria could arrange a walk in town by themselves in the evening. As they swung into view of the Acropolis, Pechlov's wife opened a box of *loukoumi* and passed the sweet candy, drowned in sugar, to Ivan and Maria and then the driver. She was crinkling the cellophane wrapper, annoyingly. He had to restrain himself from knocking the box out of her hands.

The stink of diesel fumes burned his throat, the racket bewildered him: horns tooted the opening bars of a well-known nursery rhyme; radios pulsated from every taxi; construction machinery clanked and pounded the earth; arguments raged between drivers, between drivers and police, between drivers and pedestrians. Ugly black and red graffiti, unintelligible symbols and acronyms, blighted the walls of buildings. Against all this, Bulgaria seemed absolutely pastoral.

As they neared Ivan and Maria's apartment in Psychiko, Pechlov said he wanted to inform him of two things before they separated. First, there would be a dinner party that evening at the Russian military attaché's house to welcome them on station. And second, as if relayed as an afterthought, the matter of the Bulgarian air attaché, Ivan's immediate boss. That officer had been ordered home to Sofia, and the rumor was that he would not be replaced, which meant Ivan would be running his own operation. Stunned by this news, Ivan nodded and forced a polite smile in Pechlov's direction.

They entered an elegant apartment building through a ground-floor garden. The sleek elevator ascending to the fourth floor hummed like a satisfied cat. Pechlov unlocked the door to their apartment. It swung open obediently, noiselessly, and Ivan and Maria entered the foyer, where his eye was caught by a gleaming black telephone placed on a doily, crisp and white against the polished, dark surface of the table. The walls were freshly painted. The clean windows dazzled them, letting in an unblemished light and offering a view of the marbled

Mount Pendeli across the way. In the living room, the buffed wooden floors, an expanse big enough for two families to share, stretched toward an arch. Looking through it, he could see other spaces: a dining area with a table that sat at least eight people, and a buffet stocked with china and crystal. There were two bedrooms, one so spacious that in Bulgaria it would have been split into two rooms, with its own bath, embellished with brightly colored ceramic tiles, and the other a smaller bedroom, with two beds and incredibly, a second toilet, or as Pechlov called it, a powder room, off the foyer. If that weren't enough, they had a kitchen all to themselves, an immaculate stove and a new refrigerator, standing chest-high, topped by a doily, too, this one tucked under a small vase holding a pink plastic rose and a tiny Bulgarian flag, the kind small children clutched when watching parades.

"Don't think every Greek lives in this kind of luxury, *drugariu*. Remember, you are a diplomat representing the People's Republic of Bulgaria," said Pechlov.

"Yes, luxury," said Pechlov's fatuous wife, smiling directly at the stove— no doubt expecting it to answer her, Maria joked later when the Pechlovs had left and the two of them made the rounds again and again of the five rooms and two bathrooms, as if promenading through a shimmering landscape. He fell onto the bed and tested the mattress. From the bathroom he heard water cascading into the tub and then the sound of Maria splashing about like a child and humming in the luscious hot water. He heaved himself off the bed and padded to the huge picture window that looked out on the garden of the mansion next door. Parked on the next-door neighbor's property, set in among a clump of trees, was a gleaming Ferrari, a sports car model, the color of a banana that had just ripened from green to yellow.

At eight o'clock punctually, dressed in their new clothes—he in a thick gray civilian suit manufactured in Poland and Maria in a blue wool jumper and emerald green nylon blouse made for her by a seamstress in Sofia—they presented themselves at the apartment of the Russian Military Attaché, Colonel Michail Radovski, and his wife. The Colonel, gray-haired and slightly stooped, appearing much older than was usual for an active duty officer, went round the circle of guests, introducing him and Maria first to the Russian naval and air force attachés and their wives, then to the Rumanians, followed by the Hungarians, and last the Yugoslavs. "My peers," he thought grimly, and took down in one swallow the red drink. They stood stiffly, sipping light, tangy concoctions of bizarre colors, imported from the West, he guessed, and called cocktails. The men chatted in Russian, the officers all fair to fluent in the language. But the Hungarian and Rumanian wives, who spoke no Russian, talked to each other in French, while the Yugoslav wife sputtered in broken unintelligible Russian. In the background, playing softly, was the pacifying music from "Swan Lake."

At the table, the men conversed genially, sharing their impressions of the Western attachés, dwelling on the officers from the United States—one or two of them, they suspected, were well-trained CIA plants—before turning their remarks to the British, and last to the French. While they talked, Ivan observed the old man for streaks of meanness. He detected nothing, but suspected him at least of frequent fits of irritability. Every now and then in the course of the meal, he felt the Russian Colonel's eyes focused on him.

Actually, the Colonel appeared to be a mild man, softened by a touch of harmless humor, but clearly a bore, reciting in a tired voice insipid anecdotes based on his experiences at foreign postings, while the guests leaned toward him attentively, perfect ass-kissers. At the end of the meal, Radovski waved them unceremoniously out of the dining room, leading Ivan into a small room. He shut the door, leaving Maria with his wife, shapely and hawk-eyed, strikingly younger than her husband. An obliging hostess, she had invested her prodigious energy in keeping the meal running smoothly. The Russian, grown more stoop-shouldered with the passing of the hours at table, lowered himself heavily into an overstuffed green chair and motioned to Ivan to have a seat.

"I remember"—Ivan wondered how many stories he started with that phrase—"my very first night in Athens a few years ago," he began, and droned on benignly, his eyes heavy as if he were boring even himself, and before Ivan realized it, the pointless story had come to an end. He heard the Colonel ask, "You're carrying a letter from Bereznyi?"

Ivan reached into his pocket and pulled out a white envelope, which he handed to him. The Colonel tore the envelope open and removed three pages. While scanning them, he lifted his head once to tell Ivan that he would be reporting directly to him, as if there were nothing unusual in this arrangement. Ivan had heard about all sorts of blatant intrusions on the part of the Russians, but this case, a reporting structure that skirted the Bulgarian Embassy entirely, was extreme. When he heard this second stunning bit of information, he decided that nothing else he might hear that day could surprise him. He was sure now that he stood at the very center of a Russian intelligence scheme, Bereznyi's own precious scheme to penetrate the American Embassy.

"How's the Bulgarian soccer team this year?" the Colonel asked abruptly, with intense curiosity, apparently delighted with himself that something significant had finally popped into his mind. The first joint on his index finger was swollen and bent with arthritis. Ivan noted that it was the trigger finger.

When Ivan told him, he smiled warmly and remarked that Bulgarians were damn good athletes, and resumed reading the papers, his head so low on his chest that Ivan thought maybe he'd fallen asleep. Strands of gray hair lay on the collar and shoulders of his jacket.

"The most ambitious officer in the whole army. The devil himself," said the Colonel, slumping deeper into the plush velour armchair, reading as he mumbled. "He knows exactly what he wants and how to get it. Know him well?"

"*Nyet, tavarisch.* Can't say that I do. He briefed me a few times about my mission here before I left Sofia. That's all." Of all the vicious men he had met in his life, he would place Bereznyi at the top of the list.

"I've had several communications from him about you through the pouch. The Russian laid the papers in his lap and looked directly at him. "Your mission has really caught his interest. He's all fired up in a way I haven't seen him in years, so you'd better be sharp. A perfect plum for Bereznyi, this plan to crack the

American Embassy." He rubbed his hands together energetically, alert now, his eyes alive with interest, an animation Ivan would have thought him incapable of.

"Of course. I intend to be," Ivan responded, starting to feel easier with the old man, who was now acting like a co-conspirator, but he remained wary. Hours earlier, precisely at the moment when he had introduced himself to Pechlov, he had slipped into his usual acting mode, the attitude he adopted around people of authority, especially the Russians.

"The categories of intelligence he's after are listed on that green paper. You have a copy, I'm sure. Just bring us back information about weapon systems the Americans have planted in Greece, the types of listening technology they've installed and the positioning and strength of Greek troops. You've guessed, haven't you, he's not terribly interested in your reputed primary mission, that ridiculous business of contacting the leftist elements in the Greek army. That must have been a Bulgarian plan. You can do that in your spare time, more or less. Horseshit, if you ask me, because Greece is not a priority for us. So what's the use? The United States has got the country wrapped up. Even if Andreas Papandreou, the anti-American, becomes prime minister, he won't show us any favoritism."

"I understood that from my briefing with General Bereznyi."

"So concentrate on your—let's call it, your secondary mission. That is to deepen your relationship with the Americans and set up your intelligence trading. It'll take a while to establish that. We haven't been able to crack that Embassy, but Bereznyi's convinced it can be done."

He stopped talking and looked hard at Ivan, as if it had occurred to him for the first time to take his measure. "Seems you're quite a lion with the ladies. Endeared yourself to an American woman and an Italian woman all in a few days. And made yourself a source of fascination to the American's two sons. You're more dynamic than the whole bloody Bulgarian soccer team. What's the American woman like?" He chuckled; the noise that rose in his throat sounded like the gulping of a frog.

Ivan laughed, affecting an air of ease. The Colonel's tone had been companionable, but he knew the Russian's chatting was just a ploy. Assuming that General Bereznyi had hand-picked Radovski to oversee his mission, and that Bereznyi himself had decided to bypass the Bulgarian Embassy entirely by eliminating Ivan's boss there, absurd that the General then would have turned around and picked this sluggish reptile Radovsky. Clearly, Bereznyi had passed on every detail of Ivan's relationship with the American woman and her boys. He decided to ignore the question about the American woman if he could get away with it.

"You'll report back to me the minute the deal with the Americans is set up. I'll feed you the information to trade, and I'll collect what you've brought in. Don't come near me or the Russian Embassy until you're sure they're ready to trade. If you have to communicate with me, do it through Petar Pechlov." These instructions were given in the firm voice of a commander. He caught a glimpse of how the Russian, in his day, might have been a forceful leader. He nodded in agreement.

"Now that you've been noticed by Bereznyi you'd better give him exactly what he wants."

"I'll try, sir."

"Do more than try. Or you'll find yourself floating in the beautiful Aegean waters below the cliffs of Cape Sounion," the Colonel mumbled, his chin resting again on his chest. Ivan, bewildered, tried to determine if the remark was a threat or simply his manner of speaking.

Behind a stifled yawn, the Russian spoke again, "I mean, floating face down."

The warning, so muted, resounded all the more menacingly. He stood to leave the room. He held on to the door handle for a second, testing if he could walk steadily. Then he mustered a deferential and perfectly unruffled "Good night to you, *tavarisch.* "

Chapter 17

The next afternoon, he picked up the thick blue guidebook from his desk and looked up Cape Sounion. "A precipitous rocky bluff rising 197 feet from the sea. On the highest point of the headland are the columns of the ruined Temple of Poseidon. The temple, near the edge of the cliff, forms a conspicuous and striking landmark from the sea; from a distance it presents a dazzling white appearance." In his English-Russian dictionary he looked up "precipitous and headland," but it was too abbreviated to help. Then on a scrap of paper he changed the 197 feet into meters, and closed his eyes, trying to imagine "blanched, skeletal ruins set among the rust-colored stones and the gorse" as they would look from the sea. What came to him was a vision of the tremendous drop from the edge of that cliff to the Aegean, a blue void between cliff and water; he shook his head to erase the image. Not me, Berezyni, not me, Radovski. Not this Greek, you Slavs.

He reached for the phone and dialed. When the operator said, "Good afternoon, American Embassy," he asked for Mr. Robert Baldwin's office. Baldwin's secretary answered. He lost courage, slammed down the receiver. The black instrument glistened with his sweat. He wiped his damp palm along his pants leg and leafed through the blue directory, *Corps diplomatique d' Athènes*, until he found the listing for the residence of Robert Baldwin. He dialed the number. "*Legete.*" A Greek woman answered. He asked for Madame Baldwin. In a moment he heard, "Hello. Barbara Baldwin." At the sound of her voice he was startled— so long and so hard had he thought about her, it was as if a woman he had dreamed up, a creature who existed purely in his fantasy, had sprung to life. He struggled with an impulse to hang up.

"Dimitrov here," he managed to mumble.

"Who, please?"

He cleared his throat and spoke louder. "Ivan Dimitrov, the Bulgarian officer." For a second he feared she might hang up.

"Ivan, oh, yes, I thought you'd probably arrived by now."

"I'm here. Finally."

"You and your wife are settled in? Is Maria happy here?"

"Yes. Of course. Settled."

He paused, waiting for her to speak. Her voice was friendly, had an unexpected eagerness to it. He sighed, relieved. He had forgotten its marvelous tone.

"I thought you'd call. If I remember correctly we'd promised to meet, the four of us."

"Just tell me where."

"It's a coincidence you called at this moment," she said. He should receive today an invitation to a reception at the home of the American Defense Attaché, Captain Vernon Briggs, she explained. Captain Briggs had invited the attachés and their wives from all the

184

Athens Embassies, plus a handful of other officials. She instructed him to come a half hour earlier than the time called for on the invitation. Robert and she would arrive early, too, and they'd find a quiet place to talk. "Is that O.K."?

"When is it?"

"In ten days."

"Sooner, please." She had him dangling like a paratrooper snarled on a branch.

"No. Sorry. It can't be sooner, Ivan. We've figured this out carefully, a group of us here." This she said with an unmistakable ring of finality.

No. No group. He didn't trust a group. But he was afraid to irritate her, so he said, "How are the children?"

"Fine, thank you." A new note in her voice, not exactly cold, more a touch of formality; he understood her meaning distinctly—keep away from the children.

"Very well, Madame. We will see you in ten days. We are impatient to renew our friendship."

"As the Greeks say, *kalo riziko*— you know, good roots in your new home." And she hung up, he thought, in a hurry. But could you really detect if someone hung up abruptly on the telephone? Crazy he should allow his mind to wander down such useless paths. Besides, her phone would be bugged, perhaps by the Russian Embassy, perhaps by her own Embassy. Who knows?

The Ambassador's aide, Angela Delcheva, brisk and friendly, flashed by, dropping a memo on his desk. Her fingernails were lacquered in a shade of indigo, a luxury you could indulge in when you lived abroad, what with extra allowances and an assortment of items easily available in the capitalist market.

"You're a quick one. Been here a day and received an invitation so soon," she said over her shoulder, already out of his office and headed down the hall, but not before he caught something in her backward glance. He liked the swish of her skirt, the confident way she walked; she had the look of someone with important tasks, a life with significance. In fact, he had gathered from the swirl of office chatter that she was not just the Ambassador's aide but his confidante, that "she was read into the whole operation."

He burrowed through his mail: some official correspondence from the Russian and Bulgarian Embassies, the traffic, it was called; the important Greek and world news of the day, translated into Russian; and three Greek newspapers, *Eleftherotypia*, the leftist paper, the *Kathimerini*, conservative, the one he grabbed eagerly to learn the western view of things, and the *Rizospastis*, the communist paper. Also in the stack was the *Athens News*, read by everyone in the foreign community who knew English. At the bottom of the pile was a square, cream-colored envelope, the United States seal embossed on the back, addressed to him, obviously the invitation. He tore the envelope open, removed the elegant invitation, ran his finger over the elaborate raised letters, admired the firm feel of the paper. It required an R.S.V.P. He filled out the R.S.V.P. card and put it in his box to be mailed.

Then he pulled a couple of sheets of stationery and a pen out of his drawer. Across the top he wrote:

My very dear Madame Baldwin,

I should not write to you for imediately you will see how bad my English is realy, and how I spell. One thing to talk, another to write. Also, how to send this to you without being opened? I will think of a way that is not through your Embassy. Not that it will be so privat. For I do not intend to get privat.

Firstly, I will be at the reception of the Defense Attache at the time you stated. Do not worry on that account. I am only dissapointed that we have to put off our reunion for a few days, for important matters are growing urgent.

I remember with nostalgia that we had adventures together in Vitosha for it is events like that that bring peoples together, beyond politics, beyond national ideologies. You must know the Greek saying, kato, kato tis grammis, bottom, bottom, of the line. Well, bottom, bottom of the line, you and I, we are just two souls just individuals. Nothing greater, but important also, nothing smaller. I remember also that you expressed a debt to me upon two ocasions. What I did for you and your boy and your Italian friend is what many humans beings would do. I know you appreciate me. I depend on that sentiment to expect that you will be grateful enough to agree to the following: to meet me as soon as you possibly can even before the party, at your choice of place so that we can discuss, just the two of us, our common interests. I await your call.

He folded the letter into an envelope, stuffed it in his jacket pocket, left the Embassy and had Stoyan drive him to Psychiko. In front of Baldwin's house was a cramped wooden guard shack sheltering a Greek security guard who was concentrating on his portable radio, a battered contraption transmitting through the static the excited voice of a sportscaster covering a soccer match. The shack stank from urine. The guard, totally unconcerned about who came or went, did not look at him. Ivan rang the bell at the gate.

He watched through the grillwork as the maid came down to the fence, preceded by a medium-sized white and brown-spotted housedog, a harmless animal, barking with the ridiculous ferocity of an Alsatian hound. Poking the envelope through the iron tracery, he told the woman to give the note to *Kyria* Baldwin, to be sure to put it directly into her hands, herself, and pulled a fifty drachma note out of his pocket. She stared scornfully at the money, clicking her tongue and thrusting her chin up to make the traditional sign, "no."

Three days later, she still had made no contact with him. As usual he arrived at the office early, before anyone else, to grab the newspapers. Among the many delights of being in Athens was the thrill of opening the long white sheets and having the whole world come to him via the black letters, an act of magic, about topics almost unknown to him: the structure of NATO, the developments in the European Economic Community, French movies, crimes of passion, drug problems in Holland, the American election campaign, sex scandals among the Greek clergy, the workings of Greek democracy with its political intrigues, and international and domestic terrorism.

At first there was too much information to digest, but slowly he was gathering knowledge of a few topics, gaining a more detailed sense of geography, grasping the meaning of some subjects.

He was drawn into the currents of the newspapers, where he floated for hours. The excitement. Back home, one was restricted to the Bulgarian and Russian newspapers printed by the government. Here, one never knew what catastrophe would leap onto the page, and he, the reader, stood right on the scene, just like a witness, the facts at his finger tips, the vivid descriptions before his eyes, riveting photographs. He opened the Greek language newspaper on the top of the pile.

November 17 Strikes Again
US Embassy Defense
Attaché Murdered

He read the headline a second time, a third, and again. A tremor of fury; the paper shook in his hands. "No, damn it. No." Then his eyes jumped to the photograph. In the center of page one, a picture: the smoldering carcass of a car, the windows blown out, the hood torn open, the motor eviscerated, the street littered with broken asphalt, a shoe, parts of a fence and other debris, a picture so shocking, for a time he forgot his personal disappointment. Before he continued, he squeezed his eyes shut against the carnage. Thank God, the only foreigners they're gunning for are the Americans, he thought.

The caption:

Investigators examine pieces
of American Navy Captain's
armor plated car.

His eyes went to the first paragraph.

"An explosion shattered the
tranquility of suburban Kifissia
last evening at eight o'clock, killing
American navy captain Vernon
Briggs, defense attaché of the
American Embassy. Briggs was
the third American victim and
the tenth person to be murdered
by the terrorist group November
17. The organization telephoned
the Central Police Station in
Athens at ten o'clock in the
evening to claim responsibility for
the bombing. According to police
reports, the remote-controlled
bomb was similar to a device
used in a previous assassination,
also, claimed by November 17."

Unpracticed in reading Greek, he moved a finger
slowly along the small, squiggling letters. To compare
the Greek with the English, he took the invitation out
of his shirt pocket and placed it next to the newspaper.
"Breegs," he pronounced it, in the Greek way; then
he said, "Briggs," in the English way. "That's him.
Mother of God, what shitty luck. I must be cursed."
He slammed his fist down on the desk. The meeting
with the Americans. Scuttled. Arrangements with them.
Plans that he had been formulating for days to begin the

process of exchanging information blown to shreds like the car in the photo.

> "The attaché was driving to his home in Kifissia when the bomb exploded, ripping off the car doors and hurling the body some three meters into the street. The body was blown to pieces. A woman who was returning home from the fruit store in Kifissia Square became hysterical when she saw a hand and a leg resting some five meters from the torso, and had to be driven to the hospital. The power of the explosion hurled skyward an iron fence from in front of a neighboring house like a missile. The force gouged a crater 13 meters deep in the asphalt street directly under the car. According to a police spokesman, the American officer was killed instantly. The mangled body could not be identified by colleagues, but forensic experts from the American air force base were able to make positive identification from dental records."

He searched his memory, trying to recall what he knew about these terrorist groups. He knew virtually nothing about November 17 except the name and the fact that it acted solely in Greece.

> "November 17 burst on the scene in December 1975 in Psychiko, claiming as it first victim the CIA station chief of the American Embassy. Since then, one other American victim, has been shot by the same .45-caliber weapon, and now the American attaché."
>
> "Greek authorities, who have tracked down a number of leads, have been unsuccessful in apprehending the killers. Special investigators from the Ministry of Public Order, police experts and intelligence officials of KYP (Central Intelligence Service) have not as yet come up with any breakthroughs."

He read on, straining his eyes on the Greek letters, finding a few words difficult to figure out.

> "The terrorists named their organization after the date on which the Junta (1967-1974) crushed a student uprising in

the capital at the Polytechnic University in 1973, a revolt that contributed to the regime's fall the following summer. The organization has projected itself as the people's popular avenger first by killing the American station chief in 1975, a symbolic destruction of the 'imperialist presence' in Greece, followed in 1976 by the assassination of a former Greek police officer accused of torture during the Junta days."

More difficult words. His mind wandered from the news release. What possible schemes could he dream up now to get the American couple to meet with him, what would be the new rules of engagement and what would be their frame of mind in light of this latest terrorist attack? The complexities rumbled through his head.

"In the second case, the assassin rode pillion on a motorcycle through the congested streets of Athens and when the victim's car stopped in traffic, the gunman pulled the trigger on the .45 caliber pistol. Whether the organization has links with terrorist organizations abroad such as Baader Meinhof

in Germany or the Red Brigades
in Italy is unknown."

He laid the newspaper down and smoothed it
absently on his desk. Of course, he'd heard about the
other two groups — in Germany and Italy. Terrorism
had been covered as minor news in the Bulgarian
newspapers, meriting a line or two now and then. The
subject of terrorism had been passed over lightly in his
intelligence briefing in Sofia before he'd left for Greece,
the information conveyed in a way that gave only the
most cursory details, the names of the groups, their
country of origin, their modus, their victims to date.
Terrorism was described as a destabilizing factor in the
West and in Israel, and hence a positive force for the
Soviet Union and members of the bloc. In the briefings
he had attended, terrorist information was delivered
simply as background and there wasn't the slightest
suggestion that the attachés should report on the subject
once on station, an omission that he had, at the time,
thought peculiar. He resumed his reading.

"Briggs, 50 years old, from
Middletown, Ohio, had been
posted to Greece for a year. He
leaves his wife and five children,
all resident in Athens, and his
parents in Ohio. An American
Embassy spokesman said the
family will accompany the body
to the United States within
the next few days. A memorial

194

service will be held at St. Paul's Episcopal Church, Philellinon St. in Athens, tomorrow at 10:00 a.m. It is expected that the Chief of the Armed Forces, the Chief of the Navy, the Chief of Military Intelligence, the Minister of Defense, a representative from the President's office, and the foreign attachés accredited to Greece will attend."

He realized the phone had been ringing.

"Colonel Dimitrov? Ivan, this is Barbara Baldwin."

"I just read the paper. My condolences."

"Thank you." Her voice was wavering, toneless. "Will you be at the memorial service tomorrow?"

"Of course. With my wife."

"Would you like to meet at our house after? The four of us will go someplace for lunch. Robert and I would love to see you and Maria, even though the occasion is a nightmare."

He accepted and thanked her.

He hung up and puffed his lips in a deep sigh of relief. Apparently they were eager to meet with him; considering the state they must be in, the fact that they offered him a specific invitation proved that. Tomorrow then, they would finally have their meeting. Wonderful. He had hated the thought that their first meeting was to be held at Briggs' home with other people present. Now it would be just them gathered around a table for an intimate conversation. In that sense, Briggs, in his fatal encounter, had brought him a gigantic piece of luck. This first rendezvous would be critically important to lay the ground for their cooperation. For the time being, he would set up his information trade to keep the Russians off his back. As long as he was trading, the Russians would continue to support his freedom of access to the Americans. The information trade would also bring him closer to the American couple, especially the husband, whose cooperation he would have to enlist if his long-range plan for defection, his "possibility," still a dream, as yet not fully worked out in his mind, was to materialize.

But then there was that even more frustrating problem. He was caged by regulations requiring all Eastern Bloc diplomats to request permission from the Greek government to travel outside of Athens. And, of course, the Greeks never granted them the permits. For him the worst stipulation was that all bloc diplomats were forbidden to drive in the border areas around Albania, Yugoslavia, Bulgaria and Turkey.

He stood at his desk, spread out the map of Greece for the fiftieth time and looked at the National Highway going north along the coast up past Volos, then inland through Thessaly and swinging eastward into Macedonia, through Thessaloniki into Thrace. There. . . some day, his mother's town, Xanthi, a dot on the map, there was where he belonged, there they would welcome him with all their hearts, take care of him, some day. There. . . there. . . in the forbidden border lands.

Chapter 18

The organ, like an earthquake, set the stone church to trembling. The American Embassy marine guards ushered the officials, some 150 people in dress military uniforms or morning clothes, to their places in the polished oak pews. They filled the small church. In this determinedly English, improbably Gothic building set in the center of Athens, Barbara could almost believe herself transported to England. Probably less than half the people present would know that St. Paul's Church in Athens represented an historic aspect of Greece: philhellenic Greece. Built in the 1840s to serve the British philhellenes— idealists and adventurers, a motley bunch of thieves and vagabonds, and also romantics like Lord Byron, who had come as volunteers to help free the country from the Turks—the church had served hundreds of communicants. The twentieth century members were an eclectic group of Americans, Brits, and Greek Levantines, a few of them almost as eccentric as the nineteenth century swashbucklers. She watched the congregation and the officials file in to eulogize a murdered American parishioner, Captain Vernon Briggs.

A peaked January light seeped in through the stained glass windows set high behind the altar. She noticed the glass had a milky field decorated with ruby and cobalt-blue figures, a bit faux Chartres, a creation of the nineteenth century, but in its own way striking. Beneath the windows, eight flags, one Greek, one American to honor the deceased, the rest symbols of the Commonwealth, hung limp and dust-laden from their poles. The organ had effectively drowned out the clamor of Athens traffic whirling around the church.

Seated in the first few rows were the Greek government officials. The Ambassador entered, a dynamic figure despite his handicap, flanked by two marines and supported by a lacquered black cane. He was unaccompanied, since his scatterbrained wife had returned to Texas months ago after babbling to several foreign diplomats at a formal Greek function that she found the Greeks unbearable. Next, Barbara and Robert took their places beside him in the row behind the Greek officials; the section to the right was ribboned off for the attaché corps.

The Briggs family was in no shape to attend, the wife, Lorraine, dead set against putting her younger children through the ceremony and yet unwilling to have them stay home without her. Besides, they were getting ready to accompany the body back to the States the next day. Barbara was relieved by Lorraine's decision. Out of courtesy, Freddy and Roger would have been obliged to be present at the funeral, since both of them were classmates of the Briggs children; the assassination had traumatized all the Embassy youngsters and she feared the effect the violence would have on them in the long-term.

Everyone in attendance was shaken by the murder; faces were grim. In addition, the Greek authorities bore the strain placed on them by the civic nature of the crime: the assassin's bomb had found its target in a public thoroughfare, while they, who were responsible for domestic tranquility, remained powerless. Not a few of the authorities were touched by paranoia, tormented by the question "who's next?" Were the killers members of the official Greek security guard ringed outside protecting the building, or were they seated among the foreign dignitaries and Greek politicians right here inside the church, or outside among the faculty at the University, or Cypriot hotheads entering Greece, striking and then returning to the island? No, not paranoia at all, but valid questions being scrupulously examined by the CIA, by its Greek counterpart, *Kentriki Yperesia Pliroforion*, known as KYP, and Interpol.

The priest, tall, fleshy, thin with flaxen hair and pale blue eyes, an Oxford man with a reputation for mildness, came forward in his full-length white cassock and fine white stole, exquisitely worked with colorful symbols of the Resurrection. He was presiding over a memorial service that would not be marked by tears, by personal grief. Instead, the civic nature of the terrorists' act cast another kind of pall, a collective dread that people felt when the social order was breached, when they sensed that stealth and a kind of unfathomable rot, a madness, held sway. The organ surged, joined by choir and congregation, for the first hymn.

Eternal Father, strong to save, whose
arm doth bind the restless wave

The dean of the attachés, a British brevet, Sir Harold, whose black eye patch, a result of World War II service, lent a flavor of mystery to his quick-witted personality, rose, and the other attachés and their wives, Ivan and Maria among them, who were not familiar with the Anglican service, followed his example. Behind Ivan and Maria, Barbara caught sight of Gerda and her portly husband, Günther, and next to them Louisa and her husband, Antonio. What would be in Louisa's wily mind at this moment? Would she undertake another mission after the peril of the last, detainment in a Bulgarian prison?

> O hear us when we cry to Thee,
> *For those in peril*

Ivan's eyes had sought out Barbara. His figure was illuminated by another set of stained-glass windows spilling down fragments of colored light.

> Upon the chaos dark and rude,
> *Who badst its angry tumult*
> *cease.*

She didn't nod. The solemn atmosphere did not provide the occasion for greeting.

> *Our brethren shield in danger's*
> *hour,*
> *From rock and tempest, fire and*
> *foe,*

Protect them where so e'er they
go.

Her mind was straying back and forth between the sparkling stained-glass windows and the purely utilitarian, cold, transparent glass of the Bubble, she had entered early that morning. No scintillating colors, no Chartres, faux or genuine. The Bubble: glass ceiling, glass floors, glass walls, bug-proof, impermeable to listening devices, absolutely secure. There, she and Robert had attended a meeting.

On the third floor of the Embassy, they had walked past Franklin's office down the hall to a plain wooden door. A CIA attendant unlocked that door and led them into the room that housed the Bubble. Then the attendant opened a vault-door through which they entered into the glass enclosure itself. Inside, Franklin was waiting. She'd never seen this side of him; he looked manic, his eyes deep in their sockets, black with fatigue but wild with fury, his suit unpressed, as if he had been living in it for days—actually he had not gone home since the moment he was informed of Briggs' murder. He had kicked his shoes off and was pacing in gaudy argyle socks, a celebration of color, which in the circumstances struck her—an irrational and petty observation, she realized—as entirely out of place. He should be all in black, down to his socks. She knew the stinging gossip that must be ringing in his ears: defense attaché murdered on Franklin's watch, he, a top-ranking CIA official sent to Greece for the sole purpose of finding the assassins of a predecessor, had allowed a murderer to strike right under his nose. An outrage, colossal incompetence on the part of the intelligence agents, Greek and American alike, or collusion, or conspiracy, in a small, tight country where the central government kept tabs on every citizen: each man registered for the army; baptismal records were mandatory for every Greek; all residents, Greek and foreign, had to carry I.D. cards; citizens reported to the police every time they moved their residences; passports were scrutinized at the borders; scrupulous records were kept on every child entering school. A few years ago, every horse, jackass, typewriter, radio, had to be reported to the authorities. How could Greek authorities in KYP, or the CIA for that matter, not know who the terrorists were?

Franklin, sick of pacing, sprawled in a chair, ran his fingers across his forehead to wipe away the fatigue; he bent to pick up a pair of drumsticks lying next to a practice pad on the conference table, then changed his mind. For the first time he addressed her and Robert, mumbling how fortunate *everyone* was to have her with a line to the Bulgarian Embassy just at this time. The Bubble smelled of cocoa, cloying, sickening, something only a kid would drink. When Robert started to speak, Franklin put up his hand imperiously, like a king to his lowly subject, a silencing off-with-your- head gesture that Robert heeded.

Stretching his arms over his head, Franklin yawned crudely, then took up again the thread of a conversation, telling them that "Now, for our purposes, the focus of the Bulgarian officer's mission would shift, of course. Drastically." He was prepared personally to guarantee "Barbara's Bulgarian the defection he was after. For a big price, of course."

"I thought you were offering him just that for getting messages back to the opera people in Bulgaria," she said.

He had suggested to her, just suggested, didn't she remember, that in return for getting the messages back to Bulgaria, he might consider granting him defection, but he'd never actually guaranteed defection. Big difference. She had to be very careful how she interpreted things. Then he flung at her the same silencing gesture.

He explained that there was some chance the November 17 organization was aided by the Russians, who were using the Bulgarians as their agents. He had some reason to suspect that the Bulgarian Embassy in Athens might serve as their key point of contact and that Russian messages to coordinate terrorist activities in Greece were flowing through the Bulgarian communication system.

Interrupting Franklin, the Ambassador limped into the Bubble. He seemed excited, a smile of satisfaction animated his face. Without greeting, he plunged into conversation, using his hands airily to make his points. "Cables from Washington, State, the President's Office, condolences, instructions." His right hand floated high over his head, the fingers flapping, waving at the heavens. "One actually signed by the President himself. This station is in all the newspapers today, all over the world. Not just American papers. Everyone's watching us," he said with a bounce in his voice, as if something miraculous had come to pass. "Let's give them something spectacular to see, or the press will make us look like damn fools. Let's make a name for ourselves. Lucky for everyone my predecessor isn't in charge; he'd let that gang of murderers blow up the whole damn Embassy." His words gushed like oil from a well.

In the Lord put I my trust: how say ye to my soul, Flee as a bird to your mountain? . . . the wicked bend their bow, . . . ready their arrow upon the string. . . that they may. . . shoot at the upright in heart. . .

She had been uncomfortable in the Bubble, found it disorienting—that room within a room—disturbing, a conundrum. In the terrifying reality of the new turn of events, what Franklin had demanded of her and Robert stretched far beyond the limit she had pictured less than a month ago when she had carried the magazine into Bulgaria and then agreed to work with Franklin to cultivate Ivan. The mission was no longer simply an exchange of information, no longer even a task of getting Ivan to carry messages. Robert's career, his very status, in Greece was now at risk. He was, after all, not an intelligence officer; he was accredited to Greece as a diplomat, a classification that technically forbade his working with third-country intelligence agents, using Greek space to conduct an American spy operation. She fully comprehended his current situation; he was acting without the knowledge of the Greek government, as a handler, about to ask a Bulgarian official to steal information from the communication system at the Bulgarian Embassy. If Robert were to be exposed violating his diplomatic status, he could be declared *persona non grata.* And as far as the State Department was concerned, he had no authority to work with the CIA. There was so much turmoil since Briggs' murder, Robert didn't yet know if the Ambassador had requested through proper channels permission for him to cooperate with the agency. As things stood now, Franklin had virtually shanghaied him, press ganged him like a common seaman, and set him on a dangerous voyage. Of course, until Robert, himself, could get a word to Washington, his refusal to cooperate with the agency seemed selfish in the extreme now that the stakes were a matter of life and death—the threat of violence to Americans lurking on every street corner. She recalled the words "pusillanimous bureaucrat," Franklin's old description of Robert. Robert needed time to work through his friends back at State to extricate himself. Franklin and Paige Gardner, egocentric movers and shakers, would pull every string to keep the operation moving along as they designed it, keeping Robert and Barbara in the picture. As for Ivan, their "human asset," if he wanted that defection, he'd clearly have to put his life on the line.

"So, Robert and Barbara," the Ambassador continued, "I know you'll gladly lend the station a hand. Dana tells me you have an excellent Bulgarian contact." He looked over at Franklin, who was absurdly absorbed in bobbing with an index finger the two fat marshmallows he'd plunked in a cup of cocoa. Pointing at Robert he said, "This is the wrong time to sit here worrying about the reaction back at the hushed halls of State, selfish things like your career. I'll take care of people in Washington, don't worry on that score." As he thumped out of the Bubble, Robert got to his feet; his skin was ashen.

Yea, though I walk through the valley of the shadow of death . . .

Even though she had spent a lifetime being uneasy in church, at this moment in contrast to the Bubble, she was finding the memorial service comforting. Here there was nothing to decide, no action to undertake, nothing to risk, nothing to gain. The tenor was acceptance, hope, forgiveness. The tidal rhythm of the service, the ebb and flow of familiar hymns, psalms, proverbs, human voices in unison, responsive readings, flowed in wondrous harmony. God remained fixed in his heaven, a dimensionless Byzantine icon. Tragedy arrived, tragedy passed. But the planet spun eternally in its orbit, offering humankind, at the very least, a cosmology it could count on.

An attaché from the Embassy was eulogizing his murdered colleague, calling to everyone's attention how fitting it was that Briggs be remembered in this particular church, which had served so many who had fallen on this foreign soil. He quoted from Exodus, "I have been a stranger in a strange land." And closed with, "For we are strangers before thee, and sojourners, as were all our fathers, our days on earth are as a shadow, and there is none abiding."

Ivan was bending his head over the prayer book. He would have a hard time keeping pace with the readings, the high-flying language of the King James Bible would elude him, and since he had never been to church, he would not be familiar with the text even in Bulgarian. She tried to imagine what it would be like to be unfamiliar with the Twenty-Third Psalm, to be a kind of spiritual illiterate, to hear for the first time as an adult,

206

Surely goodness and mercy shall follow me all the days of my life. . .

After the service, when Ivan arrived at their house having changed out of his uniform to a suit, a peculiar off-shade of blue flannel, they were surprised to find he'd come alone. Maria, he claimed, was busy, very busy, always, with her English lessons, and gorging herself on dozens of science books she had picked up in the bookstores.

Barbara and Robert decided to drive their guest to Turkolimano for a fish lunch to talk in the secure setting of the open air. They agreed that since the sun was warm and there was no wind, it would be pleasant to eat under a protective awning at a table facing the marina.

To her relief, Robert was professionally cordial, diplomatically correct. When they got into the car, he invited Ivan to sit in front with him "to get acquainted," as he so neutrally put it. In fact, there was nothing neutral about getting acquainted. He had about three-quarters of an hour to size up the Bulgarian before they made their pitch. He had been so angered in the Bubble at the way Franklin and Paige Gardner had bullied him, she feared he might take it out on Ivan, be deliberately unpleasant to this a poor victim who, on the one hand was guilty probably of devising a rather trite plan of exchanging information, or on the other hand was simply pro-West and wanted to defect. She felt a surge of compassion for him, his face bearing now the look of the hunted, just as she saw him the first night. He appeared strained, more guarded, eyes bloodshot, hair wilder than ever.

On the drive to the waterfront they talked about Greece—the landscape, the language, the people, the food. Ivan seemed to warm to them, spoke easily. For this encounter he seemed to have acquired a sleek veneer, a new and remarkable conversational elegance. She was pleased to hear him speak thus; it filled out his persona, made him complete. His fluency? Yes, he could speak Greek very well, he was pleased to discover, but as he had never been taught to read the language— a source of frustration— he was now teaching himself, using the newspapers for text. Fortunately, the Greek alphabet seemed to be coming to him intuitively. The countryside? Since his family had come from Thrace, a harsher, wilder area he'd heard about in stories, he was awed by the tame, majestic landscape of Attica—the purple light at night on Mount Pendeli, the extraordinary view of the sea lying below like blue fog as you dipped from that great height on Mount Pendeli on the way to Marathon. Of course he couldn't travel wherever he wanted without permission from the Greek government, a huge obstacle to learning about the country. The people? He had expected and loved the wonderful openness of the Greeks on the street. How refreshing to see people without that Slavic heaviness. And the food? Ah, well, fabulous, just fabulous, don't you agree? By the way, he had read the Greek poet Yannis Ritsos, who won Bulgaria's 1974 International Dimitrov Prize for poetry, and also for being a good communist; he made a soft, snorting sound. And thus the only Greek poet circulating in Bulgaria. Ritsos had given him much insight into Greece. Did they know, for instance Ritsos' short poem— he shut his eyes to concentrate, as he translated from the Bulgarian— it must be called "Ancient

Amphitheatre" in English. Yes, they did know the poem. They loved Ritsos. Ivan quoted the line about the echo of Greece. He felt exactly like a boy in the poem who was shouting in the ancient theatre to send forth his voice to mingle with the other voices throughout Greek history.

From her place on the back seat, she couldn't see Robert's reaction, but from the minute shift in the timbre of his voice, she knew that he was as impressed as she with the level of Ivan's conversation. They were not dealing with a rustic, not toying with a fool. In fact, she had never imagined this side of the Bulgarian's personality. If before she was motivated solely by a sense of gratitude, now she was also touched, even stirred, by his humanity; her obligation had shifted from a lofty abstraction to a personal plane with the web of emotional ties such stirring brings. She had wondered what kind of person he really was, what was locked within that expressionless facade. Now she was discovering a personality with fine sensibilities, a person worthy of her gratitude, and certainly Robert's, too.

Only after they settled at a table at Turkolimano, received their appetizers of boiled octopus, fried squid, *taramosalada* and a carafe of white wine, and raised their glasses in an unspoken toast, did they turn their chairs toward the open sea and she told Ivan Franklin's deal.

Chapter 19

He received a cable at the Embassy informing them that Maria's father had suffered a heart attack. He instructed the secretary to make a reservation for her on the evening flight to Sofia and went home. Perfect. Room to navigate freely. And just one week after he had made the deal with the Americans.

As usual, she was calm, accepting.

"He won't make it, I know. For Papa, it's over."

Her back was turned toward him as she spoke, bending from the waist over her suitcase, arranging her things. His eyes traveled from where her hair was gathered at the nape of her neck—from that unbearably smooth spot—down the length of her spine; from this perspective, his wife looked dangerously fragile, pathetically unprotected. He pitied her, he genuinely did, for the rude things to come, all of them on his account. He reached out to stroke her shoulder in a gesture of apology, but immediately suppressed the impulse. Hadn't he presented to her this gift, this fabulous couple of weeks in Greece, a chance for her to learn, to breathe the air of freedom? She said she'd never been so happy in her life. Wasn't that at least worth something? And lots more to come if she'd only agree.

What he had not given her, what she had wanted most in the world, was a child. He had told her "no" from the first day of their marriage, but she wanted a baby so much, he had been afraid she might trick him, and years after, when he had learned to trust her—not only on that matter, but on all others— he assumed she had gotten over it. He wanted no extra burdens, no suffocating web of relationships to snare him. His mother's wail at the end, calling for her people, whom he, her own son, had alienated, still haunted him. He wanted no innocents left behind to suffer for his deeds, to grow up despising him.

When he'd brought Freddy home—Maria pronounced his name "Fraidy"—she fell for the boy. As she helped the doctor take care of him before the boy's mother arrived, she crooned about Fraidy's bravery in their house, a place so strange to him; Fraidy's precious politeness when he said *molya* and *blagodarya,* little Bulgarian phrases he'd learned for the trip; Fraidy's pain in his ankle, how he stood it without complaint; Fraidy's young body, so adorably stringy, so adolescent. For a day or two after the boy left, she was for the first time in her life depressed, and he understood why, but neither of them talked about it.

While she packed, he distracted himself by reading the *Athens News,* skimming through the "News in Brief," a section spiced with vignettes of Greek rural life, shepherds in the desolate hills, "arrested for amusing themselves with the sheep," as the column so delicately put it.

"This makes everything harder, actually impossible, you know. Leaving the two of them together in Bulgaria was hard enough. But when Papa dies, Mother will be left alone there. If only I had brothers and sisters." Other than Maria, the only close relative the old woman would have left when her husband died was Uncle Vasili. But poor Vasili. As Ivan's patron—the defector's patron— he would certainly be ruined, exiled, and Jesus Christ almighty, maybe even executed. He couldn't stand to think of it. Vasili, tough, a crafty peasant boy, who during the war had slogged his way up through the Fatherland Front party ranks, who didn't lay eyes on a flush toilet until he was twenty-five, yet had the wits to guess that the country would turn left at the end of the war, took part in the communist uprising in 1944, when the Soviet Union declared war on Bulgaria, was present at the executions of hundreds of his countrymen, the so-called "war criminals"—men lined up and shot like cattle infected with hoof and mouth disease—poor slobs of the right who had not foreseen that when the Germans pulled out, Bulgaria would fall to the Russians. And the young, skin-and-bone, ragged Vasili, a member of the People's Militia commanded by Zhivkov, had probably pulled a trigger or two himself that autumn after the war, witnessed the rivulets of blood seep into the ground until the mud turned the color of a bruised body. Vasili, a saint who had taken care of his older sister and his sister's daughter, Maria, and had nourished Ivan's career. The newspaper came unfolded, some of the pages fluttered to the floor. He bent to pick them up.

"Maybe your mother can join us here. I'll look into it. No harm in finding out a thing or two even now," he said, his face concealed behind the newspaper.

Maria buckled her suitcase and turned to face him. He lowered the paper, noticed her eyes were puffed and red from crying.

"An old woman can't cope with risky adventures." There was a surprising sting in her tone, the bite of accusation, as if she had understood what he was contemplating.

He looked at his watch and told her it was time to leave for the airport. "We'll face each thing as we come to it. For now, cross your fingers that your father will pull through. Vasili will get him the best doctor, count on that."

When they stepped out onto the street, it was twilight.

"You haven't brought up the subject, not since you got your orders weeks ago. But I can read you. I know what you're plotting every minute." Her voice was quavering.

"Oh, that."

The streets lights snapped on. In the circle of light, he studied her to be sure he grasped her meaning, and answered cautiously.

"A passing dream, an innocent fantasy. Some men, the dirty bums, commit acts of infidelity, dream of other women. I dream of other places. That's the whole truth." He bent and kissed her lightly on the forehead. Her face tasted like the salt of tears.

"You know I always consider you first of all. I wouldn't do anything to make things hard on you. Trust me, *mila*, my sweetest."

She searched his face to find her own answer. Had she stopped trusting him some time along the way, maybe from the moment in the coffee house when he'd mentioned staying in Greece? No, he pushed the suspicion out of his mind, people like Maria, once trustful, remain faithful. Still, he was afraid she might find something written in the lines of his forehead, on the dark spots on his cheeks, so he hurried out of the light over to the curb, dropped her suitcase in the trunk of the car, and pulled down the door with a slam. The truth of the matter was, he thought, her absence was coming just at the right time.

Angela Delcheva, the Ambassador's aide, who adored a good time, served as a source of fascination to everyone in the crushingly dull community at the Bulgarian Embassy. From bits of gossip, a few questions, much snooping, Ivan, a trained intelligence officer, had no trouble stitching together a short but accurate bio on her. Born and raised in Bansko, she had gone to the university in Sofia and earned her diploma in archaeology with an emphasis on Thracian jewelry, a field in which she had worked for almost a decade. Her marriage to a psychiatrist, a man apparently as erratic as some of his patients, ended in divorce. Through the influence of a powerful party member on her mother's side, she wangled a job in the Ministry of Foreign Affairs, her aim being to leave the miserable marriage behind and gallivant around the world. She had been stationed in Athens for two years. Her assignment to Greece happened, he learned, thanks to family relationships: the powerful party member on her mother's side was a first cousin to the Ambassador and his powerful brother. The two potentates decided that Angela would be a real asset to the Ambassador, a lazy, somewhat disorganized, asthmatic, but generally fine man. They saw her as energetic, intelligent, not given, the men said, like most women, to moods and moping, didn't drink, her only weakness, apparently, a roving eye for the men. While the count was not exact, it was said she had enjoyed more than two quiet affairs (she was extremely discreet) at the Bulgarian and Russian embassies, each, he assumed—he had not yet traced the names—with unaccompanied or unmarried men to avoid censure. In a situation where they were sealed off from the Greeks and forbidden to mingle with the Westerners, they were bound to be incestuous, and nobody cared.

She was well-informed, and coordinated all aspects of the Embassy's activities. There was no corner of the building—even that forbidden communications room—that did not bear her managerial stamp. If you needed to locate a document, to acquire background material, to expedite your report, to complete some bureaucratic paperwork, to contact Sofia quickly, you went to her. Careful without being stealthy, she had obtained a security clearance, everyone guessed, on the same level with the Ambassador's, lending to her another dimension of enchantment.

Angela had an unusual look about her, the same air as some people he had seen in Moscow who had come from the South; the Russians said they were Armenians. Of course that was not her race, she was, as far as anyone knew, a true Slav, but that's the way she looked—soft features, huge black eyes that glowed, black hair shivering about her shoulders, maybe too black to be natural, dyed perhaps to hide the signs of early graying. She moved gracefully, quickly, like a borzoi, as if speed held its own meaning. Her hand movements were flourishes, giving her a certain lightness, a non-Slavic quality, and every week her fingernails twinkled with a different lively color. It was her laugh, an ever-ready low gurgle, that made everyone love to banter with her; in the laugh lay something that welled up from deep within her—evidence, he guessed, of hot blood. She was certainly not shaped like a borzoi; she was lusciously full-bodied, adequate, he surmised, for every purpose.

Now, with Maria home in Bulgaria, he was free to take his turn. Bundled in heavy clothes, they sat on a slatted deck bench, basking in the sun, but as the city of Piraeus grew small, resembling from this distance the white fabled city of an opera set rather than Greece's grimy largest port city, they were entering deep waters. The sea was turning rough; small, white-topped waves slapped the bottom of the ferryboat. A sharp sea wind pierced their winter jackets, now and then a fine spray dampened their hair. They slid along the bench closer to each other, then huddled together, their arms entwined, passersby would assume they were lovers, but they weren't. The alternative to huddling like this on the top deck was to suffocate inside in the stuffy, smoke-clogged lounge, among sprawling passengers, who were either seasick or dispirited.

"These landlubbers, these miserable descendants of Odysseus," Angela quipped, from under her turned up collar, "would never have survived the sail home from Troy. Not even ten days, never mind ten years."

This was not their first day trip together. The Saturday before they had driven to Sounion. He was impelled to see it. He didn't tell her why, he simply said to her one day after Maria had left, "Do I understand the road to Sounion correctly?" He took out the map and laid it across his desk. "Looks like the road goes directly south along the coast for sixty kilometers."

Yes. A very curvy, hilly road. Beautiful scenery. She went there often. Spectacular sunsets. The ruined temple there changed color with the dying light. She loved it. Would go there anytime.

And so he invited her. A few weeks after Maria's departure, Angela drove with him along the winding coastal road high above the sea, where the Temple of Poseidon swung into view from five kilometers away. A skeleton? No, more airy, more like a spirit, not a physical thing at all. A phantasma, they decided.

They went for a late lunch at the restaurant, where the ghostly ruin floated above, its elegant rectangular shape, fourteen Doric columns, like a cutout against the blue sky.

"You like Greece, I can hear your enthusiasm," he said.

"Oh, yes. I could stay here forever." The low laugh.

He watched the bemused eyes. Stay forever. She could say this because she wasn't suspect, because she had no intention of staying here forever. To her, the statement didn't signify a plan, just an expression. But maybe he ought to make a mental note of her remark, anyway. It took a long time to know people. In the beginning could you ever understand what they really intended?

"And you?" she asked.

If she was familiar with his background, she didn't let on. But of course she would have been briefed on the fact that he was Greek, that he had come to penetrate the leftist elements in the Greek army. He had no idea if she'd been told about the mission Bereznyi had given him.

"It's a fascinating country."

He asked her how she liked her work at the Embassy. She changed the subject. He tried gossip, asked if Stoyan, the driver, was as dumb as he looked.

She said, "Look at this magnificent site, forget the office. I like my weekends free of such talk."

The olives, they agreed, were delicious, as were the fried *kalamari*, and salad, so they ordered extra portions. After a dessert of *crème caramel*, they walked up the dusty path to the Temple, were surprised to see that close up the marble was yellow-veined, not the blinding white they had noted from far away. They hunted for Byron's signature carved on one of the pillars, and finally found the letters, B Y R O N. At the end of the day, the orange sun pitched into the Aegean, the sky was streaked like an artist's palette, the sea reflecting the spectrum of colors. In the second before the sun disappeared, he heard her gasp, a noise that came from deep within, like her laugh, and she reached for his hand. In the dark, they drove back to Athens.

He had gained absolutely nothing. She was shrewder than he had imagined, not about to reveal the most trivial thing. Not yet. Why should she? She didn't know him or trust him. He didn't press her. On the drive back, with the radio playing softly, he thought she fell asleep. Her head dropped on his shoulder, her hand flopped carelessly on his thigh. When her fingers began to beat time to the music there, he knew she was not asleep. Perhaps he had won. But when they reached her house, counter to his aroused expectations, she went straight in, throwing back a polite word of thanks and a cheery good night.

Now, this next weekend, they were on the boat to Hydra; this time, she had invited him. They had planned to take the regular ferryboat to the island and return the same day by the speedy hydrofoil. Apparently the propulsion of the boat, its rhythmic rising and falling with the waves, the constant motor, the hiss of the spray relaxed her. Like someone who'd drunk too many glasses of wine, she grew talkative; he considered, too, that she lived alone in night-time solitude with only two cats for company, a situation calculated, when she was in the mood, to make her jabber in company. She chatted on about her work as an archaeologist—they argued about whether the Thracians in the fifth century B.C., when they first established their kingdom, could accurately be regarded as Greeks—how she sorely missed work in her academic field.

The boat made a wide curve, and the first port of call, Poros, a humped island topped by a church steeple, popped into sight suddenly, as if the ship's captain had worked a magic trick. On the way to Methona, the second stop, a school of dolphins gamboled across the bow, rising and diving in precise rhythm. By the time the boat eased into the semi-circular port at Hydra, she was complaining about the deadwood at the Embassy, not really gossiping, but offering a professional opinion. Nonetheless, her chattering was encouraging, even though her remarks

219

were deliberately innocuous. Under her jacket, he had been kneading her back with his palm.

They took the high path that led them along the water. Across the way, the Peloponnesian mainland stretched like a giant man lying on his side. The seagulls bucked a stiff wind that was gaining force as the sky darkened. His first time on a Greek island. Where was he? He had an odd sensation, as if his body were growing lighter and at any minute he might float skyward like Ikaros, but free of those wax wings. His mother had never told him about the islands. He wondered if all the islands were this haunting.

"Listen to the gulls, they're taunting us," she said.

"Why? Are they superior because they can fly and we can't?"

"Yes, that's exactly what they're saying."

"No, I think they're saying a storm is coming."

Large drops of rain were falling. From the steep hills came the bray of a tethered donkey objecting to the downpour. The leaves on the olive trees purled in the falling rain. As they ran back to the harbor, where a crowd had gathered to inquire whether the boats would be canceled because of the storm, their coats were wetting through. Gray waves flogged the sides of the dock.

Three shore police in starched white uniforms were telling everyone gruffly that all the boats, "*malista* including the hydrofoils," were canceled until further notice. Frantic, furious people were accusing the boat lines and shore police of conspiring to strand them. One man, supporting under the arm an old woman dressed in a black dress and headscarf, complained that his mother—he thrust the frail, tottering woman forward—

had an operation scheduled in Athens for the morning. "She is ready to die right here on the spot," he crooned. A long-haired young man in a leather jacket decorated with silver studs, a beard as thick as a priest's, accused the boat lines in guttural tones of "junta-like activities." A large woman on the fringe of the crowd raised a fist and screamed above them all, "Only *Theos* will protect us," while making repeated signs of the cross.

"Let's just stay over. These storms never last more than a day. We'll go back tomorrow morning," Angela suggested.

They walked over to the hydrofoil ticket office, got tickets for the morning boat and following an arrow penned on a sign, they hurried up the hill on the narrow stone steps to a pastel- colored rooming house, an imposing old place built in the island's neoclassical style. A silver knocker sculptured like a hand, each finger distinct, was attached to the door. Angela asked the owner if the house had heat, so their clothes could dry. He asked for one room for the two of them with heat. To his relief, she did not demand a room to herself.

They draped their sopping coats over the gurgling, lukewarm radiators, stuffed their sodden shoes underneath to dry, and heard rain lash the windowpanes. The radiator took some chill out of the room, but it was the big brass bed, the woolly blanket, that offered them real comfort in such miserable weather. She pulled the blue cover over her and called to him with her deep-throated laugh.

It was years since he had another woman; he had remained faithful to Maria, except for a time or two early in his career when he'd been out with a dozen or so fellow officers, partying, and they'd chipped in to pay a couple of women to attend them all, but why even count that meaningless encounter? At first her flesh felt strange; unlike Maria's, it had a springiness to it, was scented with what he imagined was expensive French perfume. She rocked with lightness, an agility that quickened him. Aroused by the fresh sensations, he decided to dispense with comparisons to Maria, just enjoy himself. Yet, through all the hours they spent in the brass bed, what he wanted from her, what only she could give him, went unexpressed. Time. More time, he thought. Play her easy.

He kept his eyes open throughout, studied her every movement, he caught every smile, recorded every moan or cry, noted when her eyes shut or opened, the throbbing pulse in her neck, when her spine curved, when her lips parted, when she fell back. By dawn, when he heard the blasts of the morning ferryboats as one after the other they arrived and departed, he had mapped, like a good intelligence officer, her emotional and physical terrain.

In mid-afternoon he weaved downstairs to pay for the room, leaving Angela to bathe and dress. His legs were rubbery; he had come down a few times earlier to buy milk. Like a good Bulgarian soldier, he believed that drinking milk reinvigorated the body and helped replace ejected fluids; he was thinking as he remounted the stairs, trying unsuccessfully to steady his swaying legs, that the milk recipe was nothing more than an old-wives' tale. In the late afternoon, they finally caught the hydrofoil for Piraeus.

Chapter 20

She and Robert left their house at 6:30 a.m., drove to the Hellenikon Airforce Base in a bulletproof Embassy car, took off in the Embassy plane at 7:30 a.m., and landed in Thessaloniki at 8:30 a.m. They were picked up by the Consulate car and at 9:00 a.m. arrived at the outside door of the Consulate of the United States of America. They walked between the two Greek police guards to the inside door, where under the authorized photograph of President Jimmy Carter (she wondered if the President's face was really that bland or if the image had been airbrushed clean under the scrutiny of some p.r. person in Washington), the Consul General was waiting for them. Pompous, humorless, gauntly tall, with gray hair, gray skin, and wearing this morning a gray suit, he welcomed them the way he greeted every visitor who came to this historic European outpost, pronouncing in a reedy voice and through a dry laugh, "Welcome to the provinces." He led them to the conference room where Franklin, who had magically materialized from Athens, was waiting: no one asked when he had arrived, how he'd traveled up there, the normal banter that takes place among friends when they meet at a distant city. Seated across the walnut conference table from Franklin were two strong-featured but otherwise nondescript men

223

in their late forties, so much alike in appearance, she thought they were brothers. They both were unmistakably American. American? Was there an American race? An American anthropological head? She blinked away the absurdity. And their suits were almost identical, one navy blue and the other tan, as if they had been issued rather than bought. Both spoke with strong regional accents from states that hovered just south of the Mason-Dixon line.

It had been Franklin's idea to meet in Thessaloniki, an opportunity, he had said a few days earlier, "to get the hell out of this pressure cooker for a day," meaning of course Athens. A couple of his men working on the Briggs case were scheduled to meet in Thessaloniki with the chief of the KYP antiterrorist unit, Stavros Pavlides, and Franklin planned to attend. He said now that the issue of terrorism loomed so large, it would be a good idea for Robert, as the second ranking officer in the Embassy, to accompany him. Of course, Pavlides had an office in Athens as well, "But for some damn reason Pavlides prefers us all up there. A day away would certainly feel like a vacation to me. How about you two?"

She nodded her head readily, while Robert, who had been in touch with Washington for weeks via scramble telephone and cable, trying unsuccessfully to extricate himself from Franklin's and Gardner's clutches, turned an inscrutable face toward Franklin. She alone understood the expression; it was the look of a prisoner regarding his keeper, and she was alarmed at how each day Robert was turning more inward. Franklin had added that since his group was planning to meet with Pavlides—a good friend of the Baldwins from their assignment in Thessaloniki years ago—Robert's company would be helpful; Pavlides would be less formal, more talkative. Of course, Pavlides would be surprised to see her in on it, but flattered by the big American presence, he'd just swallow it. "Be good for you, too, Barbara, to hear the reports. Might put Dimitrov's information in better perspective for you."

This last remark galled her. She drew a deep breath and decided to remain silent. She was beginning to detest him.

According to her "perspective," Ivan had a few days ago given them his first "breakthrough," as she had called it, but Franklin had rolled his eyes, and said, "For God's sake, don't call it a breakthrough; the information could very well be false, a piece cooked up by Dimitrov just to have something to give to us, or a plant by someone in his Embassy."

The breakthrough had occurred one week after Briggs' memorial service, and their meeting with Ivan at Turkolimano. One evening—she had just curled up with a new translation of Elytis' poem *Axion Esti*, which she heard had been sent to the Nobel committee for consideration, and Robert was preparing a paper to deliver at a bat conference in London— Ivan arrived unannounced at their house. They had not heard from him since they had made the deal at Turkolimano. He sat stiffly in the living room, smoking and making small talk—they were used to this diversionary prelude leading up to a momentous occasion, a Balkan custom inherited from the Turks—but then he finally took an envelope out of his pocket and laid it on the coffee table. He withdrew a full sheet, carefully typed, bearing some specific details about the Bulgarian order of battle. Robert picked it up and studied the accompanying diagrams, showing the positions of Bulgarian ground forces in the Rhodope Mountains and the number and positions of Russian soldiers among them.

"This typed piece, please be aware, is the first step in the exchange," Ivan said. "To show good faith, you should give me as soon as possible some real information in exchange."

Then he withdrew from his pants pocket a second piece of paper, this one a crinkled scrap with a sliver of information, scribbled in pencil in his handwriting. He smoothed it out gingerly on the coffee table, like a man handling an explosive, put one index finger to his lips and ran the other along the creased paper. She and Robert leaned over to read it. "November 17 group to meet in Thessaloniki in February to plan Northern event. Meeting at Apollo's Restaurant, February 15. Evening."

Robert asked the key question. "May we ask where you got this?"

He shot his head upward, the Greek sign for "no," left the answer in pantomime. Unuttered.

If Ivan was truly acting according to instructions they had given him at Turkolimano, then he was bringing a message that had been intercepted on the terrorists' network at the Bulgarian Embassy.

Robert gave him information in exchange that evening, details that had been selected by the assistant navy attaché describing some obsolescent communications equipment installed at the American Naval Station in Nea Makri, which Command Headquarters in Europe used to contact the 6th fleet as it cruised the Mediterranean, not of first importance, but nonetheless, facts the Russians could not have known. It was understood by all the Americans involved, and had been made clear when she, Robert, and Ivan had concluded the deal at Turkolimano, that the exchange of information arrangement, which served as the perfect cover for Ivan, had to be carried on at a brisk pace with substantive information, or as he had said at lunch, the Russians would limit his freedom of association, or worse.

They were talking softly, almost in a whisper, when Roger, who had been listening to TV with Freddy in the rec room below, called up the stairs, "Hey, Dad, who's up there?"

Ivan turned and took a step in the direction of the voice. Robert grabbed his arm.

"It's the duty driver from the Greek Foreign Ministry, son, delivering some papers."

"Funny. I thought it sounded like the Bulgarian officer, you know, Ivan," came the reply from below.

"Course not." Quickly Robert showed Ivan out, and with a barely audible "Good night," locked the door behind him.

"My God. The scheme is actually working," she said in an undertone. "But did you have to shove him out the door?"

"I'd love to see the end of this episode," he answered.

But now, settled around the conference table in Thessaloniki, Barbara realized they were far from the end of this episode. The Consul General, puffed up with his own importance, with ceremonial dignity took his place at the head, and after clearing his throat began a formal welcome, worthy, she thought, of Bismarck opening the Congress of Berlin. As he began his third sentence, Franklin curtly waved him off with, "Sorry, Bill. No time for consular niceties," and pointed to the door, through which the unctuous host quickly exited. Franklin raised his hand in the direction of the departed gray figure, thrust his palm forward, and spreading his fingers wide in the Greek gesture meaning "go to hell," muttered, "Bloody fossil."

After some remarks by the man in the blue suit—he seemed to be concluding a report that had begun long before they had arrived—the men turned to the matter at hand, to Dimitrov, code name, "Hatchet." The man in the tan suit began to read a summary from a full report, his lantern jaw moving up and down like a nutcracker. "For the last three weeks since target has been under surveillance, target has been seen on weekends with female colleague from the Bulgarian Embassy. The first trip was a drive to Sounion for a day's duration; second, a week later, a ferryboat ride to Hydra, where they stayed together in a rooming house for a night and a portion of the following day; the third, to the island of Euboea, where again they stayed together overnight. On the last two occasions, in public, they appeared engrossed in each other, although their behavior was correct and generally guarded, except once when the female colleague was observed," the agent stopped, looked uncomfortably at her and then obviously making up words instead of reading from the text, he said, "fondling him in a compromising manner on a deserted beach." He paused and said, "Sorry, Mrs. Baldwin."

"Keep going," snapped Franklin.

"On three occasions in the middle of each of the three weeks, target was seen in late evening entering an apartment building in Kolonaki Square, where his female colleague lives. According to our sources, the female colleague is the only known acquaintance of target in that building. At each visit target left at 4:00 a.m."

The man slipped the summary back in the file and withdrew another paper. He read, "On one occasion target was observed shoplifting a trinket or two from the jewelry counter at Prisunique, either a watch or a bracelet, or both."

"Jesus Christ," Franklin groaned, and slapped his forehead with the heel of his hand.

"On a subsequent occasion, he was seen to filch a bottle of perfume at a shop in the Hilton Hotel."

"Now, look, here, I don't believe. . . ," she began.

Franklin flipped a hand toward her and motioned to him to continue.

"I simply need to add that the female colleague is the Bulgarian Ambassador's aide, Angela Delcheva, and along with the full report prepared on Dimitrov, I have included a full-length bio on her and a couple of photographs, one of them taken that day on the beach. You might not want . . ." He looked painfully at her.

Franklin reached across the conference table, picked up the files that the tan suit was holding and began skimming the contents.

"Well, looks like he's got somebody to whoopee with while the Mrs. is away," Franklin said, addressing his remarks to Robert.

Robert shook his head slowly, mulling over the report.

"Sorry," she said. "He's not the type."

"Then if not the type, what are they doing in those bedrooms, pray tell? Playing chess?"

"She's the Ambassador's aide. Isn't she privy to a whole lot?" she asked.

"Depends," Franklin said. "I understand he's a weak Ambassador, so, yes, she's probably doing most of the heavy work there. It'd be worth Hatchet's while to get as close to her as he could. According to these pictures he couldn't get any closer." He shoved the photographs across to Robert and her. Robert inspected them, passed one back to Franklin and the other to her. She slid it back across the table without a glance.

"I figure," Franklin continued, "if Hatchet's information is accurate—not the order of battle, but, you know, the harder stuff—that dame is the person feeding it to him. But I don't think his information is real."

"Is real?" she asked.

"He invented it."

She leaned forward in her chair. "I believe it *is* real. But that part about his stealing has to be a mistake," she said, rankling.

"Don't let your American puritanical values get in the way; his stealing has nothing to do with your or his moral rectitude. He's from another culture, you of all people should recognize that, Barbara. He survives by hoisting and he's slick at it, or he wouldn't have gotten this far in life. What do you think most of these human assets are like, anyway? They don't smell of frankincense or myrrh. From my standpoint, he took a stupid risk, that's all, because if he got caught, the Greeks would PNG him out of the country as quick as this" He snapped his fingers. "He'd lose everything," Franklin said, as he gathered up the files and told the two agents to drive with him to KYP so they could use the time to talk.

The Consul General was standing at the door to see his guests on their way. Franklin, adjusting the brim on his Borcellino—shaped like the one Puccini wore in the famous portrait—said in breezy self-amusement, "Keep the lid on Macedonia, Bill." Those caustic remarks, she thought, normally would have amused Robert, but he was too dejected to react.

She loved coming to Thessaloniki, this city in northern Greece weighted by history stretching to the time of St. Paul and even before. She and Robert had spent a couple of their best years there during their first overseas posting, when they were still young and fascinated by every detail of life in this exotic place. Sitting next to her in the back seat of the car, Robert wasn't enjoying this visit. To the contrary, she was aware that he was miserable, suffering.

"Robbie, look. Isn't this place fantastic?" she said, trying to get his mind off his problems.

He said to the air, "I'm a diplomat by temperament and training, in my element solving problems in a rational way, bringing adversarial parties together on common ground, searching out key host nationals and listening to their ideas to determine how U.S. interests might be effected by these foreign leaders. I'm interested in reporting to Washington in understated but articulate prose." She thought he was joking, mimicking someone, until he said, his throat catching, "That's my essence.

Don't they know I can't be anybody else? Can't be a handler for human assets?"

Snatched from the State Department's relatively open, measured sphere and swallowed into Franklin's shadowy, clandestine netherworld, her husband was becoming obsessed, hankering for his own terrain. The depth of his unhappiness disturbed her. The way Washington was treating him infuriated her. But what could she possibly do about it? She linked her arm through his and reached up to kiss him. Her own immense contribution to his distress, she could hardly bear to think about at this moment. At least he had not questioned her again about her feelings toward Ivan. Once or twice, though, she did catch a glimpse of the expression on his face that seemed to say, "You are hurting me, I'm not sure what's really on your mind."

"Why are they calling him 'Hatchet'?" she asked.

"That's his code name. I once described him to Franklin as having a hatchet face."

"Oh, my God, that's the limit. And the way they refer to him as a 'human asset,' what an irony; it actually dehumanizes him, turns him into a tool, an object, not human at all."

She was being defeated by the complexities of this whole affair: Franklin's arrogance and total lack of civility, Robert's misery, Ivan's pitiful situation. She was only too happy to turn her attention to the city as the car made its way along the waterfront, passed the rotund White Tower—a prison used by the Turks centuries ago, in her opinion the most bizarre anachronism in all of Greece—on through the sprawling, now ramshackle neighborhoods that had once seen grander days as the quarters of a great metropolis in the Byzantine era—ruins of ancient churches everywhere—and then great again, for a period, under the Turks—minarets scattered across the skyline. It was here that Kemal Attaturk, was born at a time when Thessaloniki had degenerated into a rotting backwater under the Ottoman Empire. For centuries, it was a center of Sephardic Jewry. Fifty-six thousand of them were carted in cattle trains to Auschwitz by the Nazis; only a few hundred returned, she was remembering with pain.

One of the survivors had been the children's pediatrician, a slender, gentle Sephardic, with a thin face and old-world manners, who prescribed medicine made up of half a dozen ingredients, which, like an alchemist, she had to mix together into what she feared was chancy brew. In summer, when he wore short shirtsleeves, she was aghast at seeing the blue numbers tattooed on his left forearm.

When she and Robert and the children had lived here in the mid-1960s, only the main streets were paved, the rest lay rutted, muddy, or dusty depending on the season; the city center had been backward, crammed with peasants on donkeys, swarms of scrawny gypsies with their pitiful chained bears, horse-drawn vehicles, packs of stray dogs, some of them rabid, while on the surrounding hills flocks of sheep nibbled, their bells tinkling in the still of the night. Out there too was a Farm School the Americans operated to educate Greek students, certainly the best of its kind in all of Greece. Even today, some twelve years later, Thessaloniki, the capital of Greek Macedonia, struck her as a provincial Balkan city, without a really elegant hotel, fine restaurant, park, no sophisticated European amenities, yet it was this very backwardness that put her in touch with its exotic history.

It had not been hard to love the Greeks in the old days, they had been so friendly —they used the same word, *xenos*, to mean both foreigner and guest— still clinging to the ways of their forebears, uncontaminated by the postwar forces that were revolutionizing behavior in America and Western Europe. And one of those they loved especially was Stavros Pavlides.

As the car went up Antheon Street, she kept her forehead pressed to the window looking west, hoping to spy her favorite sight—Mount Olympus, rearing across the gulf, over sixty kilometers away, its peaks decked in snow. Only when they pulled into the army post and parked by the Quonset hut, did she realize Robert had been staring at his hands, distracted.

"They've already put a rotten note in my file. My friend, John Hawthorn, you know, the desk officer for Greece, told me on the phone yesterday from Washington."

He hadn't even noticed that she had been on a different wavelength for the whole ride.

Stavros Pavlides, head of KYP's antiterrorist unit, was waiting for them on the wooden porch of the Quonset hut as they drove up. When he saw them, his face lit up in a generous smile. He grabbed them in a bear hug, and in the Greek custom, kissed each of them on both cheeks. It had been a year or more since they had seen him, although they had spoken to him or his wife on the phone several times. Always rail-thin, he had filled out some, but still exuded his characteristic energy. If he could stand, he wouldn't sit, if he could lope, he wouldn't walk, if he could swing his feet, he wouldn't sit still. She remembered him with his worry beads always twirling, and today, there they were, topaz baubles, dangling from his fingers. At the sight of him, Robert was energized as if just being near him was enough to tap into Stavros' source of electricity.

He spoke fluent English. A graduate of the elite Anatolia College in Thessaloniki, he had earned a degree in the States, where he had planned to stay, but right after university, he had been called back to Greece to watch over the family property when his father took sick. He had once told them "Fate, *moira*, that ancient Greek witch, dug her claws into my skin, and after my marriage, *moira* conspired with my wife, Aspasia, who couldn't bear to leave Greece. That sealed my future, and I stayed on native soil."

His cousin, the Minister of Northern Greece, had paved Stavros' way into the army in 1954, guiding him into KYP, which, although it was a branch of the army, was otherwise patterned after the CIA, and in those days was working closely with the American agency, really dominated by it. KYP offered a young man a secure career, since back then, it appeared the United States would be a patron state forever.

Robert had always said that Stavros was the most nonpolitical Greek he had ever met. Likable, with a good nose for opportunity—he had cooperated fully with the junta that had taken over the country in 1967 and remained in power until 1974—yet even so he had managed to stay on as a fair-haired son when democracy returned to Greece, and waves of anti-Americanism

235

saturated the country. But Stavros had remained a loyal friend to the Company and personally to Dana Franklin. After November 17 first struck in December 1975, he had been made chief of the antiterrorist unit and sent to Israel a couple of times to train in the latest methods. He often came into contact with his old friend the then-station chief in Tel Aviv, Dana Franklin, who had greased the way for the Greeks to take anti-terrorism training under the Israelis; since Greece did not choose to recognize the State of Israel, such arrangements with the Israelis were impossible without pressure from the United States. Franklin had been impressed by everything he'd heard about Stavros. "A crafty opportunist," he'd said. "He's always hedging his bets, ingratiates himself with every faction." And he'd said something else about Stavros that she couldn't believe: "He's also ruthless in the extreme."

When Franklin and his men arrived, Stavros ushered them all inside the Quonset hut, the nerve center of KYP's antiterroroist unit for Northern Greece, covering Macedonia, Thrace, Epiros, and the Northern Cylades. Stavros explained that they were now seated in the conference area. An attached hut housed electronic equipment, a third provided workspace for the agents, and a fourth was used for a kitchen, bathroom, and other conveniences. He wanted Franklin "to see the facility for yourself with an eye to sending American personnel here to share the amenities." Barbara understood this to mean Stavros was pleading with Franklin and Robert to lend support to his rickety enterprise, to beef it up. There were no windows, the place was dark, smelled of earth like a burrow that moles would inhabit.

"Let's get down to business," Stavros said. "Sorry to say, we have something really negative to tell. And then we can go for a delicious lunch." As was his habit, he followed this remark, with an ancient saying—Barbara and Robert couldn't follow the ancient Greek, and knowing that, Stavros gave the English: "If you are a rich man you eat whenever you please; and if you are a poor man, whenever you can." Like most Greeks, he had the ancients at his fingertips—thanks to Greece's tightly prescribed education curriculum—and delighted in quoting the dramatists and philosophers, especially Diogenes. "The sun too penetrates into privies, but is not polluted by them," and, "Stand a little out of my sun," Diogenes said to Alexander, the great Macedonian king, when asked if he wanted anything. These were favorites that she and Robert had managed to memorize in the ancient Greek.

Franklin and his agents reported first, handing Stavros a pile of written documents on international terrorism, focusing on the Red Brigades in Italy, dangerous elements in Germany, and terrorist camps in Bulgaria and in the Middle East, where Bulgarian and East Germans trainers were hard at work. They delivered a lengthy oral presentation based on information from Washington, along with selected bits they'd picked up in Athens. When they had finished, two of Stavros' men gave, in an annoying monotone, a half- hour rehash on the lack of terrorism in Northern Greece in the last decade and reported on peripheral activities—defectors in their zone of responsibility.

They had barely finished when Franklin jumped to his feet, red-faced with exasperation and waving his index finger at Stavros said, "That's pure crap.

Since the first murder committed by November 17 in 1975, you people have been telling me that you haven't been able to make a single arrest. That's impossible. You're not leveling with me, Stavros. Nobody in KYP is. Something stinks to high heaven. I'm convinced you guys know who's behind November 17. You guys are involved in some kind of political cover-up, and don't try to tell me you don't know who's behind those murderers, so why the hell should I pour men and money into this goddamn joint?"

"I do have one item to report, and it's a beaut," said Stavros. He waited a moment to let his words sink in.

Sleet, channeling down from Yugoslavia along the Vardaris River, began to tap the metal roof like ping pong balls. The earthy smell grew pungent.

"We've received information that November 17 is preparing to strike in Thessaloniki in March. In preparation for the hit, we learned, members of the group will meet up here next week."

Stavros was staring up at Franklin, who remained standing.

"Yeah," said Franklin softly, blowing a soft noise from between his lips. "What else?"

"Nothing, yet."

"Your source is a good one?"

"As reliable as they come."

"What's your next move?"

Stavros clicked his blue worry beads, and shifted his gaze to the mid-distance, and remained silent; he had ended his report.

"News to me," said Franklin as he lowered himself into his chair.

"You couldn't have heard anything about this. The source is Hellenic," Stavros said with a ring of pride in his voice.

Barbara felt a flush of triumph shoot through her. Franklin really was despicable. The great man was having his comedown. Oedipus learning that he'd murdered his father and married his mother. Big shot station chief, two minutes ago, he would have bet his life that Ivan was relaying false information. "He doesn't dare look at me," she thought. "How about it, Dana Franklin? Does this help put the information in better perspective for *you*?"

Chapter 21

No, Stoyan could not be as dumb as he looked. A typical Bulgarian peasant, given to calculating in his own cunning way. A schemer. This was the first chance he had to take a good look at the Bulgarian Embassy driver. Other times, Stoyan would be driving the Embassy car, Ivan would be in the passenger's seat, where he'd catch only the man's profile, or he'd be in the back seat, where he'd glimpse the driver's eyes and nose in the mirror. Now, sitting next to him in a taxi, Ivan noticed that his body, from sitting years behind the wheel, had become mushy, mostly inert, like the pulp of a mollusk. When he sat, rolls of fat collapsed into themselves, chin, chest, belly, thighs, one meaty mass. Even the bridge of his nose, his eyelids, were fleshy. This evening was bound to drag or worse, end without results, but with some luck, who knows, he might pry something out of him, this stubborn peasant.

He always pitied underlings like Stoyan. No, pity was not the right word. To be honest, he harbored an impulse to humiliate these inferiors, bully them to make them feel even shabbier, because without fate's intervention in the person of Maria and Vasili, he would have ended up exactly like these slaves. They represented an unbearable reflection of his failed self, of what he would have become if he hadn't been able to manipulate fate. He longed to belittle them, or worse, destroy them, even obliterate them, if he could. Hours later, of course, he was ashamed of himself. Only then would he pity them.

Some of these people were hypersensitive; they sniffed out insults, caught on to the slightest slur. Others, like Stoyan, whose hide was thick as an ox, could not feel the lightest prick. It would take a Spanish bullfighter driving those long, thin knives into his neck to wound him.

Now, though, at their destination, sitting across the table from Stoyan, he'd still be very cautious. The place was filling with cigarette smoke. In the space where the band was to play, the instruments were set up, but the players hadn't shown up yet. A few *putane* moved listlessly from table to table, but you could tell from their lack of enthusiasm, 8:30 in the evening was too early for Greeks to be friendly, even to whores. Stoyan ignored the women and leaned into his beer.

He had decided not to invite the driver to the Plaka—the quaint tourist-ridden section of Athens, a customary place for a night out. Too rich for Stoyan's blood, and besides they risked being seen there; instead they drove to Piraeus, the seedy Mecca for sailors serving on the ships from all over the world that berthed in this huge port. The name of the bar was written in English on a hand painted sign over the entrance— Constantine's Boar's Head Emporium; the proprietor had obviously spent time in England, and like other Greek sailors and merchant marines over centuries, had stashed away every drachma earned at sea to open a business back home. Mounted on the wall over the cash register was a stuffed boar's head, improbably crowned with an American Indian headband decorated with faded feathers, attesting to the owner's far-flung travels.

"Something stronger, Stoyan? Maybe vodka, or try a whiskey?"

"Not yet, *drugariu.*"

"Don't have to call me by my rank tonight. Just Ivan's fine."

Sailors talking loudly in a dozen languages strayed in, most of them still sober, but a few already staggering drunk after a day or two of shore leave.

On the wall behind Stoyan was a framed photograph in color of two African women, their breasts drooping like sacks, both holding babies. The picture was creased and cracked, obviously a prized memento, lugged back to Greece by one of the sailors, maybe the proprietor himself.

A blind man, his thin cane tapping, was approaching their table selling for the lottery, the tickets affixed in the usual way to a long pole, braced like a rifle on his shoulder. "*Laxio,*" he bleated out his wares in the voice of a struck animal.

"We don't want none," said Stoyan in passable Greek. The driver had been in the country for so many years, he'd become Hellenized. Ivan wondered if he had a Greek woman.

"Your Greek's pretty fluent, Stoyan. How come?"

"Picked it up. Used my ears."

"You must know your way around this city inside out."

"I'm not stupid. But I been here over ten years. Anybody would learn something in that time. How come *you* speak so good, Dimitrov?"

"Like you, I'm no idiot." He noted the "Dimitrov." Obviously, Stoyan wasn't comfortable calling him Ivan; either Stoyan was genuinely uneasy at going out socially with a high-ranking officer, or, more like it, he was using formality as a way to keep the high-ranking officer at a distance, nervous about the invitation, or guessing the truth, that the officer wanted something from him. Ivan would have to find a way to relax him; he motioned to the waiter.

"A vodka for me and whiskey for my friend, here."

The waiter demanded money for the drinks before he'd put them on the table, snarling that whiskey was too expensive to set down without prepayment. Beer was one thing, whiskey another altogether. Ivan wet his fingertips and peeled off the drachmas. He held up his glass to Stoyan.

"Well, here's to our night out," he said, successfully injecting some bounce in his tone.

Stoyan smelled his whiskey, set it down and picked up his beer instead.

A man wearing a greasy fisherman's cap flopped down convivially at their table and removed from a scabby envelope a mountain of pictures.

"How about this?" he said, shoving the pornography under Stoyan's nose.

Stoyan inspected each picture with concentrated attention. Once he laughed out loud, and Ivan bent over to see the joke, but there was no joke, just a sad representation of a shepherd engaged with a goat. When

Stoyan had finished his inspection, the man politely handed the stack to him.

"Come back tomorrow when I'm sober," Ivan lied. "I can't see straight, the pictures are wiggling in front of my eyes."

Truth was, the watered-down vodka tasted like it was drawn from a polluted well; he couldn't drink it.

"How many hours do you drive a week?" he asked, conversationally.

"Depends. Some more than others. I'm really the Ambassador's and Delcheva's driver. They get the attention. Everybody else got to line up."

Stoyan pronounced Delcheva's name neutrally. If he'd heard rumors about her and Ivan, he didn't betray it with even a blink.

"Do those two use you much?"

"The Ambassador, yes. Official rounds especially at night, but could be mid-day, too."

"And Delcheva?"

Stoyan smiled for the first time, the thick eyelids lowered as if he were remembering a sweet dream, and abruptly he opened up. "She's a good one. The best, I'll tell you that. She gets restless a lot, lonesome, wants to get out of the city. I take her for long rides. Some Sundays in the winter, when it's damp, rainy, I drive her south to the Corinth Canal, where she buys us a couple of *souvlakis* and beer and we lean over the bridge to watch the ships squeak through that narrow canal. Looks to me like the boats ain't going to squeak through. Sometimes years ago, in my village, I'd be called on to drive a big hearse down a goat path to reach a cemetery. I know what narrow is. That Delcheva. She's a true lady, that one."

No, he hasn't the slightest idea, he thought.

Two Tourist Policemen came in, their hands elegantly gloved in white, their sleeves bearing small flags to represent the foreign languages they spoke. They swaggered like visiting royalty among the clientele of sailors and sluts. To the old woman in widow's weeds behind the cash box, they gallantly touched the brim of their hats and left.

"Pretty nice place to be stationed, eh, Stoyan?"

"Damn good. An extra allowance. Fine climate. The people don't cause trouble. Had a buddy once stationed in the Middle East, one of those Arab countries. The mob there, they stole the shoes off your feet as you walked down the street."

"Your allowance, though. It can't go very far. It would cover things here, but you'll have nothing saved to take home. Too bad you couldn't find a way to earn something more."

Stoyan turned away from him and called to the waiter for another beer.

"Money's not easy for a guy like you, Stoyan," he said sympathetically. "But there are ways, you know." Finally, he had introduced it, a light hint. Stoyan didn't catch it. Then he switched to another subject.

"The women aren't bad. Get to know any?"

"No, I follow regulations, *drugariu*. I don't go with Greeks."

Stoyan's reputation around the Embassy was solid: hard worker, uncomplaining, thickheaded, polite, didn't look left or right, obliging, not anybody's particular pet other than the Ambassador's and Delcheva's, no odd habits. Background: raised in the Valley of the Roses, father worked as a field hand on a collective farm, mother in gathering of rosebuds for the industry that extracted rose oil, or attar, known as "Bulgarian Gold," a significant export product. One of five children. A grandmother's child, the typical situation where the mother worked and the children were brought up by the grandparents. No schooling beyond compulsory education. Not married. And here was a key point, Stoyan would never report any proposition that Ivan might make to him. A man like Stoyan would feel too lowly, too afraid, to inform on such a powerful, high-ranking officer. All in all, a perfect candidate to go on the take. A matter of simple bribery, not unusual in Bulgarian life. No obligation on either part. Stoyan would sell him information—a one-time deal—he would pay cash for it. For Stoyan, dirt-poor, not a stotinki to his name, anything extra, no matter how little, was a boon. No ongoing relationship. A quick transaction. As the Greeks said, *taka-taka*, over and done.

By now Stoyan was working on his third beer but hadn't touched the whiskey.

"So, you take the Ambassador to parties and Delcheva for Sunday rides. I suppose you also deliver messages around town. I guess that takes up some of your day."

"I go here and there. The messages keep me moving."

"Where mostly?"

"Wherever they tell me."

"I mean to embassies? Greek ministries? Greek individuals?"

"All."

"Are there some Greek individuals you deliver papers to often?"

246

Stoyan stood up, rubbed his underbelly, and shambled off to the toilet without answering. The driver probably sensed that he was being seriously questioned and had made a decision not to become further involved. Patience.

Over in a corner two drunks were arguing. One picked up a chair, waved it back and forth in the air like a weapon and yelled something in a harsh language, probably German or Dutch. A thug, dressed all in black, an employee of the Emporium, bolted over and in English told them to get out. By the time Stoyan returned five other sailors had joined the brawl.

"So, what were you saying, Dimitrov?"

"I was just wondering where you delivered messages in Athens. What Greeks? I mean, what non-government people."

Stoyan paused and gazed absently around the room at the mayhem. Then he said slowly, "What if I tell you?"

"Like I said a few minutes ago. I'd be happy to see you earn a little extra. Tough for a guy like you. Even if you weren't looking for more money for yourself, your people back home could use it. Think of them."

"It's something to think about, alright. But I can't jump into it. Let me think."

Stoyan put his arms on the table and laid his head on his hands.

The brawl got worse, other imbeciles joined in. The band members took their places, and without so much as a glance at the uproar, started tuning up. The microphones were turned on, emitting an ear-piercing screech; the noise level from band and brawlers made conversation almost impossible.

Stoyan picked his head up. Ivan was astonished to notice that his hair was plastered to his forehead with sweat. The poor slob had been agonizing.

"*Ne*," Stoyan said.

He could barely hear him.

"What?"

"*Ne*. I couldn't, that's all there is to it," the driver said in a muffled voice.

He heard the answer, but even if he hadn't, he couldn't miss Stoyan's vigorous head motion to underscore his refusal.

"You're plain crazy not to take me up." He was yelling now. "This is a great offer. Don't be a goddamn fool. All yours for sitting on your ass. A few addresses. Names if possible. Think what you're giving up, man. *Malaka*," he swore at him in Greek.

He'd seen the stubborn look before, a thousand times, on peasants' faces, that closing down of expression, the tightening of the lips, chin jutting. He had to suppress an urge to grab him by those rounded, sagging shoulders and shake him till his fat neck snapped. He hated him.

Why should he feel the least pity for this moron? Himself, he had bettered his lot not just because fate had been good to him—no, much more, because he had the brains to seize every opportunity that came within his reach. This nullity across from him. The trick had failed, a door had slammed shut. He was desperate for a second path to November 17, one other than Delcheva. He had a hunch that Stoyan was assigned to deliver paper messages directly from the Bulgarian Embassy to November 17. An address or two from Stoyan might have led him right to the door of one of the gang.

On the way home, they sat side by side in a taxi from Piraeus. The snail next to him had withdrawn into his shell and slumped spinelessly. Ivan, bolt upright, was hot with anger. That sensation gradually ebbed, but as his body cooled he felt his hands turn to ice. To warm them, but also to control them, he shoved his fists under his thighs and kept them locked there until they reached Stoyan's place and the silent peasant leaped out of the taxi.

Chapter 22

Wearing his dress blues, he was standing by the glass bowl, relishing the giant shrimp and drinking Campari; he had acquired a craving for this tart Italian aperitif, since his first cocktail party over a month ago. As he dipped the shrimp in the spicy sauce and devoured it whole, he bent forward to avoid slopping on his uniform. Hearing someone call "Ivan," he turned to see Barbara hurrying to join him at the shrimp bowl. He was seized by the idea that if Barbara had a flavor she'd taste like Campari.

"That's why I attend these things. To gobble the shrimp," she said, spearing a large one with a yellow plastic toothpick.

"Gobble," he pronounced. "That is a new word for me." He made some comic *g* and *b* sounds to amuse her. "But you really came here to help Denmark celebrate its national day, is that not true?" He gestured to the talkative crowd gathered at the Danish Embassy for its annual national-day fete.

"How's the job going?" She was smiling, happy to see him, he guessed, but he couldn't really know. Western Europeans, Americans, there was something so loose about them, so uncalculating; they always looked joyous in public, always kept a smile on their faces. The last time he'd seen her was at her house over a week ago, when he'd delivered the information. Then, she had seemed strained; he couldn't blame her, her thin-lipped husband had been unsociable, frowned the whole time and kept strictly to the point. He wondered what they meant to each other, this couple, how close they were. Americans never in their history had the custom of arranged marriages, a practice once common in Bulgarian society. How did they choose each other? Did passion bring them together? Did passion hold them together? She was standing next to him in a form-fitting gown the color of garnet. No doubt of her appeal.

"The job? I am trying very hard. Very hard. You appreciate that. And since Maria is not here, it makes things easier. Her father is sick."

"Oh, sorry. When do you expect her back?"

"Soon."

Oh, but you need lots more time, don't you?"

Antonio, Louisa's husband, interrupted them, waving as he approached, his sword swinging at his side.

"So, here they are, the famous ski champions," Antonio said, kissing Barbara's hand.

"Dimitrov," he said, greeting him warmly. Louisa would have loved to be here tonight to see you both, I am sure."

"Has she left?" asked Barbara.

"She is in Milano, rehearsing and working with her voice teacher. She should not be absent from Italy for even a week. She has two separate lives, you know. One with me and the other, her career."

"Well, she is fortunate to have two lives. In Bulgaria, they only allow us one."

"She and I had a delightful lunch together last week, right before she left for Italy," Barbara told Antonio.

Ivan was stung. He had called Louisa, too, some days ago. She had declined to meet him, protesting that her schedule was too full with practicing, getting ready to go to Milano, et cetera, et cetera. He checked himself. He was taking her refusal too personally. She had not accepted, he was sure, because someone had ordered her not to. She was mixed up in so much, God knows who issued her what orders.

After some more chitchat, and leaving a sentence unfinished—this was the way at cocktail parties, he had noticed—Antonio moved on to other acquaintances.

He took a deep breath, blinked his eyes as he savored his surroundings. Barbara, in the line that curved smoothly from her shoulder to her hip, reminded him of the slow, curvaceous lines on the Rolls Royces that sailed down Syngrou Avenue. Everyone at the party—that is, the Westerners, the women, the men—were chosen people, and to think he stood among them. Am I really one of them? In what sense? For a moment a melancholy swept over him; he felt like a fraud amid these free, rich, jovial people. Even the chandeliers, the tables, the food, the maroon-carpeted staircase rising to an upper floor, were select. And even among these ageless, beautiful people, she, Barbara, stood out as distinctive. He inhaled his Campari, took a sip and sloshed some around like a mouth wash, just to experience the sting of it, something to snap him back to reality.

"Robert expected you'd be here tonight. He's brought you something." She sorted through the shrimp for a large one and thrust in her toothpick.

"I, too," he said.

"You have something?"

She greeted with "*kali spera*" a portly man in a tuxedo, his black hair shiny and slicked back, who was waving at her from across the shrimp bowl, a Greek ship owner he had seen at other parties.

"Yes, but there's a problem," he said in a low voice. Before he could explain, Gerda, tonight a sedate plump matron on the arm of her husband, Günter, strolled over to them.

"*Es freut mir.*"

"She's happy to see you," Günter translated. He had a lazy eye that floated in its socket, making him appear nervous, but actually he was calm and sociable, the sort of person who had absolutely nothing to say, yet talked incessantly. He thanked Barbara "for being good to Gerda in Bulgaria," as if Gerda were a half-wit who needed special attention.

"*Ja, es war wunderbar,*" said Gerda, cocking an eyebrow at Barbara.

After exchanging a series of inanities, the couple greeted some friends from the German Embassy, and with a hearty *Grüss Gott* rushed off to join them.

"The problem?" Barbara asked.

"So far," he said, "I am unable to obtain any messages from our Embassy."

"But you did bring us one last week."

"Yes, that was for one time. A stroke of luck. This conversation is not to report, understand? I am just confiding in you. Do not mention the difficulty to your husband."

A flock of lean Chinese men and women in grayish-blue Mao suits, like hungry sea birds at the tide line,

253

were scooping up the celery stalks stuffed with caviar from a huge platter next to the shrimp bowl. There was a commotion over by the entrance. A squad of bodyguards entered, surrounding the unsmiling Prime Minister of Greece, Constantine Karamanlis, the venerable leader who had put his country back together after the fall of the junta. The Prime Minister's dour face was defined by thick, dark eyebrows. Greek officials rushed to greet him, followed by a swarm of foreigners, and soon his august figure was drowned in the crowd. Ivan was amused by the Chinese, who, fixed on the food in spite of the Prime Minister's arrival, never slowed from spearing the shrimp and other delicacies.

To get relief from the hot air and cigarette smoke, he and Barbara headed for the other side of the room toward the open windows, but were stopped by Colonel Radovski.

"So, Mrs. Baldwin of the American Embassy. Good evening. I was just talking with your husband." Radovski nodded vacantly at him as if he were someone he couldn't quite place. "He said you had been skiing in Bulgaria. A nice place, a very nice place. The people can be very hospitable."

"Just perfect, Colonel."

Radovski gave a slight bow and went on his way.

"If I am unable to get into those communications, what will you be able to do for me?"

"What a question, Ivan. What a question."

While he waited for her answer, the Campari turned sour in his mouth. She thought a moment and resumed hesitantly, "I don't really know. This whole situation is extremely dangerous. I'm afraid for you.

Maybe you can't pull it off at all. For some reason, the people at my Embassy think you can. You know I'll do whatever's necessary to. . . "

The space by the windows had been taken by the Canadian and British ambassadors, who, with their gray heads almost touching, were talking earnestly.

Breaking away from an Australian Embassy group, Barbara's husband, tall, his neck stiff in his snugly cut, impeccably starched American collar, signaled them to wait as he came across the room. Baldwin extended his hand in a formal manner without even glancing at him, and said, icily, "Good to see you, Dimitrov."

Baldwin was looking at his wife. "We'll be joining the Australians downtown for dinner after this is over," he told her. She answered, "Fine, Roger has gone to play practice so I'll just call Freddy to tell him we'll be late," and whispered something in her husband's ear. Then with a parting smile, she drifted off with a friend from the French Embassy. A group of musicians finished a round of Danish folk tunes and swung into music by Mikis Theodorakis, the bouzouki twanging the melody.

"Dimitrov, I'm heading for the toilet, the one on the second floor. Wait a few minutes, then come along after me," Baldwin told him, this time looking him hard in the eyes.

He ambled to the bar, took a handful of pistachio nuts, shelled and swallowed them and absently reached for some more. If the West was like this, he had been cheated blind his whole life. Through his body, like an electric shock, surged an irrepressible fury against the world for all his deprivations; the rage struck him with such force that for a moment he thought he'd lost consciousness. He snarled at the bartender, " Hey, you, two glasses of Stolichnaya." The man scowled, holding the bottle of vodka over the glasses, but not pouring it. The livid expression brought him to his senses. "*Parakalo*," and "*efharisto*," he added politely, as the bartender poured him the drinks. He swallowed each glassful in one gulp. With his throat burning and eyes tearing, he ascended the elegantly curved staircase, now wary. The American was growing more hostile with every meeting; that self-important bastard hated him, when for good reason he should be beholden to him. On the second floor, he found the WC. He turned the handle and found Baldwin waiting for him by the sink. When the door shut, the voices and bouzouki below were snuffed out, the room silent except for the sound of water dripping with unnerving regularity in the pipes like the ticking of a clock.

The American leaned on the door, shot the bolt, and swung round to place his back against it, bracing his feet on the floor. "Here," Baldwin said, flourishing a white envelope and handing it to him. In return Ivan gave him a folded sheet of paper.

"The exchange?" the American asked, pocketing the paper.

"Yes."

"And the other stuff? The intercepted messages for the Bulgarian Embassy?"

" Coming, yes coming."

"O.K. But when?"

"Patience. Please."

"It's been too goddamn long. The days are flying by, you know. November 17 might strike any second."

"I give you my word," he mumbled, humiliated.

"Your word? Oh, well, sure, in that case. . . " The American narrowed his gray eyes sarcastically, made a huffing sound, turned and stomped out the door, slamming it shut, leaving him standing by the sink. He smashed his fist against the mirror and heard pieces of glass tinkle as they tumbled into the sink. He washed the blood from his hand, dabbed it with wet bits of toilet paper and left the party directly, rushing out, feeling shattered like the glass when he realized that he had lost control of himself more than once tonight.

He headed on foot to Kolonaki. Baldwin was pushing him, obviously wouldn't help him at all, and worse, would probably block Barbara if in some extraordinary way she tried to come to his aid. As far as the Americans were concerned, his hope still lay with Barbara. He could trust her all the way. Angela's part was the key to Barbara; those two women represented Plan A. If that failed, his newly conceived Plan B was infallible.

Fate had delivered him last week. What unbelievable luck, when he had wandered into Angela's office and seen the message telling about the November 17 meeting in Thessaloniki. There it was, lying on her desk, where she had left it unsecured— she had fallen into this careless habit of leaving documents around, since no one dared enter the "Throne Room," as the staff called it, when she was absent. So much for luck; but what fool could trust his future to luck? The move to cultivate Stoyan— he had been somewhat hopeful—had proved a terrible flop. Now, it was time to sound out Angela. But how far could he trust her? She really had fallen for him. That was a shock, the last thing he supposed would happen to a woman like her, newly liberated from a disastrous marriage, a hot-pants, who seemed out solely for a good time. The first few times she had been writhing about in her own hot and excited world, treating him like a sex machine. In those early days, he thought with irony, just a few weeks ago, he might even have extracted payment for his generous services: I'll be overjoyed to give you this, sweetie girl, but you'll have to give me what I want in return. Back then, though, he didn't have her loyalty; the danger in the beginning was that she might betray him. But as time wore on she'd slowed down, careful to move along with him, to make him happy, a show of consideration that just might translate on her side at least, to acts of loyalty to him. And lately she had been questioning him about Maria. When will she come back? What would he do when she came back? Would he leave off making visits to her apartment? How could they manage their new relationship? Her passion for him could figure as a plus or a minus: in a crisis it could drive her toward him, but if she thought herself betrayed, it could turn her into a real bitch. He half-remembered a Bulgarian proverb, which concluded something like, "Go easy with a woman in love. Remember even a goose turns vicious when you steal her gander."

He felt in his pocket for the letter he had received that morning from Maria telling him that her father was better, that she would be returning to Greece in exactly seven days; he went over to the litter can, ripped the letter into tiny shreds and watched them float into the receptacle.

Aside from these worries, he was for the first time ever enjoying life, in this early March, in the afternoons, unobserved and free—unless he was under surveillance, which he doubted strongly, since his own people didn't have the funds and the Americans were probably not that interested in how he spent his afternoon hours. And of course, November 17 had no clue who he was and how he was working to intercept their messages. Nonetheless, he remained on his guard, but saw no traces of agents. When the office closed at two o'clock, he loved walking the great streets of Athens— the broad avenues—King George, Queen Sophia, Panapistimio, down Ermou to the Plaka, like a village in itself, nestled under the Acropolis, the revered ruin a much more dramatic structure than he had ever guessed from the grainy, prewar postcard his mother had tacked on the wall above her bed. Almost every afternoon, he'd stroll to the Plaka. There he'd dawdle, strike up conversation with a vendor, just to talk Greek, to feel at home in this new universe. He'd poke through the goods, asking what part of Greece the embroidered pillow case came from, how much for a string of worry beads, for a marble statue of Athena, a model of the Parthenon. In the Plaka he'd snitched two silk scarves and a ring for Angela, things she yearned for, stuff he wasn't going to squander his money on, not with the kinds of plans he was making; he'd need plenty of money for the future. But he'd have to quit stealing— a skill he'd perfected in childhood, the difference being in those days in Bulgaria, there was nothing much to take, just a coin, a pair of gloves, and with luck, bits of food. He felt a thrill whenever he entered the Hilton Hotel or the Grande Bretagne to experience the polish of the lobbies, the display of French perfumes, Italian leather goods, Greek jewelry, books from all over Europe and the United States in the hotel shops. He had grown used to the pounding racket in the streets; he considered the noise as the hymn of capitalism, the ring of freedom.

If his agreement with the Americans didn't work out— his Plan A—he'd make a run for Xanthi—his Plan B. There among his relatives he'd hide until he could find out how to turn himself over to the Greek authorities and apply for citizenship under the new law allowing the return of leftists who had escaped to the communist countries during the civil war. As long as he was in the Bulgarian army, of course, Plan B was too awkward. But Plan B was fine if he could wait it out in Xanthi, hidden by family. They would find a way to solve things. Soon, soon.

His sense of possibility was growing more acute. After the first few weeks in Athens new visions began to entertain him, daydreams: he'd study the faces of passers-by, searching for someone he might recognize, imagining people would leap across the street and yell, " *Yia sou,* Ivancho," or better yet, call him by his Greek name, "Ioannis, my cousin, my nephew, *agori,* you've come home, we've been waiting for you these many years." The game warmed him, salved his loneliness.

He strolled into Spefsippou Street and rang the bell at the apartment building. An automatic buzzer released the lock.

As usual, Angela was waiting for him to regale her with stories of how he'd passed the evening. He invented anecdotes, encounters with people at the cocktail party, misrepresenting the Chinese as light-hearted, the American couple as naive, the German wife sultry like Marlene Dietrich, described the mounds of shrimp and caviar, truth and absurd fiction, all mixed together into tales to keep her amused. Then she asked as she did every day: "Have you heard from Maria?"

"Yes, today."

"Well?"

"A long time yet. The old man is still pretty sick."

"What a pity. I'll have you to myself longer. I'm happy." Her fingers played with his hair, with the cleft in his chin.

He watched her enormous eyes, set deep in the oval face; dark eyes were hard to read; you had to be, like him, practiced in the art. They didn't storm or lighten with mood like blatantly transparent blue eyes, yet from their depths they could express everything—the gleam that now revealed her happiness.

"Yes, you'll have me a good long time," he said.

"How do you mean?"

"I'm working on a plan.

She got up from the couch, poured them each a cup of coffee and sat across from him.

He examined her face, scrupulously this time, to be sure of her. He noticed her cheeks were blotched, a reddening, unusual for her.

"I don't follow you. Not at all," she said.

"Maria doesn't need to rush back. I'm busy, very busy, there's really no place for her here at the moment. Maybe later. Who knows when."

He pushed a yellow striped cat, who was rubbing against his pants, off the couch; Angela came to sit beside him.

"You know, I want to keep it like it is. You and me. I want to keep it like this as long as I can," he said.

He continued to study her face. The eyes were glassy, now, she was on the verge of crying, but she wouldn't, not her; that wasn't her way to display emotion. She put her arms around him, and with her eyes shut she felt for his lips.

He held her, stroked her body, whispered to her that he could hold Maria off, that he'd keep her away as long as possible, he had a plan to stay together. She gave way not with tears, but just the way he knew she would, this time with a convulsive energy, which he was gauging very closely, her way, he surmised, to tell him she was with him all the way. They went off to the bedroom, where, finally, she wore herself out. He bent to kiss her, touched her where she loved it and started to dress. The sheet pulled up to her waist, sated, she was watching him with half-shut eyes as he put on his shirt.

"You could do me a favor," he said in an undertone, keeping the same voice he had used in bed, trying to sustain the mood.

"What? I'll help."

"I know you can."

"Tell me."

He went over to the radio and turned it up till it blared.

"If any information comes across about that organization, that November 17 terrorist group," he said, bending to whisper in her ear.

"My God, if we ever received anything like that, it would be the highest classification, Ivan. You're not supposed to know about or talk about our communication system. Be careful who you mention that to."

"I am not exactly broadcasting it, am I. I'm being careful by just asking you. I need that information that passes through our system."

"But why? What would you do with it?" She sat up abruptly against the bed pillows; with her eyes fully opened, she seemed to look through him. A striped gray cat stalked across the sheet and curled itself languidly in her lap.

Taking his time, he concentrated on tucking in his shirt. As he tightened his belt, he turned and bent to her ear.

"Angela, what were we just talking about before on the couch?"

"Maria's return."

"Did I mention a plan? One to keep us together?"

"You were just jabbering, I thought. What crazy, impossible things you were saying. I wanted so much to believe you.

"You thought wrong. Dimitrov doesn't jabber."

"I must have been mistaken, then."

"Don't ever mistake me." He bent to her ear again. "I can tell you this. That information is our passport out of here. You, me, we leave together. Just get me what I need."

He stood and looked at her.

She seemed bewildered. Then her eyes flinched with fury, just a fast dilation of the pupils, a split second's shift like the lens on a camera when the button is pushed, and then a sucking in of her lower lip. That's all. Nothing more. He caught it, read it; she might as well have screeched, "Is that all you ever wanted me for, you liar? You used me. All this time. Get out, you fucking traitor."

As he left, he saw her pull the sheet up to cover herself; it was dotted with blood from the hand that he'd pricked on glass from the smashed mirror.

Now. Nothing else to do. Now. Oh, God, Maria. He couldn't think about Maria. Not now. He had to make his move. Angela would certainly report him. Sooner or later she would report him. If it were sooner, he'd be caught. If it were later, he'd be gone, free. Now no choice but to put his alternative, Plan B, into action. Now, to move rapidly toward the possibility. He felt absolutely clear-headed, thrilled to be unencumbered, the only way for his plan to work. Those women, the hell with them. Both of them, idiot Bulgarians. Let them rot. But Angela was not an idiot. She had figured it out. Figured he would never take her.

For a moment, an unsettling idea crossed his mind. Suppose he had read Angela wrong. No. He refused to entertain it; no time now to be having second thoughts. Decisive. He had always been decisive.

Above, the black sky was unclouded, filled with thousands of stars. As he looked to the north, he saw the Milky Way spread wide, open like an unobstructed path.

He rushed on until he came to a public phone.

Chapter 23

He was cleaning his artifacts, the things he'd dug up in Bulgaria, a dozen Neolithic arrowheads his father's friend had excavated in Larissa, some authentic copies of Alexandrian coins his mother bought him at the Archaeological Museum in Athens—he loved those with Alexander the Great's noble head clearly engraved on them—five ceramic shards that Roger had gotten in eighth grade and didn't want anymore. Roger called Freddy's collection a pile of junk. With a face cloth, he dried them all thoroughly, organized them in their proper compartments in the wooden box built to order by a local carpenter when he'd returned from Bulgaria, to hold them safely for transport and display.

He stood the box up on the windowsill as an exhibit, took ten steps backward, squinted at the collection from a distance and then moved forward to inspect it close up. He was pleased, sensing he understood how Schliemann felt when the great archaeologist arranged the first golden necklaces that he had pulled from the dry earth at Troy.

He'd be up all night too excited to sleep in anticipation of tomorrow, when his class was going on a field trip across the Corinth Canal into the Peloponnese to visit the ruins at Mycenae, the actual place according to many people where Clytemnestra, Electra, Orestes, Iphigenia and Agamemnon had lived around 1250 B.C., and where Schliemann had begun his archaeology career. Next vacation he wanted to visit Troy.

Roger had teased him, said every kid who goes to the American school and had Mrs. Pappas for Greek History goes through a phase of wanting to be an archaeologist, like Schliemann, then forgets all about it by ninth grade, when Mrs. Pappas passed out of the picture. Freddy thought he'd never get over it, especially after that neat day with the Bulgarian officer digging and experiencing the miracle of discovery. Since then he was positive he'd become an archaeologist, and had even discussed with his father where to go to college to study for it. Roger had forgotten all about their day with Ivan and had long ago given up plans to be an archaeologist. He was too involved with girls and his extracurricular activities at school to notice that Mom and Dad were fighting over Ivan all the time.

When the phone rang he carefully placed the box on his night table and said into the receiver, "Baldwin's residence, Fred speaking."

"Freddy. You?"

"Yeah."

"Ivan Dimitrov."

"Ivan? Gosh. Hi."

"Look, my friend. I am going to speak fast."

"O.K."

"Can you keep a secret? Do not tell anyone I called. Not even Roger."

"Sure."

"I need a favor, please. Remember the day we went digging?"

266

"Yeah, course."

"Well, I've found a place here where I want to dig, but I am unable to drive there. My license plate will give me away as Bulgarian. Bulgarians are forbidden to go to this area. I need a different license plate. Understand what I am saying?"

"You bet."

"Does your father have an old license plate put away some place I could borrow, one of those official Embassy ones? You know, the green ones. They have a delta sigma on them for *diplomatiko soma.*

"Hold on a minute. I'll run down to look, but I don't think so. I've never seen one."

He hurried down to the garage. In the pale light, he couldn't see in the shadowy spaces, so he pounded up the steps for a flashlight. He stopped at the phone and yelled into it, "Hey, Ivan, hang on another second."

He raced back down, lugged a few cardboard boxes down off the shelves under the light, rummaged through the junk mechanically, stewing over what he would tell his parents. Oh God, don't let me find the plates because then I definitely will not have to tell Mom and Dad that he called at all. If I do find them then the fireworks begin. How could he give over a license plate to Ivan and not tell his father? But no matter how much he hated strangers, he really liked Ivan. He'd treated him and Roger like grownups, thought enough of them to take them on the dig. And he had saved his life, hadn't he?

His father had been explicit.

"Listen," his father had said to Roger and him the day after they returned from Bulgaria, "that Bulgarian officer, Dimitrov, the guy's trouble."

"He saved my life, Dad. You can't imagine what it was like lost in the snow. He'd never be trouble, Dad. Mom said I'd been dead if it weren't for him."

"Your mother exaggerates. I know how it was. And, yes, he saved you from some harm, no denying. We've thanked him. We're more grateful than words can say. But he's not the kind you can repay for his trouble. He asks an outrageous price."

"I didn't know he wanted money."

"No, that's just a way of speaking. So if he ever tries to get in touch with either of you, let me know right away. This is serious business, guys."

He was finding a slew of boxes, more than he remembered; some were piled on top of others. He stood on a stepladder and peered into the ones on top. Some he couldn't see into so he lowered them onto the floor for a better look. The dust tickled his nose, made him sneeze. Nothing. Just as well. He clattered up the stairs to the phone.

"Hey, Ivan, looks like there's no license plate. I've gone through everything."

"Thanks, Freddy. Thanks. Remember, not a word to anyone. Agreed?"

"No, I get you."

"See you soon, friend. When I settle this problem, I will give you a call and we will go digging again, the three of us. Right, Freddy?"

"See you, Ivan."

He hung up and went back down to the garage where he put everything neatly in its place and then went to bed. Nobody could tell that he had sifted through every single box.

At eleven o'clock he heard Roger pounding up the stairs to his own room. After midnight his parents came home, his mother stopping in Freddy's room as always to see how he was and kiss him goodnight. He pretended to be asleep.

He couldn't sleep, not because he was excited over the trip anymore, but because Ivan's call was affecting him like a stomachache, something heavy weighing on his body, his mind; he felt uncomfortable all over.

He hated the way Ivan had become a major topic of conversation between his parents. His father had been crabby for several weeks, not cracking his usual corny jokes with him and Roger or calling them over to help catch bats, chloroform them and then cut them open to document the number and kinds of insects in their stomachs; every time his father pronounced Ivan's name, he made a face like he was eating rotten fruit. Lately, his mother was always ready to burst out crying, his parents blabbing on in hushed, heated voices, the veins in their foreheads and throats sticking out: Ivan was a sneak, unreliable, a thug (his father); Ivan was a good person at heart, an individual caught by circumstances, needed a chance in the world (his mother); the Ambassador was an irresponsible egomaniac suffering from retarded development, and Dana Franklin was corrupted by power (both mother and father). When they weren't speaking about Ivan, they didn't speak to each other at all.

He had brought all this grief on his parents, of course. As he mulled the situation, he was thinking, "I shouldn't have left the ski school, that was all my fault. Getting lost like a two-year old in the snow, ending up in a stupid situation where I had to be rescued by a Bulgarian, that was my fault. Like an idiot, pestering Mom to go on the dig, again my fault." Now Ivan was asking for money or maybe a special favor for saving him, that too was his fault. If Mom and Dad could pay, they would, but Ivan was probably demanding more than they could afford, what with Catherine's tuition and her trips back and forth from the States to Greece four times a year. Cripes, he was so nervous he got two C's and a D in tests at school in the last two weeks, thinking how Catherine would have to leave college because of him, Catherine who was so excited about studying on an exchange program at the Sorbonne this spring. He could say he was sorry, that was the least he could do, but what good was that? Yeah, at least he'd say he was sorry. He was making them more unhappy being saved and alive than if he'd froze to death. He wished he'd froze to death, stiff as a board all laid out, that's how they'd have found him, except he hoped they found him before they went back to Greece. He wouldn't want to be stuck forever in Bulgaria, buried there in a strange country, alone. He rolled onto his stomach and hugged his pillow. He remembered once a classmate died in Athens of meningitis and they flew his body to the States on an Air Force plane. That was O.K. That's how he imagined himself now, froze dead on an Air Force plane, with GIs, not a bunch of smelly strangers, and, happily, they would all be speaking English; he was soothed by that scene.

Just as comforting was the Hodja story that crossed his mind about dying and not dying; the beloved Turkish Hodja, whose legend had spread ages ago through the Balkans, had the power to cheer everyone, and he was glad this particular tale, one of his favorites, came to him at this gloomy moment.

Once the Hodja, was sitting astride a tree limb up high chopping at it with his ax. Freddy had a picture in his brain of this scene as clear as a movie. A friend yelled up to Hodja, "Look where you're chopping. You'll fall down." But Hodja ignored the warning and kept swinging his ax. Crash, down came the limb and down came Hodja. He had been too busy to notice he was sitting on the wrong side of the cutting.

Hodja said to his friend, "You are a wise man. You told me when I was going to fall. Now tell me when I am going to die."

"After your donkey brays four times," came the answer.

Hodja, bruised from the fall, mounted his little gray donkey and started home. As the donkey thought of his manger and the hay waiting for him, he brayed. "Aman," trembled the Hodja, "I'm one-fourth dead."

Down the road they met a donkey and rider. Hodja's donkey brayed a friendly greeting. "Aman," cried the Hodja "I'm one-half dead."

The donkey trotted on, thinking of the brook where he'd soon be drinking. He let out a bray of anticipation. "Aman," groaned the Hodja at this third bray, "I am three-fourths dead."

He chatted to the donkey and patted him to divert him from trumpeting that fourth and fatal bray.

A group of men and donkeys appeared on the path. Loud and long was the greeting to his friends. Hodja toppled from his donkey, groaning, "I am dead. Dead." Snuggled under the covers, Freddy smiled. That was his favorite line.

The men ran and picked up the limp Hodja, poked him, shook him, pinched him, but he seemed lifeless. "He said he was dead," said one man, "let's strap him to his donkey and take him to his village."

On the way to the village the men began to argue about the right path to take. Hodja, irritated by the bickering said, "When I was alive, I went this way." And under the covers, he smiled again. That was his second favorite line.

The men stared open-mouthed and afraid. They scattered. Hodja sat once more astride his donkey and jogged home. That evening Hodja sat long and pondered, just as Freddy was pondering now. Dead or alive, which was he?

Poor Hodja, always in a pickle. Poor me, in a pickle. My pickle, he thought, was whether I should tell Mom and Dad about the license plate. Rat on Ivan after all Ivan had done for him? What would that do? It would be *his* fault that Ivan called him. His father would yell at him, his mother would defend him, and then his parents would get into another fight. He'd think about that on his class trip to Mycenae and decide what to do by the time he returned.

From the next bedroom, theirs, he heard their furious slamming of bureau drawers, their fierce banging of closet doors, their muffled voices, pieces of words spat out like phlegm, half sentences, the usual names, "Dimitrov," "Franklin," "the wife," "the girlfriend," "State Department," "those murderers in November 17." His mother: "I'm sorry, I never would have if I'd known . . . so terrible for you, Robbie, you can blame me for everything. I wanted something more for myself. . . and then Ivan, I still. . . there must be a way. . . if everything in the world is national interest, where is the meaning of one man, one woman, one child. Where. . . the meaning? Franklin could have. . . just granted Ivan outright. . . gesture of thanks . . .saved an American child. Your child, Robbie. Don't you owe . . .? Extend yourself for once."

And then his father flaring up. "What are you driving at? Now, what? . . .You've managed to get me trapped. Finally got an answer from Washington. . . . said they'd look into my problem. My problem, they called it, for Christ sakes. Barbara, my career, through, finished, you understand what I'm saying to you? You can't have a problem like this if you're a State Department officer. Let Franklin get his own goddamn handler for that Bulgarian."

"Then he's as good as. . . "

"You can bet Franklin's handler will screw him."

"You're being barbaric. You've got a mean streak. See it through, for the love of God."

"That's exactly what I thought. You're being selfish. Bitchy. The guy's a foreigner who's intruded in my life, turned it upside down. I resent the intrusion. You seem more interested in his welfare than mine. This is a marriage not a human rights organization."

Freddy wrapped the pillow around his head, over his ears to stop the voices. He was tempted to get up and go to their room, make them stop, but he didn't want to leave the covers, a cocoon, smooth, warm. Instead, he opened his mouth wide, and as if he were in pain, he shrieked, "Shut up," his voice resounding through the house, the windows rattling, "Shut up." The awful hissing in the next room ceased, in a second his door was thrown open. His father reached him first, sat on his bed, lifted him up from the pillow and held him in his arms. "Son, son. What's wrong?"

He poured out the story of Ivan's call and choked out "sorry," over and over. They whispered to him, to each other, their arms encircled him. He felt his parents' hands touch as they clasped around his chest, across his back.

Roger, his eyes swollen with sleep, stood in his doorway. "What's wrong with Freddy?"

"He had a stomach ache, but it's all gone now," his father answered.

Then quite suddenly, he felt the house settle peacefully into the night, like his grandfather's heeling sailboat, which after a tight tack in a squalling wind, every rope and board squeaking and straining, comes about and sails before the wind, hardly rocking, and miraculously silent.

Chapter 24

Before sunup, while the sky was still black, the moon full casting far too much light for this purpose, he climbed up the high fence, the first two meters of stone, the rest, chainlink, a barrier separating his apartment building from the house next door. Scaling the rocks, he shoved his feet and hands into crevices where the mortar had weakened. In those spots, the cement had turned to crust, and crumbled as he inserted his hands. It was taking him three times longer than he had estimated to reach the next level, the portion where the stone changed to chainlink. A sound: his fingers and feet on the metal causing a muted plink as if he were plucking a mindless tune on a *gadulka*. This part he mounted more easily, reached the top, but as he swung over to the other side, his pant's leg caught and ripped. He stopped his descent, climbed back up and carefully picked off the bit of material snagged on the pointed spikes and put it in his pocket. Hurry, I'd better hurry. As he began to climb down toward the yellow car in the next-door neighbor's garden, with his free hand he checked for the tools. Pliers, screwdriver, and small oilcan he had shoved into his jacket pocket.

The new model yellow Ferrari was parked below, moonlight glinting on its roof. Mounted on blocks, like a piece of sculpture in a museum, there it had stood ever since he and Maria had moved into their apartment building. He had noticed it from his bedroom window and kept it under observation since the first day he arrived; no one had used it the whole time. The owners, obviously travelers, had been away these many weeks; no one was even checking on the vehicle. If he stole the license plate, who would notice the theft?

Noiselessly he dropped off the fence, squatted by the license plate, took the oil out of his pocket and squeezed some on the bolts, disgusted with his useless, shaky fingers, bloodied from the climb and scored by shreds from the smashed mirror. Then he worked the pliers onto the bolts and tried to turn them. Stuck. He turned on the flashlight to be sure the oil had dripped directly on the bolts. Nearby, inside a neighboring house, a dog barked. Outside that house, floodlights flashed on, but thank God, did not illuminate the Ferrari. He shut the flashlight and lifted himself off his haunches. The aroused dog had been let out. A deep-throated bark came from what was probably an Alsatian, he guessed. The beast was tearing along the fence line, infuriated by his intrusion. He stopped, sat in silence, held his breath, but still the cursed animal continued to rage. He decided to work again and to work fast. He wrapped the pliers around the four bolts and turned with all his strength. One by one they loosened with a mouse squeak and gave way. He dropped them and the screws into his pocket and removed the plate, still holding his breath. He returned the tools to his jacket pocket and crouched in utter silence, holding the plate between his teeth. He felt the sting as it cut into his lips and tongue, then the taste of blood. The dog was lunging at the fence close by. A door opened. A man called the dog to come. "*Argo, ela 'tho, Argo.*" The dog, Argos, obviously named after Ulysses' legendary hound, unheeding, continued to charge along the fence, whipping itself into a fury. A woman's voice yelled, " *Eh, Spiro, aftos o Argos,* the stupid hound will wake the whole neighborhood."

"It could be one of those crazy terrorists out there," the man hollered back.

"*Christe eleison,*" the woman answered, her voice pitched low in her throat. A door slammed and the light went out.

He reeled; he had been holding his breath without realizing it. He exhaled through his mouth, lowered himself on all fours, scuttled back to the fence, climbed over it, the bolts jingling in his pockets, and half tumbled onto his own property. The beast growled deeply, then let out a few yelps of disappointment, the cry of an animal whose prey had escaped, and was quiet.

In front of his building, the Embassy sedan was parked by the curb just where he had told the Embassy driver to leave it, a recent but not too recent model Fiat, small, black, completely unremarkable among the thousands of *Fiataki* that sped Greeks along their accident-strewn roads. He sat on the ground to remove the official green diplomatic license plate bearing a number that denoted the Bulgarian Embassy and replaced it with the plate he had unscrewed from the Ferrari. He glanced inside the Fiat, where in the light from the moon, he made a last check to be sure he had loaded all his bags.

He dove inside the car, but before turning the key, he rested his head on the steering wheel. One more time he agonized over writing to Maria, ran systematically though all the reasons why he should and then all the reasons why he couldn't. He looked up at his apartment: that spot had never been home, even when Maria was with him, he never thought of it as home. In Sofia, their stinking, cramped apartment certainly wasn't home. That sty he grew up in with his mother was never home. Or was it? What constitutes a home? He could remember its every nook, every object, the cupboard where his mother kept the food, the pegs where he and his mother hung their sorry clothes, the picture postcard of the Parthenon, how the sun streamed through the narrow window in the morning, warming his bed, how he'd used that window, in his mirrorless society, to gauge his blurred features as he changed from child to boy, the only access he had to his reflection until he went into the army, where here and there the government provided a mirror, usually cracked or mottled, propped on a sink or hung lopsided by a string on a wall. But as a boy, he never needed a mirror to know what he looked like. He looked like exactly what he was, a skinny, famished thing, a miserable orphan. His mother spent hours after work, exhausted, dreaming and plotting how to move out of that chicken coop—she used the Greek word *kotetsi*— to find something better, to find her way back to Greece. Now he felt his eyes water, his throat convulse, his shoulders move in small spasms, movements so unnatural to him, he didn't even realize he was crying until his face grew damp. What had seized him? A nostalgia for what he'd known? It couldn't be for the desolation that had been his childhood. His present aloneness? An emptiness that exceeded by far the worst loneliness? He didn't understand.

Headlights grazed the sidewalk as a car, very slowly, was turning the corner. He ducked below the dashboard. He remembered that this time every evening a police car patrolled the street. He sprawled across the front seat and remained prone until the patrol car had made another turn and its motor faded.

A morbid poem by Yannis Ritsos, called *Eliminated,* came to him jumbled, in fragments :

> *at the end of the road*
> *he disappeared*
> *a bird screeched*
> *no one noticed*
> *lampspost*
> *between them blood*

With the back of his hand he wiped his cheeks and turned the key. The black Fiat lurched forward.

And so he entered the National Highway, north, and the road opened wide and clear. Before him rolled only a few trucks with Greek or Yugoslav plates, and now and then a speeding car would overtake him, and after a while he spotted the turn-off to Thebes, but he stayed with the highway going straight, straight north, climbed and descended along the sea, climbed and descended, always along the sea, where the island of Euboea to the east sprawled as big as a continent, blue and black at this hour, under the moon. He was fully aware that his mood was swinging mechanically like a pendulum from sobriety to giddiness to jubilation. He remained observant, scrutinizing his mirror to see the cars behind, growing even more euphoric, the old songs rushing through his head, music sung by the Greeks in Sofia—he remembered every single word—"*Kato sto yalo*, "Down by the sea, my love, my love, sleeps," and to the old repertoire he added a new song he'd just learned here in Greece, *The Children of Piraeus*—"When evening deepens, I won't find another port," took a hand off the wheel to dramatize, crooning soulfully like Melina Mercouri in *Never on Sunday.* Then Thermopylae, where he stopped at the statue of the great Spartan Leonides to read the famous inscription carved there in the stone: "Stranger, tell the Lacedaemonians that we lie here, obedient to their command."

And then northward toward Lamia, the National Highway hugging the edge of the sea, passing Volos, poised just to the east, remembering that ages ago centaurs cantered across the sands, and from where, once upon a time, Jason sailed forth in quest of the Golden Fleece. First time since he was a little kid, he called out to his dead father, Ioanni, never had called him Papa, had talked to him always as if he were another kid, but older than himself, big, laughing, strong, an imaginary playmate, friend, protector. Now, he was amazed at the movement of his own lips: "By Christ, Papa, look, look, where we are, Papa. Can you believe we're on our way?"

And then the road arced landward to Larissa, a market city squatting flat, ungainly, on the plains of Thessaly, Greece's breadbasket.

There, starved, he consulted the mirror to be sure no one was following, and pulled over to a restaurant on the side of the road, a new fancy place with large plate-glass windows shielded by maroon awnings. He scouted the parking lot. No police. Travelers? Yes. Business people? Yes. Rich families? Yes. Perfect, he decided. No peasant families asking personal questions. He chose a table by the window that offered a good view of the whole parking lot and the National Highway that stretched beyond. The children at the table behind spoke in loud, whiny voices, the mother yapped shrilly. He could have moved, there were enough empty tables, but he appreciated the unobstructed view. Besides, he was so elated it would take more than that to annoy him.

He ordered *mousaka*, fried potatoes, a salad, and a half carafe of *retsina*; he dug into the bread, *horiatico* with a tangy crust, the minute the waiter laid the basket on the table. As he finished a glass of wine, he saw an older model gray Mercedes drive into the lot bearing the diplomatic license plate—green with a delta sigma and the number 12, the number designating its country. He couldn't remember which country number 12 represented, but he could look it up on the official paper he kept in the car, a list of the countries accredited to Greece and their identifying numbers. Pray it was some obscure Embassy, people who didn't appear at diplomatic functions very often, who wouldn't recognize him out of uniform, here in his faded, sweater and shapeless, everyday pants. The sun reflected on the car window in a way that obscured his view of the passengers. When the car doors finally opened, a man and woman climbed out, and smoothing their rumpled clothes, headed for the restaurant. He turned in his chair to make out their faces Thank God. He had never seen the couple before,

Scandinavian, perhaps, bent slightly forward to make themselves inconspicuous; they'd be quiet people, would take their seats and wait humbly to be served, not the type to search the other patrons for familiar faces to shout to and wave at.

When he faced front again, he found that a stranger had seated himself at his table, across from him, his face hidden behind the menu. He surveyed the restaurant and noted three or four empty tables where the man could have sat rather than with him. Still, weren't Greeks like that, gregarious, hating to be alone? From behind the menu drifted a plume of cigarette smoke.

"*Kalimera,*" he said coolly to his new tablemate.

The man returned his greeting, as he lowered the menu.

"Where you headed?" the stranger asked

He didn't answer, but raised his hand high in a waving motion that meant straight ahead.

The man grunted, inspecting him. The waiter came over and the man ordered toast with honey and coffee.

"I'm not very hungry," the man said conversationally.

He shrugged and sized him up. Ageless, his face was flabby, features soft, the bland appearance of, say, a bureaucrat, perhaps a civil servant who sat slumped for eight hours, six and a half days a week, smoking, drinking coffee, picking his teeth, no work to do. He wore a light blue dress shirt, the collar button open, the right cuff slightly frayed, and a blue and brown tie loosened at the neck. The man removed his heavy horned-rim glasses and rubbed his eyes, the habit of a person who spent his life shuffling papers. He was remarkable in his blandness.

If he ever saw the stranger again, he thought with irony, he would recognize him by that empty quality.

"You meant north, right?" the man said.

"Exactly."

"You got an accent. Where do you come from?" the man said in a voice that was expressionless, yet with a certain edge to it.

"Born in Alexandria. We came back to Greece when Nasser nationalized," he lied.

"Alexandria. So. Egypt." The man stopped rubbing his eyes. "Like not being Greek at all. A stranger." The man took out another cigarette, while the butt of the first was still smoldering in the ashtray.

He wanted to eat, be on his way, escape. He called to the waiter impatiently.

The man was drinking his coffee but pushed the toast aside.

"Knew a guy once from Alexandria, really rich. Fabric merchant. Linen, cotton, wool, everything. He was a Hellene, too. He didn't sound anything like you, Mister."

He thought about moving to another table, but was afraid of creating a commotion. Who knew what the man would do? Follow him to the other table, make loud comments? The last thing he wanted was to start trouble, call attention to himself. Who knew what menace was buried under that dull veneer?

By the time his food came, he didn't want it, but ate anyway, shoving it down till it lumped in his throat. He gripped his knife and fork tightly to keep his hand steady, had to force himself with all his being to remain seated. As he chewed, he kept his face half hidden by angling it toward the window.

"Where you been, eating so much, so fast?" the man asked

"Athens," he said indistinctly, his mouth stuffed with food.

"You got excellent road to the north. But where north are you going? Thessaloniki? Thrace? Further still?"

He got the bill and stood up to go.

"Yes, correct," he said, and hurried away. As he unlocked his car door, he glanced over at the restaurant. Standing in the window observing him, his face pressed against the glass, was the stranger. The euphoria of the day evaporated leaving him with a heaviness in his stomach, in his legs, a weight, a pulsing in his skull, a feeling akin to dread, the fear he associated with the curse his people had laid on him years before.

So he continued north, slowing to ogle Mount Olympus, an awesome mass, its two glowering summits draped with snow and bound in a light, swirling fog, where gods and goddesses might well be cavorting, but here below there was only this spectacular view and on its flanks there seemed to lie a deadly stillness. He turned on the heater.

At Katerini, a town lying close by the sea, he parked the car and walked toward the shore, stretching his stiff legs and breathing deeply to clear his lungs with sea air. In town, he bought some food supplies to avoid stopping again at a restaurant, and cruised along the shadowy floor of the gorge at Tembe, the nine kilometer-long valley where the Peneus River ran and where the ancients believed Apollo had purified himself in the river's water. Toward evening, his spirit lifted; he pulled over into a clump of pine trees, where hidden from the road, he enjoyed the bread, *spanakopita*, and *tiropita* he had bought in Katerini. Then he bedded down in the back seat of the car, cramped but almost pacified, and slept.

The next morning he pushed onward through the noise and traffic of Thessaloniki, then headed due east through the peninsula, Kalkithiki, the Aegean Sea always glistening beside him. After Kalkithiki, he would leave Macedonia and finally enter Thrace. After he shifted down to a crawl through the bustle of Kavala, the Greek port on the sea—in school they had drummed into their heads that Kavala really belonged to Bulgaria and what an outrage that it had been ceded to Greece—the road veered north, at last leaving the sea behind.

Inland. I've made it home, just coming to the outskirts of Xanthi. Home. My dream has come true. I've made it. As he slowed for a traffic light, he glanced in his rear view mirror and saw the motorcycle draw up beside his car. The driver had a cap pulled down almost to his eyes, and a scarf tied around his mouth and chin. But the man riding pillion was bareheaded, his face distinct. As the motorcycle came abreast so close it almost sideswiped his door, he recognized the fatuous features. The smug civil servant who yesterday in Larissa had ruined his meal, was pointing a gun at his head.

Chapter 25

When the doorbell rang early in the morning, the dog went wild, waking her. Alarmed, she thought, no one ever rings at this time. Ourania wouldn't be up, but Robert would be, and he'd probably answer it. She listened, propped up in bed on an elbow. A moment later she heard a car drive away from the front of their house, and then Robert's footsteps sounded on the stairs, so slow and halting—his tread was normally strong and rapid—for a moment she was frightened it was someone else.

"Barbara," he said, even before he entered their bedroom. His voice was low, odd.

"What?"

"I really cannot imagine this. I cannot."

In his hand he was holding a paper with a message, a couple of lines written in ink.

"Who ever was at the door at this hour?"

"One of Franklin's goons."

"At this time of day? My God." She looked out the window to the pale sky, a sickly sight, compared to the painted, boastful streaks of light that would soon appear as day dawned over Mount Pendeli.

He was silent, his head bent, reading and rereading the letter as she watched him; he read it five or six times.

"Robert. What is it for heaven's sake?"

He glanced down at her, shook his head in disbelief and said, "You're not going to figure this out, not in a million years. He took off, the goddamn fool, heading north on the National Highway."

"Terrific. But who?"

"Oh, sorry. Your Bulgar."

"What?" She got out of bed and snatched the paper from his hand: "For Your Information: Hatchet left Psychiko at 4:30 this morning, heading north on the National Highway. Come by my office on your way in this a.m. D.F."

"Where did you get the idea he took off? Franklin writes only that he left Psychiko heading north."

"By the tone. I read it to mean he's flown." He made a flying motion with his hands.

"I'm going."

"Where?"

"To Franklin's office, too."

"No, I don't think I could take it," he said, but half joking.

"You go ahead, I'll drive down in a half hour or so. I need time to get dressed."

"Barbara, remember, we're one hundred percent together on this Hatchet affair. We promised last night after we calmed down Freddy. We can't have the children distraught over this ever again.

"Yes, right. But Robbie, darling, just please lay off calling him Hatchet, O.K.? A hatchet is a tool, a blunt instrument you wield. The name doesn't sit right with me."

Within the hour she joined Robert and Franklin and one of his agents in the Bubble.

"Glad you're here, Barbara. Robert told me that Freddy got a telephone call last night. Lousy thing to do, scaring the kid. My surveillance guys report that some time after Hatchet hung up, he went over to the neighboring house, stole a license plate from a jazzy Ferrari and took off in a Bulgarian Embassy car. Too bad. Just when he was getting useful. Wonder what prompted this extensive jaunt?"

He cocked an eyebrow at her.

"I haven't a clue. Maybe he's just gone on an archaeological dig some place. Might be on a mission for the Russians."

"Wrong," he said smugly. "The stolen license plate. That's more like an individual act rather than a sponsored one. He's headed north along the National Highway. Lucky him. In a few hours he'll be getting a great look at Mount Olympus if he continues north on the National Highway." Franklin opened his eyes wide, as if he were taking in a spectacle, then snapped his hands out as if he were throwing something. "Zeus or some other god might hurl down a thunderbolt. Poof, he's a plume of smoke. What a fantastic view that mountain is from the highway. His route, you'll note, makes no sense if he's poised for defection. Heading north puts him in transit to the following borders: Yugoslavia, Albania, Bulgaria, hardly on the road to freedom, unless he veers east to Turkey or west to Italy. People like him, rodents, like your bats, Rob, probably have adaptations to help them. What do you call that special adaptation that bats have so they can see more acutely?"

Echolocation, explained Robert, is an added way of seeing. Bats emit high-frequency sounds that bounce off distant or invisible prey and come back to them as echoes.

The agent sat there silently, his hands clasped on the conference table, like an obedient elementary school child in the classroom, shaking his head in agreement with Franklin's analysis and listening respectfully to Robert's bat lecture.

Again Franklin looked at her, angled his head, encouraging her to comment.

She herself was dumbfounded by the news. She had never imagined this scenario. Heading north. Something clicked in her memory. Ivan's mother was from a town in northern Greece. Definitely some place in Thrace. Where was it? Komotini? Drama? Didimotiko? Xanthi? She couldn't recall just then, but it would come to her. He'd once told her exactly, probably that time he'd taken Freddy and her back to the lodge from his in-laws' house in that broken down jeep. It occurred to her how fascinated she'd been by his story that day, how she'd felt an unexpected attraction to him—pity? something else? Her emotional reaction had so overwhelmed her that she had dismissed him from the lodge rudely, only to be disgusted with herself an hour later for her rash behavior. After, she had made a pact with herself not to think again about that particular surge of feeling for him. Just let it be.

"Any idea why he'd be going north, Barbara? Go ahead, take a wild stab at it," Franklin was goading her, as if just at that moment he'd read her mind.

Hadn't she already mentioned that she had no idea? What was this, a grilling? Deliberately, she crossed her hands across her chest and looked up at the ceiling.

Robert asked, partly with the aim of taking the heat off her, what action Franklin planned for "Dimitrov's little excursion," then what the Greeks would think about his trip and of course, the important question, what line had the Bulgarians slash Russians taken?

"Let's look at it this way. First, what does Hatchet's roving the countryside mean to us? Not a hell of a lot. We may be losing a really promising human asset; normally we protect our assets so nothing happens to them, but in this case I'm not sure, am I, what he's up to, so I'm in no rush to protect him." He shook his head solemnly like a doctor delivering the worst prognosis to a cancer patient's family.

And again she felt the intensity of his eyes as he studied her.

"One outcome: he gets caught by the Greeks and announces that he's been trading information with us," continued Franklin. "Or they break him down and he spills the beans about some access he might have to November 17 communications at the Bulgarian Embassy. These are non-events, really. Stavros couldn't care less what Eastern Bloc people we're running. In fact, he expects us to be running them, and in some cases we and the Greeks are running the same ones as a joint effort. Stavros could even be sympathetic to him."

"Why would Stavros be sympathetic to him?" she asked quickly.

"I didn't say *would.* I said *could.* He might regard him as an asset and protect him exactly the way we would, especially if he believes the Bulgarian has information about November 17."

He was impossible to talk with, she thought, smug—testing her. They had arrived at a total breakdown in their relationship. There was no way she could help Ivan through Franklin. That was now perfectly clear.

One of Franklin's men, whom Franklin introduced as the director of the surveillance team, came into the Bubble to report an update on the subject's whereabouts. Hatchet was still driving north on the National Highway, had pulled off the highway at Karmena Vourla and was wandering casually along the water. It appeared that so far neither the Greeks nor the Bulgarians or Russians were tagging him.

"The Bulgarian and the Russians, now that's going to be a study," Franklin said. "When they realize he's flown they'll want to nail him as quickly as possible but, obviously, they don't have the freedom to roam the countryside to find him. They'll have to use their Greek agents, but the ones in their poor pay are so sleazy, they'll report it all to KYP." Franklin put his head back and guffawed, enjoying the vision of the frustrated enemy.

Then, claiming he had nothing more to say "until I can put two and two together," Franklin swept them collegially out of the Bubble.

"I know you'll call me immediately, won't you, Barbara, if you hear anything," were his parting words, the "won't you," inserted not as question but with the biting quality of a command.

She left the car in the Embassy parking lot and started to walk as fast as she could, hampered by the high heels she had put on this morning before she realized her day would include a speedy walk downtown. She felt anxious, had a sudden, sickening premonition that something terrible was going to happen. Her mind leapt to Catherine: something wrong with Catherine? No, Catherine would be fine. What could happen to her on the Dartmouth College campus in pristine Hanover, New Hampshire? Not easy to have a child thousands of miles away. I'm getting crazy with all of this, she thought. I'd better call Catherine this afternoon, though, just to reassure myself. She was overjoyed that just yesterday DIA had sent her a proposal to write an historical overview and contemporary analysis of Albania for their 1979 annual report, a welcome diversion to settle her down with good, wholesome work, lots of absorbing research.

On the way downtown, she came to the American School of Classical Studies, a cluster of buildings including the Gennadion Library, where she spent hours in historical research. Usually, she delighted in reading the message carved into the stone portico above its imposing entrance. The original Greek, or even a casual English translation, *Kaloundai ellines* . . . "They are called Greeks, all those who study Greek culture," was touching both in its significance and poetic rhythm. But today, bent on other business, she entered the Gennadion without glancing up at the words; she proceeded to the phone booth in the entrance hall.

After her number went through, she asked for Stavros Pavlides. When he answered she asked if he could meet her right away at Zonar's.

"Of course, Barbara, of course. I can be there within half an hour." She hung up and hurried on her way, and still the anxiety persisted.

Ivan's bolting, if indeed that's what it was, of course—Franklin was usually right about those things—had come as a shock and was forcing her into a deeper realization of the drama that was pulling them along—her, Robert, Freddy, Roger and by extension, even Catherine-the strange and accidental twists in the course of events. Yes, she herself had put the train in motion, yes, she had acted as the locomotive, driving her family and Ivan along a track that coiled round and round, perilously. She had chosen to act, to enter into the fullness of life, but what she hadn't anticipated were the runaway consequences of her early decisions—Robert's turmoil, Freddy's misery and now Ivan's precipitous reaction. A truly unsavory factor was her own deep emotional tie to Ivan's dream of freedom, an obsession that was upsetting her family's stability and that, she had to admit, she could not tame. There was little doubt in her mind that Franklin had detected her weakness for Ivan, regarded it as a security risk, the reason for his prickly reactions to her.

Entering Kolonaki, she picked her way carefully to avoid the piles of dog stuff; Greeks didn't pick up after their dogs, and more dog owners, it seemed, lived in Kolonaki than any other quarter of Athens.

Her thoughts rolled on. What, after all, had been gained and what had been lost since they had come into contact with the Bulgarian some six weeks ago? What had been lost was clear. For her family, it was peace. They had been shaken from their privileged, idyllic world, made to face up to an obligation they owed a stranger, someone who by accident of birth was infinitely less privileged than they, and this obligation was tearing at them. But was that really a loss? Suddenly she couldn't separate gain from loss, they had become a muddle, messed up in a ledger where gain and loss were entered in the same columns in the same color ink.

This morning in Kolonaki Square, the pageant of the week was in progress: the *agora*. Heaps of fruit, vegetables, flowers, plastic kitchen items, real sponges, all manner of brushes, cages imprisoning frantic wild finches lay displayed on tables; sweaters, slippers, house dresses fluttered like scarecrows from hangers. The haggling voices of the women shoppers, the lyrical calls of the barkers, gave the scene an air of conviviality, a kind of raucous merriment, a riveting theatricality like a street scene from a medieval play. She hurried along, itching with pleasure.

She rustled through her purse for her wallet and counted her drachmas. Then, one by one, she went down the line of birdcages, opening the tiny doors. Some of the creatures flew away immediately, others fluttered in their prisons, not sensing that they were free. A group of dismayed shoppers gathered round her as she proceeded along the line of cages. The vendor, at first dumbstruck, suddenly came to, clenched a fist, and then brandishing it in the air, plunged toward her. She plunked down enough drachmas to assuage the infuriated birdman, one of those beaux gestes, magnificent and completely possible, which, she thought, must occur to many people often, but for some reason, they always let pass, unrealized. She opened the last cage, reached in to guide a cowering bird to the door, and glancing back to be sure the cages were all empty, she continued on to the flower stand where she bought some daffodils.

As she passed a vegetable seller, he picked up a cucumber and performed a suggestive motion with it. "*Angouri*," he leered at the passing women, "the hardest and best in all of Greece."

So, all of this was life, all of it inescapable, the turmoil, the misery, the obligation, the inability to control consequences, the savage drive toward freedom, the dog messes in the street, the daffodils, the caged birds, the responsibility to set them free, the raw humor of the vegetable seller, a man whose expression of mirth was so Dionysian, he hardly differed from a pagan. And finally, there was this absurdity in front of her eyes—this parade of human beings spending a precious portion of their nanosecond on earth in frivolous pursuits, buying potatoes and scrub brushes. And wasn't she too part of that parade? Not buying potatoes or brushes, nothing so practical, but daffodils, and rushing to meet Stavros Pavlides, spending her precious nanosecond doing what? She had not even figured out what she should say to him.

Stavros "might regard Ivan as an asset and protect him," "could even be sympathetic to him." These were, more or less, Franklin's words, the words that had set her on the path to Pavlides.

She walked alongside the Grande Bretagne, crossed the street and entered Zonar's, the best-known coffee house in Athens. Dozens of politicians, businessmen, and idlers, many well past their prime, sat in the Greek male posture, one thigh crossed over the other, at the dark little tables, fingering worry beads. They peopled the smoke-filled emporium, an historical landmark, famous as a meeting place for coup plotters; there, Athenians generally agreed, of the series of political upheavals that rocked Greece in the twentieth century, at least some phase was hatched here. Here and there small clutches of Kolonaki matrons were relaxing after a morning's shopping; around their feet their bulging plastic bags were piled like sandbags. Yet for all the conversations, the atmosphere was typical of those ubiquitous Greek establishments, a strange blend of excitement and torpor.

She wove around the tables until she saw a hand shoot up from the back of the buzzing, somber room. Stavros stood to greet her.

"Well, surprised to hear from you, Barbara, but pleased. Drinking coffee with you is a great way to break up a boring morning."

As they ate a *rizogalo*, they talked aimlessly of this and that, whereabouts of old friends from Thessaloniki, mutual American acquaintances. She'd learned long ago the etiquette of Balkan procrastination and was waiting for the exquisite moment when she could come to the point. They recalled momentous happenings they'd shared: the time Catherine's high school class had been stranded in an outlying village on the day in 1973 when Military Police Brigadier Ioannidis performed a countercoup against the dictatorship. Movement throughout the country was immediately forbidden, under penalty of death, the terms of martial law. How to get Catherine and all the kids home safely? She and Robert went crazy with anxiety. Stavros contacted a Greek general who owed him a favor and succeeded in prying from him an armed convoy to escort the kids back to Athens. Now, recalling those more dramatic times, she and Stavros agreed friendship was friendship, and nothing should be spared to help a friend, even in a revolution. He had proven himself a real friend in 1973, one both she and Robert trusted with their lives.

He recited an ancient Greek phrase.

"Please translate," she said.

" 'Without friends no one would choose to live, though he had all other goods.'Aristotle."

How ironic that she was more comfortable with Stavros than, say, Dana Franklin or dozens of other Americans that she could name.

"But did you really call me to talk over old times?"

Putting the question so directly was totally un-Greek, a sign of how Americanized Stavros was in some ways. Taking note of the perpetual twirling of his topaz worry beads, she admired how gracefully he straddled two cultures.

"I merely want to ask you a few questions. Informational things, procedures, stuff like that. You might be able to answer in general terms without compromising anything." She spoke tentatively, not sure yet of how much she should reveal.

"Let's hear them."

"What do you do when you learn an official from a bloc country is driving around Greece without permission and may be heading for the borders? I mean, how important is this to KYP?"

Stavros beckoned to the waiter and asked for the check.

"That one is easy to answer. Depends somewhat on who the official is and what he's looking for. But, on the face of it, we'd consider this a national security issue."

He paid the check, and helping her to gather the daffodils strewn across the table, suggested they move out into the fresh air. They strolled along in front of the Parliament building, where the Evzone guards in their blue skirts and pompom clogs were strutting in front of the tomb of the unknown soldier, and then headed over to the National Gardens to sit on a bench and continue their discussion.

She had decided earlier on her walk downtown, on the stretch from the Grande Bretagne to Zonar's, that she would not be explicit with Stavros, she would present him with veiled facts, disguised personae, just to get his reaction. But now when she asked questions, he could not respond: her information was too vague, he claimed, too scanty.

So she began all over, and this time, still holding back a little, she told him about a Bulgarian officer of Greek ethnicity, accredited to Athens, who had saved Freddy's life and to whom she was indebted.

"He's a good man. He's someone who's suffered from an outrageous fate and who wants to defect." She skidded off on a tangent about the worth of an individual pitted against issues of national security, then recognized her mistake in discussing these kinds of abstractions. When Stavros, in his supercharged way, began pacing in front of the bench she steered her remarks back on course. To make himself valuable to the Americans the Bulgarian officer had been exchanging information with Franklin, but for some unknown reason, the Bulgarian officer had suddenly taken off and she was afraid the Bulgarians would get him, harm him was how she decided to put it.

"Has he got something on him? Is he carrying anything to anybody?"

"No, not that I know of. Franklin had discussed having him get some messages to people in Bulgaria, but they haven't started that program yet."

"Is that all? Because Franklin certainly isn't going to hand him a defection for that Mickey Mouse."

"What do you mean?"

Stavros sat down next to her on the bench, picked up a long stick and doodled in the thin winter grass. "Exchanging information. That's interesting. What sort of stuff?"

"Low level. Obsolescent technical information from Nea Makri. In return, he gave us the Bulgarian order of battle information from the Rhodope area."

He laughed. "If that's what Franklin wanted, he would have come to me. That's not what he wanted. We share that junk with each other on a daily basis."

He took the stick, and in a patch of mud he etched slowly and deeply. She bent over and read the two squiggles. The numbers one and seven appeared in the dirt.

She winced.

"Do I surprise you, Barbara?"

"No, I guess not."

"That's all Franklin wants. Absolutely nothing else attracts his attention. He's in heat. I'll tell you honestly. There are so many theories about the identity of this gang that it's driving us all crazy. So, I'm guessing, if I know Franklin, the Bulgarian's activities have something to do with November 17."

"The Bulgarian had nothing to do with November 17," she said steadily. She hated the lie, pricked herself with the thought of the other vices a liar would possess—greed, vanity, selfishness, God knows what else.

"Barbara, you're in charge here. But if the Bulgarian officer was squealing on that elite band of assassins, you'd better say. If November 17 gets to him before I do, he's finished. A .45-caliber bullet through the car window straight into his head. You know, I'm in a position to get to him faster."

Stavros "might even be sympathetic to him . . . regard him as an asset. . . protect him," again fragments of Franklin's remarks trailed through her head.

"What would you do if you got to him first?"

"I honestly don't know till you tell me more."

In the budding trees, yellow finches flew from branch to branch; she thought of the empty cages. They'd be filled with birds again tomorrow, but at least she had acted, had to obey the prompting, call it conscience.

"All right, Stavro," and she told him of Franklin's arrangement with Ivan—that he'd grant Ivan defection if he could penetrate the Bulgarian Embassy communications, which might concern November 17.

When she had finished, he stood, raised his right hand high, and a young man approached from a neighboring bench. Stavros told him to bring the car around quickly to the side of the Parliament building, they were going to drive the *Kyria* to the American Embassy.

When she got out at the Embassy, she said, "Stavro, give him a chance. Right?"

"Barbara, don't worry. As we say in Greek, *myn stenehoriese.*"

"But of course I'll worry. Till you tell me he's safe."

300

Later she thought of the finches and wondered what kind of gesture it really was to set them all free. Seen from the crowd's point of view, she would be a rich, spoiled American tourist, foolishly tossing away hundreds of drachmas on some stupid birds.

Chapter 26

She was strolling along a gravel path that twisted through the formal garden at the front of her house, bored with the uniform rows of daffodils and straight, soldierly lines of rosebushes, buds still tight in the early spring. In the center of the garden grew a square of cropped grass. The precision of these formal gardens, the prescribed kinds of flowers, the paths curling round and then back in on themselves, she found tedious. Why did the Greeks, given to disorder and whim, both as a people and as individuals, ape the formality of French gardens?

A wind had burst in from the south, as brutal as the summer's Meltemi, which every August buffeted across the Mediterranean up from the African desert, churning the sea and scattering a coat of red grit on everything in its swath—on the orange tile roofs, on forsaken seaside tables, on the smudged windshields of the blue and white buses. People griped about the grit in their mouths, the grinding noise between their teeth. In March, though, with the approach of Easter, no such raging wind was slated to ruffle Greece. And with it came drizzle.

She pulled a hood over her damp hair. Such a miserable morning; she ought to go inside before she got a sore throat, a weakness she succumbed to in damp spring weather, a legacy her mother pinned to a childhood bout of scarlet fever. But the house was too confining, its nervous twittering—the doors and windows straining against the wind—seemed to echo her own turmoil. Sitting in a stuffed chair would make her more tense. Her eyes were too tired to read; she couldn't muster the concentration to work on the DIA report; the living room was too yawning, the sitting room too cramped; she couldn't bear listening to music, it would press in on her; she couldn't stand the effort of visiting friends.

She was afraid, too, that if she went inside the scenes would start. Scenes, that's what she called them; scenes, how else describe them, those day-time nightmares that racked her brain. They came on like an aura from a migraine, a white light from an explosion filtering across the background of her mind, followed by perfect silence. Then a tornado of red dust gyrated toward the foreground, whirling round a humbled, broken man sitting on bare dirt, his head resting on drawn-up knees. When he lifted his face, she saw Ivan, exhausted, horrific in his hopelessness, like an inmate in a concentration camp.

Go someplace, get away from yourself, she thought, as she hunted in her pockets for her car keys: an excursion to hike on Mount Parnitha, a ride to Glyfada to stare at the sea. No, she didn't want to be away from the phone. From the other side of the hedge out by the street she heard music, the wail of *rembetika*, coming from a radio in the guard shack.

In the last two days since Ivan had left, she'd received, via Robert, reports from Franklin on his whereabouts. She had begged Robert to go to Franklin's office a couple of times a day to keep abreast of the updates from the surveillance team. Each time, Franklin told him that the Bulgarian officer was moving north, recent reports had him leaving Macedonia and entering Thrace. "He can't be going back to Bulgaria, so he must be headed for Turkey," Franklin said. He added that he was getting bored with the whole thing and might recall the surveillance team.

"He's not telling you all he knows," she told Robert.

"He never does. But don't expect me to probe," he said.

Thank God, Robert had relaxed since Ivan's departure, and was actually after these many weeks almost himself. For one, Ivan, like inflamed tonsils, had been removed from his life; but equally important, he'd received a long cable from his friend John Hawthorn, in Washington, who had spoken to the Assistant Secretary for European affairs. A close colleague of Hawthorn's, the assistant secretary told him that Robert's record was outstanding, that he, the assistant secretary himself, had put a memorandum in Robert's file carefully explaining Robert's predicament—that is, the compassionate circumstance of thirteen year old Frederick Baldwin's rescue from certain death by freezing by the Bulgarian officer—and he had stressed the state of mind of Mrs. Barbara Baldwin (DIA analyst) over the rescue of their son, and Ambassador Paige Gardner's zeal to join with the station chief to exploit the situation for intelligence purposes.

A couple of hours after she'd enlisted Stavros' help, Robert came home and said, without the usual acid in his tone, "I hope Dimitrov keeps going. Never comes back. I don't wish him harm. Really, I don't, Barbara. Never did. But he doesn't belong in our lives, because frankly there's nothing we can do to help him. You see that now, don't you?"

"What difference does it make anymore what I see? Our role's over, done with. I won't kid you, Rob, I'm terrified for him. I've gone as far as I can go for him. But now I'm relieved of responsibility, aren't I? It's been no picnic for me either God knows."

"I'm glad you've come to that. Yes, it's over. Say it to yourself again and again until you believe it."

Where was the poor man? Was he safe? Why had he taken off like that? The questions continued to plague her, because of those unnerving scenes invading her mind at least twice a day, she feared for her own stability. She resolved not to torment Robert with the Bulgarian anymore. Enough for both Robert and her and Freddy, too. Now on the second day of his disappearance, she was looking forward late in the day to driving to Thebes with Robert to escape from the whole affair. They had decided that a day or two away would be a healthy change. Yet she could hardly subdue an opposite tug to remain by the telephone.

They were bound for the pre-Lenten celebration, the *Vlachikos Gamos*, an annual parade the Thebans had dreamed up eons ago, satirizing the marriage customs of the Vlachs, a tribe of nomadic shepherds who had roamed from lands around today's Rumania into Greece during Roman times, before the concept of borders and nationhood had turned these ethnic groups into "minorities." Most of the Vlachs, through the centuries, had integrated into Greek life but retained some of their ancient customs, and many of them could still speak their Latin-based language. She loved the *Vlachikos Gamos,* recalling the country-bumpkin aspects, the swipes of crude humor.

As they entered the National Highway and headed north toward the Thebes cut-off, she thought how Ivan had just taken a portion of this very route. She rode silently beside Robert, trying to fasten on the scenery. With each kilometer, worries for the Bulgarian officer would dull, and she convinced herself, those nightmarish scenes invading her mind would fade. Yes, they were going to the Thebes of Oedipus and Jocasta —she could never get over that, the actual site of the powerful myth; also, the city figured prominently in the period of the Macedonians, Philip and Alexander, although now it was a forlorn, one-horse town without as yet a single material trace of its ancient history, only the *Vlachikos Gamos* to lend it a mark of distinction. And, of course, an added thrill: you could drive out further past Livadia, along the lonely rise toward Delphi and stand at the crossroads where, it was believed, Oedipus killed his father. By immersing herself in the ever-looping legend of Oedipus, she could distract herself entirely.

She began to rerun the tangled ancient myth through her mind, the impossible, absurd story, which Freud wove into his modern science of psychiatry. Laius, King of Thebes, warned by the Delphic oracle that any child born to his wife, Jocasta, would murder him, abandoned their infant son Oedipus on a mountain. He was found by a shepherd and brought to Corinth, where he was adopted by the King and Queen. As a young man, Oedipus learned from the Delphic oracle that some day he would kill his father and marry his mother. Believing that the King and Queen of Corinth were his parents, he ran away to avoid the tragedy. Later, on the way to Thebes, Oedipus fell into a heated argument over right of way at a crossroads with Laius, King of Thebes.

In a theatrical voice, declamatory like a Greek chorus, she began to recite the story out loud for Robert to amuse him. "With his whip, the king lashed out at the young stranger, who had failed to make way for the royal chariot. But as fate had determined, Oedipus in a fit of hubris killed Laius. At the entrance to Thebes, Oedipus was the only person able to answer correctly the riddle posed by the man-eating sphinx; disgraced, the sphinx killed herself. As a reward for the destruction of the hated sphinx, the citizens of Thebes offered Oedipus the recently widowed Queen Jocasta as his bride. With this union of mother and son, the prophecy was fulfilled"—she reverted to her natural voice—"which in good Greek fashion, set in motion yet another chain of tragic consequences."

She was totally immersed in tracing the next sequence of events in Oedipus' life when she felt Robert's hand cup hers and press it.

"He's dead."

"Are you thinking of Laius or Oedipus?" she whispered.

Silence.

"Dead," she continued, "or do you mean the brothers? Remember that sickening part of the myth

307

when Antigone—Irene Papas plays the part in the movie—keeps reburying her dead brothers?"

"He's dead, Barbara. Dead." His voice was as gentle as she had ever heard it, and she felt the pressure of his hand increase until it hurt her. He pulled off the road, walked around to her side of the car, and guided her out. She leaned against him, fighting back grief, anger and rising hysteria.

Arms around her, he led her into a meadow full of wildflowers, all dipping this way and that in the wild grass. Beyond the Theban plains, in the dusk, rose the snow-glazed shoulders of Mount Parnassos. He was still holding her hand. "Don't say it again," she quailed inwardly, "don't make it true."

"He's dead, sweetheart."

"I knew all along. Where?"

"Right outside Xanthi."

"Xanthi, his parents' village. At least we know now where he was headed. How?"

"Bullet through the car window. Two thugs on a motorcycle."

"My God. November 17."

Robert agreed that was exactly the modus used by November 17, and the ballistic studies being done by the Greek authorities would reveal if the bullet was from the terrorists' own weapon. "Unbelievable that they got into the act." He told her, too, that Matilda and Franklin would be joining them at the hotel in Thebes tomorrow; Matilda wanted to see the procession. But, to give the devil his due, Franklin knew she'd be upset and wanted to fill her in. "Wasn't that oddly kind of him?" he said. Franklin had reconsidered and kept his surveillance team on Dimitrov until the end. His team had reported that Stavros appeared on the scene, too, with his agents, and watched across the way as the murderers struck, the whole gang of them observing. "Must have been like an operating theater with the audience seated around for observation."

She sat back down again in the car, tilted her head back against the seat and closed her eyes, agonizing over how to explain Ivan's death to Freddy. She fabricated a half dozen versions of the truth, to tell him, each softened by major distortions and outright lies. It was only then, as she tried to construct a story of Ivan's life suitable for the telling to a youngster, that she realized how truly merciless was the human condition.

Neither of them said another word until they reached Thebes' premier hotel, a small uninviting, three-story building in the center of the town.

Franklin and Matilda arrived, Matilda unsubdued by the provincial appearance of this remote town. If she had arrived in London, New York, Paris or Beirut, Matilda's expectations would have been the same. Approaching the Theban plains, stepping into the geography of a myth that underpinned the whole sweep of Western civilization, hadn't stimulated *her* sensibilities at all. Certainly, large, spacious accommodations, a full restaurant, a boutique, and as a minimum some setback from the main street were the least amenities the hotel could offer a stranger, she complained, settling herself into one of the unbalanced wooden chairs, first inspecting the seat for scum. Robert had put the chairs on the third-floor balcony outside his and Barbara's bedroom, a cramped but convenient place to view the wedding procession at a safe distance from the crowd, which thronged boisterously along the street below throwing confetti, blowing into carnival horns and whacking each other on the head with plastic hammers.

Franklin shook Robert's hand and surprised Barbara by kissing her on both cheeks, European style. He thanked them for making the hotel reservations for them, he was sure Matilda and he were in for a great experience, so unusual for them to get out into the countryside, he felt terrific just being there.

"I know how *you* must feel today, Barbara. This whole affair has been a real bummer. Maybe I can answer some questions, put your mind at ease a little bit," he said in an attempt to commiserate. She was astonished at his sincere demeanor. He is actually sorry for *me*, not *Ivan*, not the person who was murdered

"Thanks. It's a relief it's over. Not to have him dead. I mean just not to be responsible for him anymore. For his freedom, for things like that."

Below, the police were pushing the crowds back from the road onto the sidewalk. Heads were swiveling up the street in the direction of the music drifting in from a distance. She was grateful to Robert for engaging Matilda in conversation so she could have Franklin's full attention.

"First off, I wanted to tell you he didn't know what hit him. There were two guys, one behind the other on a motorcycle. The guy in the back shot him point blank when he stopped at a traffic light at the edge of town. Dead on impact." He snapped his fingers smartly. "Stavros was there in a flash, grabbed the body, got the scene cleared in a minute. As a result, the media won't get hold of it. Hush-hush, in everybody's interest to keep it quiet."

No memorial service for him, no one to intone a passage from the Bible, no traditional hymn to bind the mourners in common grief, no eulogy to praise him. Hush-hush. Stavros had taken care of that. She remembered the story of Ivan's father's death, how they crammed his corpse into a mountain crevice and marched on to be forever tormented by the unburied body.

She nodded her head in acquiescence to the force majeur.

Below, the music was growing louder, the crowd parting to open a pathway for the procession as it straggled into view, led by the musicians in traditional village finery, rambling toward the town's center, banging on their shallow drums and playing their string and wind instruments. Matilda stuck her fingers in her ears and made a face of disdain at the musicians. Robert turned from her to Franklin, who remained standing, his back flat against the wall. Every few minutes, he surveyed the crowd, his eyes sweeping from left to right with a searching, concentrated look; he was not an aimless onlooker. He probably had brought along enough bodyguards to protect the capo of a Mafia family. For a moment she thought she saw his Israeli house servant on the edge of the sidewalk, but his figure was obliterated by the shifting masses of people.

"Where were the Russians and Bulgarians through all of this? They're the ones who'd want to hush it, who stand to lose the most if it got out that their attachés roll around the county like loose cannons," Robert said.

"They weren't following him, that's for sure. My inside sources tell me that they didn't even know he'd taken off. Seems they assumed he was busy when he didn't show up for work, and they simply went trustingly about their business. You know, he was given all that freedom so he could be out currying *our* favor. In fact, they may not know even yet. Delcheva's at her desk, working as usual. If she knows anything about his plans, apparently she hasn't told a soul, according to my sources there."

Matilda was pointing below to the procession, which was now livening up. A ragged formation of misused donkeys, harnesses decorated with bells, pompoms and braids of wildflowers, clomped past, laden with bedding, rugs, flapping chickens tied by the feet, pots and pans, an assortment of furniture, and to the glee of onlookers—for this was after all a mock wedding—bedpans and toilet plungers. Trudging behind were sheep, goats and mules, representing the dowry. Guarding the treasure were the men of the bride's family wearing sheepskin capes slung over one shoulder. They were carrying rifles, which in playful menace they pointed at friends in the crowd.

"How did Stavros get into this?" Robert asked.

"Remains a real mystery to me. Though he does have informers all over the place. Even more than I do, and in some cases, I hate to admit, higher quality."

Barbara stood up and grasped the rail of the balcony. The parade had become a blur, a welter of animals and people. She didn't want to know any more; she wished Robert would lay off questioning.

Next on foot came the groom, accompanied by his family, the men mounted on donkeys and work horses,

312

the women walking. The groom, waving at the crowd, strutted extravagantly, swinging a shepherd's crook. He was dressed splendidly in a black traditional suit, white shirt, wide maroon cummerbund, embroidered and fringed headband, breeches, and knee boots. But he hadn't shaved, his shirttails hung out, and he dangled a cigarette from the corner of his mouth.

"Want to hear my theory about Stavros' role in all this? Barbara, you'll hate this part, I bet." She remained at the edge of the balcony, her back to Franklin, acting the fully absorbed spectator.

"Of course, Dana. Tell us," she said absently, and asked Robert to call down to order some cold wine and something to nibble on.

She reached for the binoculars that Robert had brought. The bride appeared, standing atop a great mound of hay, all heaped on a rumbling cart drawn by two oxen. She was enormous, made to appear even more so when the wind slid under her bridal gown, billowing her skirt. From beneath her headpiece, tipped askew, beamed a bloated face. She was smiling broadly, displaying, Barbara could see through the binoculars, a row of blacked-out teeth. Some men approached the cart, and peered under her dress when the wind tossed it up. Matilda giggled, and getting into the spirit of things sent the contents of four bags of confetti sailing down on the bride.

"What's peculiar in all of this is how anyone fathomed Dimitrov's interest in November 17. I have a theory about that, which I'm sure would test out true," said Franklin.

He asked them to recall who knew about the Bulgarian officer's disappearance. He reminded them that, "We were the only ones to know at first," he reminded them. My team took off right behind him. Then the next day, Stavros joined the hunt, the only other person with the capability of learning that Dimitrov was heading out. I know for a fact that Stavros had been informed—God only knows where— about Dimitrov's interest in November 17, because an informer from his unit reported to us that Stavros in the course of a briefing told his squad that he expected two men on a motorcycle, someplace along the way, to take out the Bulgarian, and Stavros gave them instructions on how to grab the body, remove the car from the scene and allow the motorcycle to make a clean getaway in one fell swoop."

"So what are you saying? That only you and Stavros were aware of Dimitrov's interest in November 17?"

Franklin nodded his head vigorously.

Two local gallants emerged from the crowd, folding back their sleeves, conspicuously exhibiting their muscles. They linked hands, formed a seat to lower the bride from the cart, staggering clown-like under the heft. Another band of musicians, this one with modern instruments, struck up the popular *Pao yia ipno, Katerina,* while the bride threw kisses at the crowd. The ox cart lurched forward without her; she tottered after it, hurling crude curses at the oxen, words that, normally, only the men would dare pronounce.

"So let me advance my elegant theory. Your dear friend Stavros, I believe, in an effort to ingratiate himself with November 17 and any politicians who might support the terrorists, somehow reported to them that the Bulgarian officer had been snooping on the organization. Whether he actually knew this for a fact or dreamed it up, I don't know yet. You know, it might have been just a fantasy, but Stavros used it to perform a perfect act of opportunism. Now, Stavros is a decent figure in his own world, of course; is scrupulous about whom he betrays. Dimitrov was exquisitely dispensable. Why not betray him? I can assure you it's not easy for Stavros to find sacrificial lambs; but discovering a despicable Bulgarian to pitch into the cauldron is a gift from Zeus and Hera."

The waiter brought a tray with a bottle of lukewarm wine, only three glasses, one of them cracked, and a charred heap of melted cheese and ham on toast.

Franklin said through a mouthful of the burnt offering, "He might need a favor from those November 17 guys some day. Who knows? After all, Stavros played ball with the junta and when it fell in 1974, he then inserted himself seamlessly into the new democratic government. He did it by pleasing all sides; in fact, you could say he's master of that art, and like Machiavelli, he could write the standard text about it."

She had not turned back to face Franklin. She couldn't face him, any of them. His theory was amazingly correct, and she held the pieces of information to fill in the missing parts of his argument.

Robert was handing around the wine. In the street some men and women dancing the *hassapiko* were weaving through the crowd.

By telling Stavros all about Ivan in the hope of enlisting his help, she had unwittingly become an accessory in Ivan's murder. She'd tried to save him. Whatever she'd done, she'd done because of an inner imperative born of gratitude that later became concern for a human being, and she knew that faced again with a similar situation, she'd act. Robert's way was not her way, and Franklin's way was not her way. And neither was Stavros' way. Franklin, the most guilty, could easily have saved him by granting him defection. And now he was dead.

She left the balcony, groped her way downstairs, rushed out into the street. She swayed in the pressing crowd. A group of dancers hollering "*opa* " leapt alongside and yanked her into their circle. People on each side snatched her hands and held them aloft. The music coming from some place, as if oozing from the atmosphere, no, from a dozen places all at once, from the clusters of musicians up and down the street, each playing different songs, revving up to a frenzied pace—she felt the music, only the music, and those hands soaked with sweat, holding hers, as she took off, her feet leaving the ground. And wishing she could dance forever, she danced her despair. Once she stumbled, came to her knees, but the hands lifted her. Her chest was heaving as she tried to catch her breath. Sweat ran off her brow into her eyes and blurred her vision. She glanced up at the balcony and saw Robert in a mist, his eyes glued to the binoculars, peering at her. She wanted to call to him, to have him join her in the dance. But he couldn't hear; for the moment they were too far apart.

*

Flanked by the same heavily armed guards who had escorted her into the prison two weeks earlier, she walked out of the courtroom down the corridor to the exit, where she was met by a throng of reporters and television people clustered under the sizzling Athenian sun. They shouted at her in Greek and English, a boisterous interrogation.

"*Kyria* Baldwin, how much did your government support the junta?"

"Madame, did your government help install the military dictatorship in 1967?"

"Mrs., do you believe members of your government like Henry Kissinger should be tried as war criminals?"

"Why did your government not stop the Turks when they invaded Cyprus?"

"Do you agree your country suffers from a bad case of *alazonia*, arrogance, *hubris*, whatever you want to call it?"

"Tell us the truth about why your president really wanted to march on Iraq?"

She made a half gesture of lifting her hands to cover her ears but lowered them quickly. Obviously, the press had taken into account that over many years she had been accredited to the American Embassy in Greece. It passed quickly through her mind that they assumed because she had been outspoken at the trial—some might even condemn her for being disloyal to friends and country—she might now offer titillating tidbits to the aroused public. She took a deep breath, straightened her back against the onslaught. She felt humiliated.

She had expected to face shame, but in private spaces, at the CIA, at State, among friends and others when she got home. And worst of all waiting for her was Robert, of course, Robert. But for some reason she hadn't reckoned with the vehemence of public reaction on the streets here in Greece. Greece, where since ancient times, avoiding shame was a basic commandment. She was remembering Homer. "She has brought shame both on herself and on all women who will come after her," repeating the line to drown out the shouting. But she had come to Greece to make sure that the story of Ivan's death was told, and to insure that Stavros' role in his murder was a matter of record. At least, she had been able to grant to Ivan a kind of funeral service; it was, for her, a kind of solution. If necessary then, let this rude chorus call it out, "*Anathema, Anathema.*"